Reunions, Reflections, and Reconciliations

Book 2: The City of Nis Trilogy

P.J. Fenton

Acknowledgements

The author would like to acknowledge the works of Dante Alighieri, particularly his masterpiece, *The Divine Comedy*, for the inspiration that it played in the writing of this story.

Thanks also to Roberta J. Buland, Editor, Right Words Unlimited, for her professional editorial guidance.

Dedication

This book is dedicated to my nephew, Seth, and niece, Madison

Table of Contents

Part 1: The Emissary's Journey Through a City of Light

Chapter 1

"Dan-te, wake up." A voice whispered; a hand shaking her shoulder. "The airship is preparing to land."

Dan-te, a member of the Remnant of the Tribe, one of two ancient civilizations living under the ground beneath them, woke quickly from her sleep and was soon ready for action. Taking a quick stretch, she was easily taller than her companion. Yet height was not the only difference between them. Dan-te, like all members of the Remnant of the Tribe, was a pure white color from having evolved with no real exposure to sunlight. Her eyes looked to be made of two shimmering shades of silver, her ears stuck out long behind her head, and around her head were two horns—one gold and the other silver—that formed a coronet and culminated in a horn on her forehead. The person waking her was her companion, Virgil of the Hy-mun race, a race of beings who lived on the planet's surface. He also had fair-colored skin, but with a slight tan to it. His eyes were also white and blue-grey, he had black hair, and no horn. It was just one of the many ways Dan-te learned Hy-muns could appear. The two of them had met under some of the strangest and chanciest circumstances imaginable.

The events leading to Dan-te and Virgil's meeting began back when she and her brother Ice came to the city of Nis as part of a group protesting the completion of the Tribe of Shadows' Third Great Attempt. Through their ability to *Know,* an ability to see and experience the world around them not only by their sense of sight, but also with all their senses, combined with study, they could see and feel the land's fear over the Third Great Attempt's completion. It was an attempt meant to darken the skies of the surface so that the Tribe of Shadows could march on the surface and retake it for themselves.

Upon arrival at the Tribe of Shadows' home, the city of Nis, their group was predictably captured. Neither Dan-te, Ice, nor any member of the Remnant expected the Tribe of Shadows to listen to them, but the amount of fear they *Knew* from the Land was more than compelling enough to make them want to try. Yet even though they were captured, the two of them had privately made their own plans.

"We want to become gladiators!" Ice had shouted, surprising the other members of the Remnant, and Don-ati, the head jailor of Maestri, the First Circle of the city of Nis. Since there had never been a Rodent—as members of the Remnant were often referred to by the Tribe of Shadows—to *willingly* volunteer to become a gladiator. Let alone two.

The other members of the Remnant quickly realized that Ice and Dan-te must have been planning something but said nothing to help hide whatever secrets they were carrying. Dan-te and Ice planned to reach the Grand Coliseum and steal the First Envy's Veil of Shadows to contact the surface and warn its inhabitants, the Hy-muns, about the Third Great Attempt. They hoped that once the Hy-muns knew about the danger lurking beneath their feet, they would be able to do something about it. Neither one of them could go to the surface directly because of the lethal effects sunlight had on their people. Nor could they use the current veils, they were tied to the Tribe of Shadows and the other blood. A bloodline that had become a part of the Tribe of Shadows' lineage ever since the Tribe of Shadows' ancestors, the Greater Tribe, joined with Lord Tanas's Legion of Shadows. They needed to use the Veil of the First Envy, a former member of the Last Council of the Ancient Tribe, and one whose blood was still the same as theirs. Along the way, they encountered a Hy-mun girl named Reye, a captive of the Tribe of Shadows, driven mad by grief and sadness over the death of her brother at the Tribe of Shadows' hands. Reye was looking for revenge and inviting her into their plans—even if she hardly listened to them, gave them the opportunity for Dan-te to snatch the Veil in the Grand Coliseum, and use it to reach the surface, but not without it being damaged.

Once on the surface, Dan-te found herself in a room filled with shelves and books. She quickly discovered that the damage to the Veil had altered it in several ways. It still protected her from sunlight, but now she could "physically" exist on the surface world instead of the Veil's shadowy Reversed State. But thanks to that, she was able to meet Virgil, the occupant of the room she chanced upon. From Virgil, she learned many things, the most important of which involved the true identity of Lord Tanas, the Tribe of Shadows' leader, and how the Third Great Attempt was a danger to them all. She also learned her original plan to come to the surface was doomed from the start because of political forces acting on it, and that Virgil—nudging her shoulder to wake her up—was the best, if not only, friend she would find on the surface. Coming quickly to full consciousness, Dan-te made her way out of the hammock.

All of those evacuation drills had their benefits, Dan-te thought to herself, remembering her home underground, the tent city of Rem. Growing up there, she and her brother, Ice, quickly learned the art of waking up and being ready for action immediately. It was a necessary skill to learn, since every member of the Remnant needed to know how to pack up the city and evacuate quickly.

Rem, Dan-te, and Ice's home, was first built generations ago by two members of the Last Council of the Ancient Tribe, The Seats of Hope and Courage. Shortly after the division between the two Seats and the rest of the Last Council resulted in it dividing into two factions: The Remnant of the Tribe and the Greater Tribe. However, no member of the Remnant, either now or in the ancient past, blamed either the Seats of Courage and Hope or the other Seven members of the Last Council for that split. Nor did they blame the Tribe of Shadows for treating the Remnant like Rodents. The real blame for those actions could be traced to an older event and a single entity.

It began with "The Coming," Dan-te remembered coldly. She heard the stories dozens of times from the elders; so many that if she was not ready for them, pieces of them would blink into her mind. *All was peaceful, the Glow spread across the land, but then Light appeared, shattering our ability to* Know, *burning the Land and our people in its wake, and from that Light came fiery wheels carrying the Beings of Light, and their leader, the Light Bringer, who began slaughtering our people in the name of their Lord and Master.*

Dan-te shivered briefly, remembering the story about the Beings of Light. "The Coming" might have been the event that led to the shattering of the Ancient Tribe, but its orchestrator, the Light Bringer, was a far more terrifying creature, and really the one responsible for the destruction of the Ancient Tribe's home and dividing the Ancient Tribe afterward. Yet the *real* frightening thing was that It, and It's influence, was *still* alive and active through the Tribe of Shadows.

After coming to the surface using the Veil of Shadows, and meeting Virgil, Dan-te learned that the Light Bringer who led "The Coming," and Lord Tanas, the seemingly immortal ruler of the Tribe of Shadows, were, in reality, the same being.

It was him. The whole time it was him. The Light Bringer has been leading the Tribe of Shadows! Dan-te had cried, after learning that Tanas, the ruler of the Tribe of Shadows, and the Light Bringer who directed "The Coming" were the same person. It had felt like a cruel and sick joke had been played on the members of both the Remnant and the Tribe of Shadows for thousands of generations. After seeing Dan-te break down, Virgil suggested that they compare notes, exchanging information about both their people's respected pasts, Dan-te could still remember parts of that conversation.

Following "The Coming," our Ancient Tribe split into two, the Greater Tribe who wanted to pursue vengeance against the Beings of Light and our Remnant of the Tribe who sought to rebuild and live in peace. Twenty years after the division, the Remnant sent an emissary named Rill to the Greater Tribe to see how they progressed. Her account tells not only about how the Greater Tribe had fallen into decadence and depravity in the name of pursuing vengeance but also about something far worse that happened to the Greater Tribe. What was that? Dan-te remembered Virgil asking.

They joined the thing they wanted to kill most of all! Dan-te shuddered just remembering the conversation. Thinking of Tanas was scary enough, knowing now that It was also the Light Bringer who led "The Coming," remembering the stories about how It charmed the Seven and the Greater Tribe into letting It and It's legions join them merely added a new depth of terror to It's name.

They all became the willing servants to Lord Tanas and It's Legion of Shadows. Lord Tanas, a creature of nothingness, promised them a way to strike back at the Beings of Light that the Greater Tribe hated in exchange for letting It and It's legion join the Greater Tribe. Lord Tanas, the Light Bringer, wanted to use the Greater Tribe to attack It's own people after slaughtering ours. The Greater Tribe agreed, becoming the Tribe of Shadows in the process. The Tribe of Shadows, from that moment onward became the servants of Lord Tanas in exchange for a way to strike back at the Beings of Light. But even now, after succeeding in driving the Beings of Light from the surface, Lord Tanas and the Tribe of Shadows still aren't satisfied. At least the Tribe of Shadows won't be until they live on the surface again. They still fight, now against the Hy-muns residing on the surface, and also increase the size of their city, regardless of how it affects us.

Growing up in Rem, it was common knowledge that the Tribe of Shadows sought to expand their city and wipe out the Remnant. But every time they got close to Rem, they found that the Remnant of the Tribe had already moved it deeper into its subterranean realm.

Reunions, Reflections, and Reconciliations

The founders of Rem, the last Seats of Courage and Hope from the Ancient Council, recognized that our home might come under attack, either from the Tribe of Shadows or from the Beings of Light if they found us again. So, they decided our city should be built from tents, making it easy to pack up and carry away at a moment's notice—that if we ever had to leave again, we could take our homes with us.

I lost count of the number of evacuation drills me and Ice practiced, Dan-te remembered, thinking about how she and her brother trained to get up and be ready to move quickly, after only a little sleep in case an attack found its way to them. *At least it made me used to getting up fast and working at full strength after only a short rest, because who knows how much rest the two of us will be able to get once we're back on the ground.*

So far, Virgil had guided Dan-te through Spectral Academy, the Platinum Throne, Minos Airship Port, and then onto an airship bound for Wonton City; that is where they would continue their journey. The damaged Veil of Shadows still allowed Dan-te to travel in Virgil's shadow, just like a normally functioning veil would, but now while in his shadow she could touch and talk to Virgil directly. Without that advantage, Dan-te knew that her voice would only sound like a whisper to him, and only when that whisper matched whatever Virgil was feeling would he be tempted to act on that whisper.

I wonder how many more Tempters we'll encounter once we're back on the ground, Dan-te asked herself as she refitted herself with the Veil of Shadows. *Just traveling between Spectral Academy and the airship I lost count of the number of Tempters active on the surface. At least three of them noticed something suspicious about us before we reached the carriage that took us to Minos Airship Port. Who knows how many more might see us once we're back on the ground?*

Dan-te often spotted Tempters, members of the Tribe of Shadows active on the surface in the Veil's reversed state while she was hidden in Virgil's shadow. To fool them while at Spectral Academy, Dan-te—wearing a disguise under the Veil—acted like a Tempter with Virgil acting along every time she said the word "Tempter" to keep them from being noticed. Once they were both alone, rested, and aboard their airship, Virgil was able to don his own disguise, one that they expected would keep both inquisitive Tempters *and* Hy-muns from bothering them.

"Dan-te, have you seen my cane?" Virgil asked putting on his own clothes.

"It's over there by the door, Virgil. Your hat is also on top of it," Dan-te replied, pointing toward the door of the cabin that they shared.

"Thanks, Dan-te," Virgil said as he walked over to the door and picked up both the hat and cane.

Virgil's idea was for him to fake blindness. He told Dan-te that, "No one pays attention to the blind." Fully confident that once in his disguise, he would become all but invisible to the Hy-muns around him. Dan-te also liked the plan, remembering her time back in Nis where she heard that Tempters did not bother with people who had disabilities since they wanted Hy-muns that they could influence in *every* way possible. All he needed was to get into disguise.

Since Virgil's eyes were already sensitive to light, he always carried large, dark, sunglasses wherever he went. To complete the costume, by Hy-mun standards, he produced an extendable cane, specially marked with tape to indicate that he was blind. To top off the disguise, he would place a large sun hat over his head, making the costume complete. Virgil planned to begin playing the part of a blind man once they left the airship, and then they would be off on the next leg of their journey.

"I still don't understand why you need the hat," Dan-te asked as Virgil took a small pin out and checked to see if it was fashioned securely to the hat.

"Sun hats like these are common in both the Yellow and Green Dominions, wearing one will make me more unrecognizable. As for this little *addendum* Dan-te, it is going to be what gets us help along the way."

"Add a what," Dan-te asked, noticing Virgil just slipped a word of Platin, an old and nearly extinct Hy-mun language he spoke, into his comment.

"*Addendum*, it means 'an item to be added.' Trust me, you *Know* I know what I'm doing."

"That I do." Dan-te chuckled. She *Knew* that Virgil was telling the truth through her ability to *Know*. Virgil's words rang with truth like a gentle bell while he was pulsating blush honesty from his face. If he said the pin was going to get them some kind of help, then at the very least *he* believed it.

"I just hope you're right," Dan-te slightly fretted, not as confident as Virgil. *Considering what we are going up against we are going to need all the help we can get.* But, she also *Knew* that the pin Virgil fixed to his hat was no ordinary decoration, the moment he took it out of his pocket, a spark of white mental energy flashed over his head.

That pin has something to do with Virgil's past, Dan-te guessed. She *Knew* Virgil was still uncomfortable talking about his past and family. The little bit he did tell her, involving his friends with the Alien Astronaut Movement who were massacred by the Hammers of the Orange Light was hard enough, but much of his own personal history was still unknown to her. However, Virgil still generated the same blue energy of compassion, and the indigo energy of loyalty, from when they first met in Spectral Academy. Dan-te *Knew* he felt nothing but both those emotions toward her, and someone like that was not going to intentionally put them in harm's way regardless of what their family situation might be.

I just hope he'll soon be more comfortable with his past to tell me more about it, Dan-te thought until a voice came over the loudspeaker.

"Landing complete, all passengers please disembark, welcome to Wanton City in the Yellow Dominion."

"It's time to go Dan-te," Virgil said, putting on his sunglasses.

"Yes, it is," Dan-te agreed, disappearing back into Virgil's shadow and slightly tugging his hand, signaling him that she was ready to go. With the signal received, Vigil opened the cabin door and walked out with Dan-te invisible by his side into the main cabin of the airship, and then into the light of the Yellow Dominion.

The Yellow Dominion, for the most part, was a vast desert created when the Nag-el, the Ancient Tribe's Beings of Light, first arrived on Prism during "The Coming." The palaces making up the Dominion were scattered across it and determined by the location of the desert's few oases. The single main river, The Great Line River Ty-xs—or just the Great Line River as it was commonly called, started at the Grand Oasis (the location of the Citrine Ziggurat) and extended to the Grand Delta where Wanton City was located. The Grand Delta also contained the most fertile land found in the Yellow Dominion, making it the home for much of the Dominion's agricultural industry. Immediately after leaving the airship, Virgil and Dan-te were greeted by the Yellow Dominion's heat. Usually, the Veil of Shadows would not only have protected Dan-te from light but from the temperature as well, keeping her comfortable while in the Reversed State. But in its damaged state, she could feel every bit of it—made worse from actually *wearing* the Veil.

"How do you do it," Dan-te asked, panting from the heat, as they crossed through the checkpoints to the main terminal.

"Do what?" Virgil whispered in reply, trying not to draw attention to himself, in case anyone found it strange that a man—apparently alone—would be holding a conversation with himself. Or if a Tempter noticed them and realized that he was talking to Dan-te instead of being tempted by her.

"How do you put up with this heat? I *Know* that it's bothering you, so tell me how you put up with it?" Having grown up in the cold caves deep underground, with the only source of heat coming from either magma flows or heated springs, Dan-te never experienced the intense heat of the sun before— especially the desert sun. Collapsing for a second onto Virgil to steady herself,

Virgil hunched over a bit from her body weight, she took a few deep breaths until she was ready to go.

Virgil himself was not that much better. Dan-te could see the silver life energy slowly washing off him, feel its rippling rhythm as she steadied herself on Virgil's back, while the heat washed over both of them. She recognized the experience from other members of the Remnant, always when they were tired, strained, or extremely exhausted.

"It's simply mind over matter," Virgil answered. "As long as I don't mind, it doesn't matter. Besides, complaining only makes it worse." The Indigo Dominion where Virgil grew up might have been mostly islands, but those islands were far to the north and were often mild to cold year-round. It was also one of the other reasons why he stayed in his dorm room as much as he could, it was cooler there.

Dan-te, on the other hand, *Knew* that Virgil was being both serious and slightly humorous with his answer, the tone of his voice mixed with both funny and thoughtful sounds. She *Knew* that his response, in a strange way, made sense. Once Virgil mentioned the heat, he began emitting gray stressful energy, until he stopped talking about it. Trying it herself, she found that when she stopped mentally complaining about the heat and accepted it, it became a little more bearable.

"On a different note, how many Tempters are around?"

Dan-te quickly scanned the area, checking other passengers from the airship, as well as ground crews around it. She quickly realized something very peculiar.

"Virgil, there are almost no Tempters around us at all."

"Really," Virgil asked, confused because he remembered how many times Dan-te needed to use the "Tempter" keyword at Spectral Academy; as well as how many Tempters Dan-te later told him were around Minos Airship Port. For there to be almost no Tempters at the Wanton City Airship Port, which was bigger than Minos, did not seem to make any sense.

"Do you think something could have happened back in the city of Nis?" Virgil asked.

"Maybe," Dan-te whispered, unsure about the answer herself. "When I escaped, I left my brother Ice fighting in the Grand Coliseum alongside Reye. But the two of them alone couldn't have caused the amount of trouble needed for the Tribe of Shadows to recall almost all of their Tempters while we were flying on the airship, could they?"

Virgil's reply was a shrug of his shoulders and a flash of white mental energy and cream uncertainty from his head. He did not know what Reye could do any more than Dan-te, but he did know what was happening to her since she lost her brother. That kind of pain could drive people to lengths they have never gone before, a notion Dan-te quickly realized herself from Virgil's uncertainty.

"They're probably just recalling everyone before the start of the Third Great Attempt," Dan-te rattled.

"All the more reason for us to move," Virgil whispered, noticing a gap in the crowd, and making his way through it. "If they're getting ready to start the Attempt, we have to pick up our pace."

"So, what do we do now?" Dan-te asked.

"Once, we get through this last checkpoint, I can get into costume," Virgil replied, approaching the customs counter to give them formal entry into the Yellow Dominion. "After that, we take a city transport through Wanton City, and then on to the Hotel Avery. That's where we'll meet the sand ship that will take us to Tri-Dominion City. I just hope there aren't any other problems."

There were no other problems. The two of them not only walked through the rest of the of the port's custom counters and checkpoints without any trouble, but also without Dan-te spotting a single Tempter attached to anyone.

Something must *be going on back in Nis,* Dan-te thought to herself. *There should be Tempters here, there should* always *be Tempters on the surface. What could possibly be going on back there, are they preparing to start the Third Great Attempt, or have we run out of time and it's already started?* Dan-te quickly shook the thought from her head, if the Third Great Attempt *had* begun, they would know about it—along with everyone else on the surface. *It must be something else, they probably are just finishing their preparations.*

Passing the customs officer, Dan-te and Virgil entered the main terminal. Quickly finding an empty restroom, not an easy task, Virgil ducked into an empty handicap stall with Dan-te to get into his blind man costume. Taking off his shirt and pants, revealing a second pair underneath, he completely changed his outfit. Next, he folded all of his paper money into different shapes—letting him tell how much each one was worth without looking and putting his coins into the various pockets scattered within his new pants; that way it would look like he was reaching into any pocket he wanted for money without actually having to *look* for it. Finally, Virgil took out his dark wraparound sunglasses, and his decorated hat, and put them onto his face and head, finishing his disguise by extending his marked cane out in front of him.

"Are you ready Virgil?" Dan-te asked, retaking his hand as soon as Virgil finished putting his unneeded clothes back into his bag and slinging it across his back.

"I'm ready, let's go."

Virgil opened the door to the stall, tapping in front of himself with the cane as he walked to the door until it touched it. Feeling for the door with his hand, as if he really were blind, Virgil walked out of the restroom entirely in character.

"Wow," Dan-te whiffed, amazed by the change in the way the other Hy-muns reacted, or perhaps didn't react, once Virgil emerged in costume. *The Hy-muns, it's like Virgil's just become invisible to their own eyes. Or maybe it's actually the other way around, he's become so visible to them that he just vanishes from their recognition. I Know Hy-muns are aware of the other Hy-muns around them, even if they don't focus or talk to one another. It's the same with us in the Remnant; there is always a slight amount of latent energy, a brief acknowledgment, a way of saying, "I see you as a being." But once Virgil started walking among the other Hy-mun, portraying the image of being blind, that small bit of energy simply disappeared.*

From the moment Virgil walked out of the restroom and back into the main terminal, Dan-te noticed a sudden and instant sense of both recognition and avoidance from every other Hy-mun in the area. The energy directed toward Virgil first acknowledged his presence, but that was all it did. All the other energies slid off him like water over a rock immediately afterward, Virgil was now less Hy-mun and more "object to be avoided." Dan-te quickly realized what this meant, what the other Hy-muns were doing was *not* noticing, or even being aware of "Virgil the Hy-mun" at all. He just vanished from the presence of everyone, slipping into a place between existent and nonexistent, leaving only an obstacle to dodge. Virgil, however, was carrying on confidently. Generating pearl colored energy of confidence, he moved through the crowds as naturally as if it was how he had always done it.

This can't be the first time that he's pulled this trick, Dan-te guessed. The energy he was generating was not just confidence, there was also a powder calm energy mixed with it. It was not sharp and erratic from fear, stress, or anger—like how she felt Reye's horrible red energy. Nor was it vastly overflowing, or turning teal pride, the way it had when the Ancient Seat of Humility had died and become the First Pride. Dan-te *Knew* that Virgil had been trained to do this a long time ago, and he had done it before to get out of trouble. His confidence came from experience.

"So how many times have you done this before?" Dan-te finally asked once the crowds started to thin at the entrance to the terminal.

"Quite a few actually. My mother often said, 'abundans cautela non nocet,' that means 'abundant caution does no harm.' She wanted me to learn the quickest ways I could *disappear* if I ever ran into trouble, and this was one of the handiest." Virgil allowed himself a smirk thinking about how often people would walk right by him, believing him to be blind, never guessing he actually had 20/10 vision. "By now, you've already *Known* how Hy-muns—thankfully not all Hy-muns—generally view someone who's physically incapacitated. That's why this makes for such an effective disguise."

Dan-te did, and Virgil was right; his new persona was an excellent disguise. The other Hy-muns quickly ignored them, blotted them out of their minds, wherever they went. As for the few Tempters on the surface, they did not bother to glance at them.

The few Tempters that are still around probably think I am being punished, Dan-te thought to herself. While it was true that Tempters *usually* didn't bother Hy-muns with disabilities, it did not mean they left them alone. She had heard that they sometimes went after them when they were being disciplined.

Virgil, however, played the part of a blind Hy-mun perfectly. Tapping his cane in front of him to make sure his path was clear, he looked like he had done it for most of his life. He probably would have kept walking, oblivious to everyone around him, until he let the cane bump against a signpost. Reaching out with his free hand, he began rubbing the post, feeling a series of dots and bumps at the bottom of the sign.

Those markings on the sign must mean something, Dan-te realized. She *Knew* that while Virgil was focusing on the sign's words, which said that the transport to the Hotel Avery would arrive here every ten minutes, he was also fixed on its markings. Virgil's white mental energy popped around his head as his hand rubbed each pattern. It did not take Dan-te long to realize that he was reading it the same way he read the sign's words. Once he took his hand off the sign, Virgil walked over to a bench, tapping with his cane all the way, and then sat down with Dan-te at his side.

"Those dots on the sign," Dan-te whispered, "were they some kind of writing?"

"Yes," Virgil answered. "It's a type of writing called LB script. It was invented for blind people so they could read and write. Once we board the transport and get through Wanton City to the Hotel Avery, we'll be able to get a sand ship—that's a special kind of ship built to hover above and travel long distances across the dessert—that will take us to Tri-Dominion City where we can start making our way back underground. Actually, I think I hear the transport coming now."

This transport looks like some kind of weird combination of a carriage, train, and boat. All propelled by a massive fan behind it, Dan-te thought to herself as the vehicle stopped before them. When the conductor noticed Virgil in his disguise, he walked directly over to him and put his hand on Virgil's shoulder.

"Are you going to the Hotel Avery?" the conductor asked.

"I am," Virgil answered. "Could you please lead me somewhere I can sit?"

Never taking his hand off Virgil's shoulder, the conductor led Virgil to a private area with marked seats sectioned off at the front of the transport; Dan-te, maintaining her invisibility, never left Virgil's side or let go of his hand. Once the conductor took the destination fare from Virgil, he left them alone. The rest of the passengers boarded the transport soon afterward, taking seats throughout the vehicle. After that, it began hovering slightly in the air, moving away from Minos Airship Port and into Wanton City.

Chapter 2

The transport moved steadily through Wanton City. Special lanes allowed only it and others like it to move relatively unrestricted from the regular traffic of Hy-muns and vehicles that crowed the streets. Yet even though they were traveling quickly through the city, Virgil hadn't heard Dan-te whisper "Tempter" to him once since they left the airship. Virgil could also feel Dan-te's hand tremble as her grip tightened the more they made their way through the city.

"What's wrong Dan-te?" Virgil whispered. "You're nervous about something. Are you worried about what could be going on back in Nis since we haven't seen any Tempters, is it that we're just not moving fast enough, or both? You've had to realize by now, but this is the fastest way to travel through Wanton City. If we tried using the regular traffic routes or just walked, it would take us two to three times the length of time needed to get to the sand ship."

"It's not that," Dan-te replied. "Well, not *entirely* that, I do wish we could move faster, and I am worried about why I haven't seen any Tempters and what could be going on back in Nis. But right now, I just want to get out of *this city* as fast we can."

"Oh," Virgil replied, as the simple answer behind Dan-te's trembling hit him so hard he realized he should have guessed it sooner. Virgil remembered that Dan-te, after passing through both Spectral Academy and the Platinum Throne, described them as, "a gloomy, stressful place that lacked belief," and that the experience was slightly disturbing for her. At the time, he had worried about how she might react to *Knowing* the rest of the Hy-mun world on their journey. Now, as they were traveling through another Hy-mun city, Wanton City, she seemed to be reacting to it even worse than before.

"How do you *Know* this city? It's different from the way that I do, isn't it? If so, tell me what's wrong with it. Please don't keep it to yourself."

Dan-te waited for a moment before answering. "Tell me, how do you *Know* it," Dan-te asked.

"I have always known it as a bustling city," Virgil answered, peering out the window through the corner of his eye to the streets crowded with Hy-muns and other vehicles moving throughout the city. Since he was playing the part of a blind Hy-mun, Virgil did not dare look directly out of the window, he did not want anyone to think he could actually see.

"Back in the outer sections of the city, you'll find shops for almost all of the businesses which are found throughout the city. People come here from all across the continent and the Platinum Throne to trade, conduct business, and also to have fun. Right now, we are moving through the busiest parts of the city, home of the best amusement centers on the continent. Hy-muns of all ages gather here to have one kind of fun or another. Those reasons are why *anyone* decides to come to Wanton City. You see, Wanton City is one of the newer cities to develop following the devastation of the Great Rainbow War. The buildings are mostly constructed out of the stones excavated while cultivating the Grand Delta. They reach about five to seven floors in height, and they don't show any outward signs of destruction that other cities do. The roads, for the most part, might be unpaved, but they're still not blown open and full of both holes and repair crews. Transports, like this one, are able to move on specially constructed lanes that were part of the city design instead of using the normal streets, so people are able to move relativity easy from place to place, instead of being delayed by normal traffic and reconstruction teams fixing the battle damage."

Virgil had already visited Wanton City before, so he was not surprised about the scenery as he passed by. All of the activity and energy he remembered from his last visit was still here, and as he saw the other Hy-muns enter and exit the transport at its various stops, he could still feel some of that energy. Dan-te, however, was another matter entirely. Virgil found her grip tightening, and her trembling getting worse. He could tell that she was becoming increasingly disturbed over how she *Knew* the place.

"It's lustful," Dan-te finally said. "This place, it's even more lustful than the Third Circle of the city of Nis, Lust Atrophied. Everywhere is a storming torrent of lustful rosy energy."

Lust Atrophied, Dan-te remembered. *All the female members of the Tribe of Shadows are kept there so the males can mate with them to produce offspring. When Ice and I were taken through there, the first thing that hit me, harder than any gladiator, was the intensity of the rosy energy of lust beating throughout the circle. The energy alone felt like it was pounding me relentlessly, which I know is a strange yet appropriate comparison considering what goes on in that circle. I actually was almost separated from Ice so that I could be turned into a breeder when I passed through that circle. Thankfully the Warden rejected me because "the Rodent doesn't possess the right qualifications for a breeder," meaning they didn't want to take a member of the Remnant unless she physically appealed to them. Thankfully, because of that, I could stay with Ice all the way to Wrath Eras.*

Virgil couldn't see Dan-te while she was veiled, but he could feel her hand trembling violently in his. After hearing Dan-te compare Wanton City to Lust Atrophied, it did not take much imagination to figure out what was making her so nervous.

According to the Stories of Rill, the stories about Lord Tanas's appearance and the growth of the Tribe of Shadows, the Tribe of Shadows—then the Greater Tribe—established the practice of forced and rapid breeding after both "The Coming" and the two Tribes' separation. However, it was under Tanas's leadership that it took on the newer and more extreme measures that led to the establishment of Lust Atrophied. When Dan-te first told me those stories, I actually wasn't too surprised about them, a fact she quickly noticed. I had to explain to her that in the Alien Astronaut Movement, one thing we talked about was what could happen in the event we found the Nag-el, and they turned out to be hostile.

"Oh, they're hostile," Dan-te, had mockingly laughed out loud.

I told her some of us tossed out ideas about how we could adapt, and one of the ideas that came up was breeding; combating the new, invasive, species by making sure that there was more of the native one. The Tribe of Shadows seemed to have the same idea. Still, I don't understand how Wanton City could be compared to a place like Lust Atrophied, especially the way Dan-te described it.

"How is Wanton City more lustful than Lust Atrophied?" Virgil asked, the question now burning in his mind. "I don't doubt that you *Know* it is lustful, but I don't understand why. Nor do I understand the comparison; this city isn't full of Hy-muns coupling with each other indiscriminately to make more Hy-muns, so how does it compare to the Third Circle of Nis?"

Dan-te *Knew* Virgil was trying to understand, but could not, the question of "why" burning in his head with white mental energy. She also *Knew* that he didn't *Know* Wanton City to be a lustful place. Virgil's own energy did not change to a lustful rosy color, a transformation she noticed on both the Hy-muns leaving the transport and the ones on the street. If anything, Virgil's energy—like all the other Hy-muns' energies—felt lighter and more energized from the energy, sounds, and smells surrounding him; but the city was not a distraction for him. Virgil knew they were only passing through on the way back to Nis, and that getting to Nis in hopes of stopping the Third Great Attempt was the important thing. Yet she could not help recognize the same transformative reaction to the ambient lustful energy, a response she *Knew* in Lust Atrophied and needed to make Virgil understand—if she could.

"The people," Dan-te began. "The people are a torrent of the same rosy lustful energy that I *Knew* throughout Lust Atrophied. Just like the Tribe of Shadows' energy, it's erupting from the Hy-muns surrounding us, propelling them from building to building, place to place, and fueled by nothing more than pure lustful desires, charging and saturating the air itself. But unlike the energy in Lust Atrophied, the energy isn't locked in a self-contained kingdom, it's free. All the different energies of lust are spiraling together in a seemingly never-ending vortex. Pushing Hy-muns further into lust and turning them around toward newer lusts.

Reunions, Reflections, and Reconciliations

"Some of the Hy-muns are lusting after new food and tastes, others for thrills, and others—like the Tribe of Shadows in Lust Atrophied—for the pleasures of the body. But that ever-present rosy lustful energy is like an infesting wind, blowing throughout the city in response to its inhabitants' lustful desires, infecting Hy-muns, and changing their energies to match the surroundings. It's no different from what I witnessed in the gladiatorial pits and halls of Lust Atrophied. Warriors and spectators alike, radiating with an infectious rosy lust for combat, for women afterward—almost always for women, and the desire to satisfy that lust. Only now, it's everywhere, not just in one contained circle, and no one seems to be able to resist being affected by it, not even…"

Dan-te stopped abruptly, realizing what she was about to say. Virgil never interrupted her. Not only for the sake of his disguise, but he could tell from her voice that this was hard for her to relate, so he wanted to make sure he paid attention to every word. He also realized what she was about to say before she stopped herself.

Not even me? Virgil thought, glancing out at the city again, and his reflection in the glass, trying to imagine how Dan-te must *Know* the people, Wanton City, and his own reactions to it. *If I could* Know *like Dan-te, would I* Know *Wanton City the way she does, or would I* Know *it more the same way that the Tribe of Shadows* Knows *their Lust Atrophied? If I came here on a regular vacation, would I change and appear no different than any other Hy-mun walking the streets now?*

While Virgil doubted that Wanton City and Lust Atrophied were *exactly* alike, he did try imagining how they could have been the same in the way Dan-te *Knew* them to be.

The definitions of "lust" are either "sexual desire" or "eagerness." The former description doesn't seem to have much bearing on the outer appearance of Wanton City, Virgil realized, thinking a little harder about both the second definition, and the way Dan-te *Knew* things. *But the people are definitely eager, and for many reasons. Remember, the way Dan-te* Knows *something, or someone, isn't just based on the outward sight and appearances alone. It's also based on smells, tastes in the air, sounds, and the energy radiating off it; which she, the Remnant of the Tribe, and the Tribe of Shadows can see with the intentions drawn from those emissions based on her own skill at reading those emissions.*

Virgil thought back to some of his previous visits to Wanton City. To say that the people were eager about what they were doing was an accurate description for the Hy-muns who lived and visited there every day. Virgil understood that eagerness as just a part of city life, never once thinking of it as being lustful. He always associated lust with the type of actions and behaviors that would have been most common in Nis's Third Circle of Lust Atrophied, especially the way Dan-te described it. However, Virgil had also come to understand Dan-te's abilities to *Know* as being far more accurate than any Hy-mun perceptions could ever be. The more he thought about it, and the more he tried to picture what it was that Dan-te was both seeing and *Knowing*, the more he realized how little he might have understood about his own people and how much in common they might have with the Tribe of Shadows.

Dan-te is Knowing *lust,* Virgil told himself, trying to Know the same way as Dan-te. *But for her, it's manifesting itself physically through energy, intentions, and her own reading of it. Unlike me, who is trying to picture lust in my mind. Throughout Wanton City, Hy-muns are moving left and right and going wherever their fancy takes them. Dan-te is* Knowing *that lust through their bodily desires and intentions. To her, the emotion is radiating off them, just like Reye's horrible red energy, and letting her read it like a lit-up sign. If the Hy-mun lust is that powerful, more powerful than the lust the Tribe of Shadows displays following their own desires in Lust Atrophied, how much more alike could we be? I just wish I could understand.*

"You are understanding," Dan-te said to Virgil, knocking him out of his contemplation.

"Yes, I am," Virgil snorted in slight amusement. "I understand that you *Know* Hy-muns to be more lustful then I do, something I should have already been aware of."

Virgil realized he could understand all he wanted to, but it still would not allow him to *Know* things the way that Dan-te could; that was her ability alone. He also realized that if Wanton City could produce this much of a similarity to Nis for Dan-te, then the difference in how she would *Know* things on the surface would be at best different from the way that Hy-muns perceived them, and at worse as an upgraded version of the Tribe of Shadows.

I need to get Dan-te home sooner rather than later, Virgil thought to himself, considering what might still happen on their journey. *The longer that she stays on the surface, witnessing Hy-mun civilization, the more culturally shocked she could become. I can't let anything happen to her until she's safely back home.*

"I can handle being shocked, Virgil," Dan-te whispered quickly, catching Virgil off guard. "I *Know* that you're worried about me. Your mind is sparking with mental white, and fearful pink energy, both directed at me, so I can tell you are worried and scared for me. I'm not going to pass out or faint over anything like this. No matter what I've seen up until now, it's still *nothing* compared to the city of Nis and its gladiatorial arenas. Fighting in those areas, from the First Circle of Maestri to the Grand Coliseum in Wrath Eras, I think have made me more than tough enough to take anything, including whatever arenas you Hy-muns could cook up."

Virgil felt a little relieved over Dan-te's assurance that she would be alright, but he did not overlook the fact she said "I think" instead of "I know." He also realized, moving through the bulk of Wanton City and toward the Hotel Avery, that they still had a long way to go. Anything could go wrong with either one of them before this journey was over. Regardless, Virgil knew he had to make sure that he was always there to look after Dan-te as long as she was in his care, whether she thought she needed it or not, and he did not mind if she *Knew* it as well.

Chapter 3

The Hotel Avery, one of the bigger hotels in Wanton City, acted not only as a hotel but also as a port for sand ships. Resting right where the delta met the desert, the ships regularly came and went to both the mountains of the Violet Dominion and Tri-Dominion City. The hotel also boasted a singular marquis that no other hotel in Wanton City possessed; three beast-like heads on either side and above the main entrance, each one with a sign next to it with a speech bubble in it saying that they "wanted you to stay" and would "chase all crooks away." The transport carrying Dan-te and Virgil to the Hotel Avery arrived with just enough time for them to be guided through the hotel to the sand ship port on its opposite side. Virgil, helped off the transport by the conductor, with Dan-te veiled and invisible next to him, was led to a waiting area near the marquis where an attendant from the hotel would come and lead them to the port.

"If these heads are supposed to make Hy-muns feel secure, I have mixed opinions on their effectiveness," Dan-te whispered, looking up at the beast-head marquis and into the main lobby of the hotel. The figure made her uneasy, a lingering taint of hateful red and tawny brown colored energy of greed from its creators was wrapped around it as it looked down upon Dan-te. On one level it did make her feel like it "wanted her to stay," but she could not tell whether as a guest or a captive; and on another, she definitely felt threatened by it, regardless of what it was.

"They're not supposed to be scary," Virgil whispered in reply. "They're just for decoration, pay them no mind."

Dan-te tried to ignore them, but it was hard. Thankfully, she was distracted by a female Hy-mun in a uniform walking up to them with a stack of papers in her arms.

This Hy-mun is generating so much stress I'm surprised the Tribe of Shadows isn't *around to capitalize on her.* The female Hy-mun was pulsating with grey stressful energy, so much that it seemed that any spark, regardless of the source, might set her off. As she approached them, she quickly straightened herself up, put on a smile Dan-te could tell was forced, and began to act cheerful, only creating more internal stress for herself in the process.

"Can I help you, sir," the Hy-mun asked, putting her hand on Virgil's shoulder to let him know she was talking to him.

"Could you please take me to the sand ship port?" Virgil asked in reply, immediately placing his cane hand on top of the other Hy-mun's hand so it would look like he was feeling for whoever touched him.

"Allow me to take you, sir," the Hy-mun said, taking Virgil's hand and leading him to the entrance of a long hallway. "We will have to walk straight from here. We will pass the mud baths, the gym, and the sports arena." Virgil felt a slight grip on his hand from Dan-te at the mention of "arena."

"You'll no doubt be able to smell the mud baths; the Hotel Avery supports some of the finest facilities in Wanton City. You will also be able to hear the arena, there is a wrestling match going on today, and the audience is just as feisty as ever. Once we are past the arena, we'll reach the doors leading out of the hotel. There is a station there—for someone in your condition—where you can wait for the next sand ship. Just don't let go of me and try to ignore the noise."

The noise was about the only thing Virgil and Dan-te *could not* ignore. From the moment the Hy-mun led them into the hotel they were bombarded with noise from guests, machines, and other uniformed Hy-muns like the one leading them now—all under extreme stress.

"And I thought the Hy-muns back at Spectral Academy were under stress," Dan-te whispered as they walked down the hallway. "The Hy-muns who work here make the stress they were under seem like nothing."

"I doubt it could be helped," Virgil whispered in reply and resignation. "Concierges, porters, and all matter of hotel staff like the usher directing us now deal with hundreds of people day after day, so it often makes them overly stressed. After that, dealing with a 'blind man' is just one more aggravation."

"Is there a problem sir?"

"None at all," Virgil quickly replied, realizing that his and Dan-te's conversation was being overheard despite the din from the hotel. "Just mumbling about how you must deal with hundreds of people day after day, it must make you overly stressed."

"You learn to live with it," the usher answered. "If you can't, you won't last very long in this industry. Now please maintain contact with me, we'll be reaching the mud baths soon, and it gets crowded there. You *do not* want to get lost."

Virgil simply nodded in reply as the usher continued to take them through the hotel.

Dan-te *Knew* that the usher was concerned for him, she generated the same blue caring energy that Virgil did; but with it was so much grey stress, tinted with crimson anger, that she was not surprised by the slightly hostile tone in her voice.

This usher is worried about Virgil, Dan-te thought to herself. *But she can't hide the intimidating nature in her voice. Are mud baths really so terrifying a place that we have to be threatened to avoid getting lost in them? Or is this usher merely reaching a point where she won't last much longer in this hotel?*

Virgil, on the other hand, was not letting the noise from the hotel or any of the usher's stress or anger get to him—nor could he allow it to. Even when their conversation came close to being overheard, he was able to quickly cover it up.

And he didn't even lie when he did it. Dan-te thought to herself, slightly amazed by Virgil's quick thinking. *He said he was mumbling about how she handled hundreds of people every day and the stress that went with it, and that is precisely what we were talking about.*

Dan-te *Knew* that Virgil's current focus was to get to the port and from there to their next destination. They both knew there were far more important matters that they needed to take care of, so becoming distracted because of something as minuscule as an overly stressed usher would be a waste of their time. Still, the usher's warning did bring a question to Dan-te's mind, one she realized she had to ask. "So, what is a 'mud bath,'" Dan-te whispered, wanting to know what it was before they reached it and wondering why she would feel threatened about it.

"You'll see, or perhaps you'll *smell* soon enough," Virgil replied, a bit quieter this time to reduce the chance that they would be overheard again. "Mud baths have a particular odor to them that you'll be able to smell once we get close enough."

Virgil was right. Just after he finished talking, the usher led them through a set of sealed doors. A strange odor quickly filled the air, becoming all-consuming as Virgil and Dan-te walked out onto an overpass overlooking the Hotel Avery Mud Bath.

The mud bath was huge. The overpass that Dan-te, Virgil, and the usher were walking on took them over a segment of the hotel dedicated entirely to the mud bath. Everywhere they looked, Hy-muns were bathing, getting out, or into the mud bath.

"That smell," Dan-te whispered, her face twisting from the bath's fumes.

"The mud that makes up our baths comes from volcanic ash, peat, and partially decayed plants, which are mixed with mineral water," the usher explained, leading Virgil down the overpass and explaining the mud bath to him as if he were just another tourist. Virgil simply nodded at the usher's commentary as they walked, trying to be polite and attentive, but he was worried about something else. Even though he could not see her, Virgil could tell that Dan-te was troubled. Her hand was tightening and trembling from the moment they entered the bath. It was not only the smell of the mud bath that was bothering her, it was also something else. She was *Knowing* the mud bath as something else.

"Decaying plants and ash, Hy-muns enjoy sitting in this rotting filth and mire?" Dan-te whispered again with a gasp. For her, the baths were a cesspool of mossy green, decaying brown, and sickly yellow energy—three colors of spiritual and physical decay—given form, and the smells from the bath were filled with just as much rot and decay. As for the Hy-muns in the bath, they were just as rotten. Each of them emitted gluttonous dark-green energy as they continued to happily wallow in the sludge around them, unable to get enough of it.

"Personally, I don't get the reasoning behind why Hy-muns enjoy mud baths either," Virgil responded.

"Would you like to know the reason why our guests enjoy mud baths?" the usher asked, turning around to face Virgil.

"If you could," Virgil politely answered, silently chastising himself for letting their conversation be overheard again. *This usher has* excellent *hearing, I guess she needs it to hear the guests calling to her in this hotel.*

"Most of the reasons are for medical purposes," the usher explained. "The mud baths remove stress from the body, detoxify it, soften the occupants' skin, and improve their blood circulation. But there are also mental reasons as well. I'm confident you don't know many people who could say that they bathed in mud before."

"No, I don't," Virgil answered kindly with a chuckle. He had already heard some of those reasons before, but still, the idea of sitting in mud and bathing oneself in it seemed more like the kind of thing that a farm animal would do; and *not* something he would do.

"Well you just met someone who does," a haughty voice bellowed from behind them.

Virgil quickly turned around, tapping his cane in a gesture to look for the source of the voice that just spoke to him, and suddenly discovering that it came from a portly man in a robe—partly covered in mud—who must have come from the bath. But for the sake of maintaining his blind act, Virgil continued to act like he could not see or figure out where his voice was coming from.

"I'm just behind you on your left," the man said again, allowing Virgil to tap him with his cane and grasp a dirty outstretched hand.

"Ha ha ha," the man laughed with a snort. "I appreciate the gesture of politeness and courtesy, but if holding a muddied hand is weird for you then you can let go."

Thank you, Virgil thought to himself, quickly letting go and rubbing the mud off his hand. Virgil knew that the man's hand was muddy before he grasped it, but for the sake of his disguise he could not let on that he knew that.

"And you Miss Janney, it's not often that I see a pretty young lady like yourself in this part of the Hotel Avery."

"And for a good reason, Mr. Ciacco," Miss Janney, the usher, replied. "Whenever you and your business cohorts stay here you almost exclusively spend your time either in our mud bath or our gym facilities. Now, if you don't mind, I need to take this gentleman to the sand ship port."

"Then it's lucky for all of us," Mr. Ciacco bellowed. "I am also heading in that direction. I have a workout scheduled at those beautiful gym facilities you just mentioned, and I am making my way there now. The three of us can go together."

"Of course," Miss Janney replied, smiling courtly. "Right this way, sir."

"You are a Nag-el," Mr. Ciacco joked, taking up a position on Miss Janney's side opposite to Virgil and Dan-te. "And as for you young one, I didn't get your name."

"Woody," Virgil answered using an alias that he decided on while he and Dan-te were still on the way to Wanton City.

"Well, Woody, you really should try the mud bath the next time when you are here if you have the time. They do wonders for you. Also, there are plenty of people among the hotel staff who would gladly help someone with a condition like yours so you can safely enjoy one."

"I'll consider it," Virgil replied, trying to be polite, and to not be affected by the smell coming from Mr. Ciacco, now that he was standing next to them. Virgil did not notice it at first, but Mr. Ciacco stank of the mud bath—if it perhaps was not his own natural odor, and he did not need to see to know that their usher, Miss Janney, was even more disturbed by his presence than anything else.

I can only imagine what Dan-te must be Knowing about Mr. Ciacco, Virgil thought to himself as the group of them passed over the mud bath. Dan-te had become silent ever since she asked him about how Hy-muns could enjoy wallowing in a mud bath. However, he still felt her steady grip on his hand, tightening ever so slightly the more they continued onward.

I'll bet she wants to talk but is afraid we might be overheard again, Virgil realized, remembering how they had already been heard twice now. Looking out of the corners of his eyes, Virgil watched as Mr. Ciacco swaggered heartily on the other side of Miss Janney, Dan-te, and himself.

At least he seemed good-natured, although a bit large and stinky, but a good-natured one none the less. So why do I feel threatened?

Virgil could not shake a slight feeling of uneasiness from having Mr. Ciacco around, and he was sure Miss Janney was uncomfortable around him; he was making glances at her every chance he could get.

"Excuse me, Miss Janney," Virgil finally snapped, stopping mid-stride. "Is there anywhere coming up where I can relieve myself?"

"Of course!" Miss Janney exclaimed, a bit more happily than Virgil would have expected. "There is a lavatory just around the corner with special facilities just for you."

Miss Janney led them to an alcove with three doors, and opening the one in the middle, she herded Virgil inside.

"I'll be waiting right out here until you're done. Mr. Ciacco, why don't you continue on, you don't want to miss your gym appointment."

"Nonsense," Mr. Ciacco laughed. "I have time before my appointment. I'll stay out here and keep you company."

"Thank you," Miss Janney replied sarcastically, closing the lavatory door behind Virgil and Dan-te, leaving the two of them alone. Virgil did not need to use it but found his way over to the urinal and began acting like he was going to use it in case there were any cameras in the lavatory. What he wanted was a private place where he could talk without being overheard again.

"Are you okay Dan-te?"

"No, not exactly," Dan-te whispered, her voice trembling as she talked. "I'm still on my feet, sorry about not warning you about that other Hy-mun, Ciacco, approaching us. But after realizing that the usher, Miss Janney, could hear you whispering to me, I didn't want to take another chance talking to you until we were someplace private. That said, is there any way you could have thought of a better place for us to hide, especially from that oversized glutton Ciacco, then here?"

Walking through the mud bath, ripe with its scents of decaying plants and volcanic ash, mixed with the different energies of physical and spiritual decay— peppered by gluttony—left her more nauseous then she wanted to admit. Being pulled into, what Miss Janney had called a lavatory filled with the lingering odors of urine, excrement, and vomit was one of the last places she would have wanted to be.

"I'm sorry Dan-te," Virgil puffed. "This was the only place I could think of. At least it's private."

"Mr. Woody, are you all right in there," Miss Janney called, knocking at the door. "I thought I heard you talking to yourself. Are you all right?"

"Nuts, she has good hearing," Dan-te and Virgil whispered together, sharing a brief laugh together immediately afterward.

"Yeah, are you okay in there?" Mr. Ciacco also asked.

"I'm okay," Virgil answered back. "I just take a while in the lavatory, talking to myself often helps me."

"That oversized glutton trailing us definitely likes to hear himself talk," Dan-te slightly hissed. "Do you think there is a way we can get rid of him?"

"Mr. Ciacco? No, I think we're stuck with him until we get to the gym."

"Great," Dan-te puffed, not even trying to hide her displeasure over his following them. The tone in her voice and the way she called him a glutton all told Virgil the same thing, that Dan-te *Knew* Mr. Ciacco to be a very different person than the happy-go-lucky Hy-mun that he presented himself to be.

"Dan-te, how do you *Know* Mr. Ciacco? All I can tell about him is that he seems to be some form of businessman, a bit fat for his size, boastful, definitely lacks a few manners—he couldn't even clean his hand before shaking with it— and he obviously makes Miss Janney uncomfortable; I figured that out right from the start. But how do you *Know* him? I am guessing that there is more to him then what I am seeing."

"There is," Dan-te whispered directly to get her point across as clearly as possible. "I *Know* this Hy-mun, Mr. Ciacco, is definitely a glutton to the bone, and it's not just because of his size. There is a storm of gluttonous dark-green energy pulsing and swirling around him forming a monstrously hoggish form. Then there's the smell, and I'm not just talking about the mud, all that does is try to cover it. It's his breath, it reeks of dead plants and rotting flesh. He's a Hy-mun that eats and continues eating, everything he can as ravenously as possible. Not just food either, but also people, trusts, relationships, and resources; he would devour them all and excrete them like they were just rotten waste. It's the reason why Miss Janney is so uncomfortable around him and has been trying to get away from him, or just make him move on of his own accord.”

“She’s aware of Mr. Ciacco’s ‘true intentions?’”

“Indeed, when we met him, Mr. Ciacco acted like he was playfully flirting with Miss Janney, but there wasn’t a note of honesty anywhere in his words or actions, and she was completely aware of it. The moment Mr. Ciacco saw her, his gluttonous energy flared up even more as he started projecting it toward her, while her own stressful grey energy rolled around her forming a shell to keep him out. The truth is, Mr. Ciacco doesn’t want anything to do with Miss Janney, beyond devouring her and throwing her away, and she is *completely* aware of that. In fact, almost all the Hy-muns in that mire you called a mud bath were not that much different from Mr. Ciacco.”

Virgil did not try to challenge Dan-te’s comments, he knew he could not. Dan-te’s way of perceiving, of *Knowing*, went far beyond the surface perceptions that he, as a Hy-mun, was accustomed to, or the body mannerism and speech tones that he knew a person could learn to identify to tell what another Hy-mun might be feeling. Virgil also did not try to question Dan-te’s estimation of Mr. Ciacco for one other reason as well, because he did not doubt she was right.

How many men, like Mr. Ciacco, did my brother and me secretly watch our father meet over the years? Virgil thought to himself, thinking back to before he joined the AAM when he and his brother spied on their father and his dealings with the various businessmen who met him. Dan-te also *Knew* that Virgil was thinking about what she had said about Mr. Ciacco, the Hy-muns they passed in the mud bath, and something in the past too—his drifting white mental energy told her that much at least. However, all of their thoughts were suddenly broken as Mr. Ciacco suddenly knocked on the door.

“Hey! You okay in there?” he bellowed.

“I’m fine,” Virgil answered, turning around to face the door. “I’m coming out now.”

Feeling Dan-te’s hand in his own, Virgil and Dan-te left the lavatory and rejoined Mr. Ciacco and Miss Janney.

Chapter 4

"Do you always take that much time in the restroom?"

Mr. Ciacco's mode had turned inquisitive ever since Virgil and Dan-te had rejoined them, and the four of them had restarted their walk through the mud bath section of the hotel. Virgil was polite with his answers, but Dan-te *Knew* from the tone of his voice and the slivers of stressful grey energy he was producing that his patience was beginning to wear thin.

"As I told you before Mr. Ciacco," Virgil explained again. "I just have trouble relieving myself."

"You should see someone for that, or simply eat more rich foods. I can tell you from experience they make the digestion process a whole lot easier."

"I'll think about it," Virgil answered again as their group came to another set of self-sealing doors like the ones they passed through to enter the mud bath area. With a whoosh, Miss Janney and Mr. Ciacco both pushed the doors open, and all of them were soon out of the mud bath area and into a long hallway partitioned by a long pane of glass. On the opposite side were weight machines, barbells, treadmills, stair machines, and dozens of other types of exercise equipment.

"Well, this is my destination, the Hotel Avery Gym," Mr. Ciacco laughed, walking away from the group and toward a door in the glass separating the hall from the gym; Miss Janney exhaled a long-held breath the moment he started walking away. Virgil and Dan-te also noticed the change in their usher. Virgil could feel her grip relaxing as soon as Mr. Ciacco walked away and Dan-te quickly noticed her energy becoming more comfortable and less erratic.

"Plutus is going to be starting his workout sessions soon, I just have enough time to say hello to a few friends before he begins. Mr. Woody, it was a pleasure meeting you, just stick close to Miss Janney and you'll reach the sand ship port in no time. All you have to do is keep walking down the hall alongside the gym, and you'll eventually reach the sports arena, you'll know you're there from the noise the crowds are making in it, behind that is the sand ship port. Have a safe journey." Mr. Ciacco then went through the door and left Virgil and Dan-te alone with Miss Janney.

"Well, he was an interesting person to have along with us," Miss Janney stated, clearly happy that they were finally rid of him. "It's time to continue on, your ship won't be there forever."

Matching Miss Janney's pace, Virgil and Dan-te quickly walked down the hallway. Even though he had Miss Janney guiding him, Virgil continued tapping his cane in front of him to continue his illusion by making sure that the way was clear. But no sooner had the two of them started walking again, then he could hear Dan-te whispering to him.

"I'm sorry, Virgil, I know that if you reply Miss Janney is going to hear you, and the last thing we want is another curious onlooker like Mr. Ciacco, but what do Hy-muns use this gym for?"

Virgil could tell that Dan-te's whisper was pleading. He realized that she must either *Know* the gym or the Hy-muns inside, as something different entirely then how he knew them. However, he did not want to leave Dan-te wondering what was going on around her, nor did he want to try the bathroom idea again. Thinking fast, he came up with a solution. "Excuse me, Miss Janney," Virgil asked, turning his attention to Miss Janney. "How big is this gym, and how many different functions does it serve?"

"Our gym here at the Hotel Avery is one of the biggest and most advanced in Wanton City," Miss Janney replied, switching gears slightly from usher to tour guide, and making Virgil extremely grateful that he guessed right, that she would answer just about any question about the hotel.

"Our patrons use the gym, its equipment, and our staff and professional trainers—like Mr. Plutus, the trainer Mr. Ciacco was talking about—to develop their bodies into whatever goal they might have set for themselves. Whether their goal is losing weight, or reaching the best physical state of their lives. Does that answer your question?

"It does," Virgil replied. "Thank you for answering my question about 'how do you *know* it?'"

Miss Janney looked at Virgil oddly for a moment, but quickly shook off his reply and continued leading him down the hall. Dan-te, however, did not miss the way Virgil asked, "How do you *know* it," nor did she miss the way he squeezed her hand when he asked the question. She knew *that* question wasn't meant for Miss Janney, but for her.

"This gym is a den of greed," Dan-te whispered to Virgil, continuing to walk alongside him, watching the room pulse with tawny brown greed. "The Hy-muns inside, they're just erupting with so much greed I don't know how this one room can contain them and keep them from rushing out and trying to acquire what they don't have. They're greedy not just for what they want, but for the means to get it, too. Do you see the group over there, coming up on our right, pushing up those heavy stones?"

Virgil shifted his gaze slightly to the right and quickly found the Hy-muns Dan-te was referring to. She spotted some weight lifters doing bench presses and using freestyle weights, each one lifting massive weights, Dan-te's "heavy stones," up against their bodies and over their heads.

A number of those weight lifters have got to be lifting more than their own body weight, Virgil guessed, looking at the lifts, mentally estimating the total weight of some of them, and imagining how much the weight lifters lifting them must have weighed.

"Those Hy-mun already have more than they need, but they are still greedy for more. Each one of them is radiating tawny brown greed; an avarice that desires more wealth, better bodies, more of everything. They are almost the same as the Hy-muns in the mud bath we passed earlier emitting the gluttonous dark-green energy. The only difference is that the gluttonous Hy-muns shined with an uncontrollable hunger to eat and keep eating, whereas these Hy-muns simply desire more *things*. How can there be Hy-muns like this on the surface when… when…"

When there are no Tempters from the Tribe of Shadows around to influence us, Virgil guessed, trying to finish Dan-te's sentence for her. *Or perhaps it's when you've already met a Hy-mun who's like me.*

Virgil never carried a high opinion of himself. He knew he was—among many things—the oddball in his immediate family, a loner at Spectral Academy, and a heretic in the eyes of groups like the Hammers of the Orange Light. It was the main reason for his monastic lifestyle. He knew he was filled with his own good and bad points just like any Hy-mun. But he also knew that he was the first Hy-mun Dan-te met on the surface. She was impressed by him, and he could guess she must be judging other Hy-muns they met since their first encounter against him. Now it was getting complicated.

Dan-te is getting both upset and shocked from Knowing *the Hy-muns we've encountered and our culture*, Virgil realized, thinking back to her reactions toward Spectral Academy when they first started their journey together and wondering then how Dan-te would *Know* the Hy-mun world.

I think I can understand why she would look at the large groups of Hy-muns we've seen so far both relaxing in the mud bath and working out in the gym and would Know *them to be nothing but a group of gluttonous and greedy people. The Hotel Avery is a resort hotel, and every resort hotel I've ever visited has people who, as part of their vacations, would spend their time eating, partying, and/or working out in the gym to try and lose whatever weight they might have gained. Dan-te described Mr. Ciacco as someone who "eats, and continues eating, everything he can as ravenously as possible," that was the gluttony in him as well as the others in the mud bath. Miss Janney also mentioned that they were businesspeople. How many businesspeople have my brother and me playfully spied on that can never seem to stop stuffing their faces whenever they were at a banquet?*

Virgil's thought of him and his brother sneaking around when they were younger put a playful smile on his face. He could still remember some of the men, like Mr. Ciacco, visiting his father and gorging themselves whenever they got the chance. However, the memory also gave more weight to Dan-te's argument.

As for the greed Dan-te Knows, *it could easily be fueled by the greed for a more physically fit or attractive body. In the case of the weightlifters, Dan-te might* Know *their greed for new limits, to be* that much better. *But if I'm thinking about everyone, then the greed she* Knows *could even be taken further, not only for health and sports reasons, but also to impress women for the sake of having a better body. If they are all like Mr. Ciacco, all businessmen, then their greed extends to the material world as well.*

Regardless of what Mr. Ciacco or the other Hy-muns in either the mud bath or the gym were doing, Virgil realized Dan-te had given him plenty to think about when he got the chance to sit down, mostly concerning the way she *Knew* the world and the way he saw it—or perhaps did not see it.

Once we are on the sand ship, I am also going to have to think about how to help Dan-te be less troubled about everything she Knows, *sees, and encounters. I realize* Knowing *and understanding are two very different things, and as it stands I can't* Know *the way she does, but if I could only understand a bit more like her…*

"You are understanding…" Dan-te whispered to Virgil, breaking him out of his thought. "I *Know* you are."

"Really?" replied Virgil, a little confused.

"Really what?" Miss Janney asked.

"Really, are we almost to the sand ship port," Virgil covered, silently cursing himself that he forgot Miss Janney was still guiding him.

"Now, please, don't get yourself in a hurry now Mr. Woody. All we still have to do is walk through the sports arena, and then we will be there. It won't be that much longer now."

Virgil was glad that they were almost to the sand ship port, and he suspected Dan-te was too. But more immediately, Dan-te's whisper that Virgil *understood* her way of *Knowing* after experiencing the greed from the Hy-muns in the gym did give him one realization about Dan-te's way of *Knowing* things.

Dan-te, perhaps all of her people, live in a world where there are no grey areas, Virgil thought, considering Dan-te's perspective. *They just know something as that one thing, be it either wholly good or wholly bad. There's no way something bad, like greed, can be used productively. I doubt someone could be greedy for love, joy, or hope, without it turning bad.*

Virgil also remembered Dan-te's story about "The Coming," the events that happened after it, and his own notions about the changing of the definitions of "right" and "wrong."

I bet I'm right. That simple, yet extreme viewpoint is what Dan-te, her people, and the Tribe of Shadows are living with all the time. If that is the way that Dan-te Knows things, either wholly one way or another with no space in between, then she must have Known exactly what kind of person I was from the moment we first met; still, Knowing what she does about me, she put her total confidence in me, a complete stranger, to help her.

That moment of realization was actually a little overwhelming and caused Virgil to stumble on his feet.

"See, you understand more and more even now," Dan-te whispered, watching Virgil radiate white mental energy as his thoughts came together. "But do *you* now need a moment's rest," she added sarcastically.

Virgil would have laughed at the joke, but a sudden roar drowned out both of their voices.

Chapter 5

"What is that?" Dan-te shouted.

"The sports arena," Virgil answered, the sudden burst of noise drowning out Dan-te's voice—just a whisper while veiled—to a point where it was almost gone.

"Yes, it is the sports arena," Miss Janney confirmed, shouting herself, and taking Virgil's statement for a question. "Don't let go of me. In this noise and excitement I doubt anyone would either hear or notice you trying to get to the sand ship port. Just stay close, we are almost there."

Virgil merely nodded in reply, the noise quickly growing by the second. Another thing Virgil noticed, Dan-te's grip was tightening again, harder than he ever felt it before as the group of them walked through the sports arena.

"An interesting fact about the Hotel Avery Sports Arena," Miss Janney shouted, still acting as both tour guide and usher. "The sports arena is actually a converted quarry pit. The quarry was originally used to mine stone and resources that were used in the construction of both the Hotel Avery and other buildings in the local area. When construction was completed, and the quarry mined out, the hotel's owner at the time decided that instead of decommissioning it, it would be better off recycled and converted into an arena for sporting events that would be hosted by the hotel. Around the quarry, bleachers were built to hold the spectators, and above it, a large tent was raised to keep the wind, sand, and rain off. Currently, we are hosting the Central Continent Division Mud Wrestling Finals."

"I can hear," Virgil shouted, acting like he could only hear the noise around him when he could see it all with his own eyes.

Mud wrestling was not the most popular sport in Hy-mun culture, but it did have a strong following. Virgil himself had never been much a follower of it, the whole concept of purposely wrestling around and in mud never appealed to him. As for the spectators that Virgil and Dan-te passed, they were eating the entertainment up, cheering and howling for their favorite wrestler as he or she gained or lost the upper hand in their match. Dan-te, however, was not reacting to the competition as impartially as Virgil. The howling crowds, the wrestlers fighting for the joy of the masses, and the energy and smells filling the air were bringing back bad memories from when she was still a prisoner in Nis.

The same, Dan-te whispered to herself, unwilling to say the words out loud, because she was afraid it would make it even more real. *It's the same, this stadium, the Hy-muns, they're the same as the Tribe of Shadows!*

The stadium was radiant with the same crimson red energy of anger she witnessed in every coliseum throughout Nis from the First Circle of Maestri to the Grand Coliseum in Wrath Eras. Every Hy-mun, both the ones in the stands and the wrestlers in the stadium, were alight with the same energy, extruding the same sharp-smelling fear and excitement that had become so familiar to her. She then saw a slight that made her blood run cold.

"Tempter!" Dan-te screamed.

It was the first Tempter Dan-te had seen on the surface since their arrival in Wanton City. Looking around, Dan-te soon noticed that more of them were scattered throughout the stadium. Hearing the word "Tempter," Virgil quickly reacted.

"Mr. Woody, are you alright?" Miss Janney asked, seeing Virgil suddenly stumble to one knee, his hand going to his face.

"I just need a minute to rest," Virgil replied, waiting for Dan-te's signal for them to move again. "The noise, it's just a bit much."

"Okay, we'll wait right here."

Virgil nodded in reply, still waiting for Dan-te's signal, but it did not come. Dan-te's attention had been caught by an even more shocking revelation than the appearance of Tempters.

They're not tempting, they're watching*!*

Everywhere in the stadium, the Tempters from Nis were just watching the Hy-muns mud wrestle. As far as the Tempters were concerned, it could have been just another gladiator match anywhere throughout Nis. The Tempters were cheering for their favorite wrestler, booing the one they were against, and seemingly enjoying themselves right next to the very Hy-muns that they were dedicating themselves to destroy. Worse, the whole sight, Hy-muns and members of the Tribe of Shadows cheering together, looked so *natural* that it was unnerving.

I always believed that the Hy-muns were created by the Beings of Light, Virgil's "Nag-el," Dan-te thought, trying to make sense of what she was witnessing. *They were then tempted to do wrong by the Tribe of Shadows' Tempters. But then, aren't the Tribe of Shadows also a Nag-el creation, partially from "The Coming," the hatred it sowed, and the Nag-el bloodlines introduced through Lord Tanas's Legion of Shadows. Are the Hy-muns in the end really no different than the Tribe of Shadows, is Virgil just some rare exception, could there even be exceptions in the Tribe of Shadows too?*

Dan-te had thought that she could take whatever Hy-mun civilization could dish out to her. But witnessing this spectacle, so similar to what she experienced in Nis, and seeing members of the Tribe of Shadows enjoying it right alongside other Hy-muns as if they were family, had utterly unnerved her. She did not know how to process it, or what to make of the Hy-muns in general.

"Dan-te…" Virgil whispered, worried as to why she had not signaled him yet. Daring to find out, knowing full well that the gesture might be noticed by Tempters in the area, he tried to tug on her arm, suddenly feeling the whole weight of her body fall right on top of him.

"Are you alright Mr. Woody," Miss Janney snapped as Virgil suddenly collapsed to the ground.

"I'm fine," Virgil puffed, the weight of Dan-te's larger form pressing down onto his back and almost pinning him to the ground. "I'm fine, I just need to get myself back on my feet and to the sand ship."

Being careful not to throw Dan-te off his back, Virgil staggered back on to his feet as best he could. Dan-te's size hunched him over and made him drag his feet with every step. While Miss Janney's hand had returned to his shoulder, leading him toward the port, Virgil could feel her eyes, and possibly more eyes, boring into him, wondering what—if anything—was ailing him. As for Virgil himself, he was more concerned about the unconscious Dan-te now riding on his back.

She must have passed out from Knowing *the arena, or at least that's what I* hoped *happened*, Virgil guessed, trudging through it. *Once we're out of here and on the ship, I'm going to have to do something to try to wake her up and fast. Thankfully, it seems that besides Miss Janney there is almost no one around or at least no one that I can see who cares. The Hy-muns like me are mostly focused on the mud wrestling championship, and if anyone does notice me, all they would see is a blind man shuffling through the back of the stadium. But Dan-te said that there were Tempters in the audience. If anyone of them notices us and tries to hold us up, then there will be problems.*

Virgil already knew that while veiled, Dan-te, nor any member of the Tribe of Shadows, should be able to physically interact with him. The only reason why Dan-te was able to do so was because of the damage the Veil sustained during the escape from Nis. Worse, Dan-te had fallen in an awkward position on top of Virgil. Even if he could not see her, he could feel her, and what he was feeling right now was making him embarrassed.

If any Tempters from the Tribe of Shadows see us like this, they'll Know *something is up*, Virgil realized, moving as fast as he could. *I have to get going, that's the first thing that needs to be done. I have to get us both moving faster, especially since I'm now carrying her, and get us to the port so we can catch that sand ship.*

So, with as much speed as Virgil could accomplish under the extra burden of Dan-te's weight, he lifted her up more onto to his back and continued to let Miss Janney lead him through and eventually out of the arena and onto the sand ship port. Never once being questioned by another Hy-mun about the reason for his hunched state, or feeling Dan-te stir from where she rested on his back.

At least I know she's still where she fell on top of me, Virgil thought to himself, relieved to be close now to a place where he would have privacy again.

If something did happen to her, I definitely would have felt someone pull her off me. Giving her an extra shove onto his back, Virgil continued onto the sand ship port.

Chapter 6

"I'll be leaving you here Mr. Woody," Miss Janney chirped, depositing Virgil in a yellow painted area of the port for Hy-muns with disabilities and sounding happy to finally be done guiding him. "I hope you enjoy your trip."

"Thank you for your help," Virgil replied, slightly winded and moving sluggishly from carrying the unconscious Dan-te on his back. "I'm sure I will."

"Are you going to be boarding the ship alone or is someone going to meet you here?"

"I'm expecting someone from Land Break City. He should be on the ship now and will be meeting me once it comes into port to take me on board."

"Well then, have a good day."

Miss Janney walked away immediately after that, leaving Virgil alone with Dan-te in the sand ship port. The port was far quieter, and nowhere near as active a place, compared to the arena. Only one ship named the SS Phlegyas entered it. The vessel traveled in a loop from Wanton City, to Tri-Dominion City, and then to Land Break City in the Green Dominion. All Virgil had to do was wait in the appointed area. Thankfully, he did not have to wait long. The SS Phlegyas arrived soon after Miss Janney left Virgil in the loading area. Once the ship had docked, the entire mood of the port changed instantly.

Hy-muns rushed from the ship in droves. The port quickly became a flurry of activity as workers sought to hand people luggage and direct others to the hotel, arena, and back to Wanton City. With everyone moving quickly, no one seemed to even glance at Virgil in the disability area—exactly how he wanted it. But as he looked over the Hy-muns rushing about the port, he could only think about Dan-te slung over his back.

Humph, a part of me is actually glad you're out right now Dan-te, Virgil mused, thinking about both the unconscious Dan-te on his back and the crowd before him. *I wonder how you might* Know *all of these Hy-muns? Probably that they are creating a storm of lustful and gluttonous energy, each one being pushed by those emotions toward whatever it is they want to do here in Wanton City.*

After finding out that all it took for Dan-te to pass out was *Knowing* a sporting event, a new sense of worry had begun building in him over what else she might find disturbing in the Hy-mun world; he also realized that he might not even know his own world as well as he believed.

When you wake up, I am going to have to talk to you about what you Knew *in that arena. You need to tell me what it was that knocked you out. Not just for our own sake, I can handle carrying you, but it's going to create another problem we* can't *have.*

With Hy-muns leaving for Wanton City en masse, Virgil knew that there was a good chance there could be Tempters from the Tribe of Shadows mixed in with them, especially after Dan-te alerted him that there were Tempters in the sports arena.

If any more Tempters happen to be in the crowd and notice the two of us, we'll be in big trouble real fast. We can't let this happen again.

Virgil knew that the longer he supported Dan-te over his back, the longer he held up a sign to any observant Tempter that said, "We can touch each other," something that *should not be possible* with a properly working Veil of Shadows.

"Come on, where are you?" Virgil whispered to himself, trying to find one particular face in the crowd.

"Do you need help, sir?" a ship attendant asked, spooking Virgil by coming up from behind him.

"Oh, ah yes," Virgil replied, stumbling and almost letting Dan-te slide off his back. "If…you…can…"

"I'll take care of this gentleman," a tall, dark-skinned man in a business suit interrupted, placing his hand on Virgil's shoulder. "Why don't you see if you can take care of someone else."

He began to lead Virgil slowly away from the disability area and toward the ship. Once they were out of earshot from the attendant and finally mixed with the other boarding passengers did the man talk to him again.

"Nice disguise and acting, Master V," the man whispered, snickering as he talked. "When I received your letter back in Land Break City telling me that you were traveling in disguise to Tri-Dominion City I admit I didn't believe it at first. Ever since leaving the Indigo Dominion again, I honestly didn't think you would ever travel unless it was to one of your parent's preapproved destinations. Yet here you are. If not for that pin on your hat I wouldn't have realized it was you. Bending yourself over like you've either got a heavy load on your back or a severe case of kyphosis is a really nice touch. If it weren't that attendant's job, he probably would have just ignored you completely. Now, is there any place specific you want for a cabin?"

"Just someplace dark, Leslie," Virgil answered, extremely grateful to see Leslie again. "It needs to be a place where no natural light can get in. Also, I can't explain why, but no one can disturb me until we get to Tri-Dominion City."

"Alright then," Leslie replied, a little confused over Virgil's request. "I have a single cabin reserved in the bowels of the ship. I reserved one on each level since I didn't know what you would be asking for. Also, you will be happy to know that your escort is waiting for you in Tri-Dominion City. He will be looking for the hat ornament, too."

"Excellent, thank you for everything, and pass it along that I am to be called 'Woody' during my trip."

"Yes, Woody, I'll see to it that he knows; now, let's get you to your cabin. Also, one more thing."

"What's that?"

"It's good to see you again."

"Likewise."

Virgil was happy to see Leslie again as he led him onto the sand ship and down into its lowest parts, leaving him in a small cabin furnished with a desk, chair, no windows, and one bed.

"I hope this suits you," Leslie asked.

"Perfectly," Virgil replied, shuffling into the room and turning around to put a "Do Not Disturb Sign" on the door and to face Leslie. "I'll see you again once we reach Tri-Dominion City."

"Until then, Woody, take care of yourself."

Closing the door, and slightly more confident that he was now alone, he turned off all the lights in the cabin until it was completely dark before setting the unconscious and veiled Dan-te onto the bed. A slight moan escaped Dan-te lips once she hit it, and she finally woke up.

"Did you enjoy your nap?" Virgil asked humorously.

"Nap," Dan-te moaned before realizing what had happened, grasping Virgil's hand and springing from the bed—almost taking his arm with her.

"Burn it all," Dan-te shrieked, forgetting for a moment that she was supposed to be traveling in secret. "What happened to us? Where are we? Why do you sound so calm? How *can* you be calm, especially after walking through that arena? What I *Knew* in there, what I *saw* in there…"

"Tell me," Virgil said, part asking and part demanding as a serious expression crossed his face.

"It was wrath," Dan-te began, also removing the Veil of Shadows so that Virgil would be able to see her. "So much wrath; the arena, the combatants, the spectators—they were all erupting with wrath. It was no different than the coliseums that I had to fight my way through to reach the Veil of Shadows back in Nis."

Dan-te's voice turned hollow, trembling as she talked, and now that she was visible again Virgil could also see it in her eyes. They were growing wide. Her reaction quickly reminded him of the day they met and what he had heard on the radio just before returning to his room and finding her there.

She sounds similar to Sol, Virgil thought to himself, remembering Sol's interview and his reactions to the "accident" that claimed the lives of Reye and everyone else on the Demp Cavern Mining Project.

But Dan-te sounds more genuine. *When Sol gave his interview, he spoke the words and gave the physical cues, but it seemed scripted, acted like he performed it. But, Dan-te, her words are stuttering,* she's *trembling, the way her eyes are moving, looking past me back to Nis. You can't fake that.*

"Every coliseum throughout Nis was the same," Dan-te continued. "Hordes of warriors screaming for me, Ice, and the other gladiators to fight and die; the *gladiators* were screaming for their own deaths. All around us, an addictive frenzy of crimson wrathful energy and sharp-smelling scents of fear and excitement constantly bombarded us as relentlessly as the physical attacks from the gladiators themselves. A few times, it made me almost want to give myself over to the frenzy and become just as wrathful as the gladiators just so I wouldn't have to keep resisting it. Your 'sports arena' was the same as the coliseums in Nis. The energy, the smells, the reactions of both the mob and the combatants, it was all the same. And it wasn't the only thing I witnessed."

What more could there have been, Virgil thought to himself. *What else could you have* Known?

"You remember how I told you that there were Tempters in the arena?" Dan-te asked.

"Yes," Virgil answered. "I started to act stressed out and in pain like we practiced, but you never signaled me that they moved on. Instead, you passed out on your feet, and when I pulled against your arm, you collapsed onto my back."

"Ah, yes, sorry about that," Dan-te apologized. "But what I saw, the Tempters in the arena, they weren't tempting anyone. They were *enjoying* the Hy-mun spectacle as if it were no different from one of their own gladiator matches. The Tribe of Shadows is always preaching about The Plan, retaking the surface, and destroying and/or banishing the Hy-muns to beneath the surface; so, how could they enjoy a Hy-mun activity alongside Hy-muns as if they were their own people, especially when generations upon generations of talking by the Remnant couldn't."

"Until you witness Tempters acting like Hy-muns and Hy-muns acting like gladiators from the Tribe of Shadows. All of them enjoying themselves over a common event, where otherwise you *Know* they would have torn each other apart," Virgil concluded, trying to piece together what Dan-te was feeling.

Dan-te nodded to Virgil, signaling that he was right. He already realized that there were no grey areas in her ability to *Know*. Every emotion, smell, action, and spark of energy that radiated from the body lent itself to being only one thing. Also, that one thing, existed on either one extreme or the other. Good or bad, order or chaos, something was either one thing or a different thing; and while energy, emotions, smells, thoughts, and sensations mixed together, there was no middle ground for any of them.

"While you were still in Nis, you *Knew* the Tribe of Shadows desire to return to the surface, The Plan they had devoted themselves to, and the goal of defeating the Hy-muns, the 'final enemy,'" Virgil began, remembering how the Tribe of Shadows referred to his people. "You *Knew* their anger and wrath, their need for the war. However, once you saw that stadium, saw Tempters finding common ground—something that usually wouldn't exist in their culture—with their self-appointed enemy making them give up tempting—even for a moment—where countless attempts by the Remnant of the Tribe have failed, it just blew your mind."

Again Dan-te nodded, but this time she did not stay silent for long.

"What *are* your people? How can they be no different than the Tribe of Shadows? How can the Tribe of Shadows find peace within such a wrath-filled environment? How?"

Virgil did not have an answer. He always tried to find the right words to fit whatever problem or situation someone presented him with, but he knew that this was unlike anything he had ever been given before.

The sports arena we passed reminded Dan-te of the gladiatorial arenas she had fought in while a prisoner in Nis, Virgil mused, crossing his arms, racking his brain, and trying to find a solution to Dan-te's question. *She already told me how she and her brother had fought in various arenas—what it was like in them, leading up to the Grand Coliseum, where she met Reye and stole the Veil of Shadows she used to reach the surface. The spectators, both here and in Nis, definitely were excited about the action. The same could be said for the gladiators and the wrestlers themselves. I'm guessing they would be on an adrenaline high, feeling both a rush from the crowds and the excitement that went along with any kind of competition. Unfortunately, this is still only* my *view of it.*

Virgil knew his viewpoint was still the *Hy-mun* viewpoint, and despite how much he might have come to understand Dan-te's ability to *Know*, it did not mean that he would have been able to *Know* the spectacle the same way she did.

Dan-te, Virgil realized, *would have* Known *both the arena and the spectators in it through the composite image created by their sight, sounds, smells, and the energy they radiated. So, what were those emotions? And how are those emotions so much the equal to what the Tribe of Shadows feel that they can find peace with their self-appointed enemy?*

Virgil both watched and participated in various martial arts competitions—all using an alias—before coming to Spectral Academy. He remembered the rush from winning one, listening to the spectators cheer the name he was using, and the pleasure of putting what he had trained himself for into practice. One thing he had always remembered hearing from some of his instructors just before the competition: there was a point where "the only thing that matters is cutting down the opponent in front of you." He heard that line the most in sword classes and while prepping for cutting contests to put himself into the right mind-set. Both the memories of those events, and the mentality he put himself in, started to make him think about what the arena's spectators, both Hy-mun and members of the Tribe of Shadows, would have been feeling in the first place.

To compete in a mud wrestling arena, the wrestlers would need to summon up all of their focus to take an opponent down, Virgil thought to himself, trying to compare the situations. *While this might be a different type of event then what I'm used to, the mind-set is the same. The goal, especially in sparring matches, is to beat your opponent, and I've seen plenty of fighters focus anger and wrath on doing that.*

At the thought of "wrath," Virgil remembered Dan-te's description of the Grand Coliseum, and the Fifth Circle it inhabited, "Wrath" Eras.

Dan-te described the Grand Coliseum, all the coliseums actually, as being filled with spectators from the Tribe of Shadows. The spectators were always animated, extruding scents of adrenaline as they both anticipated and watched the matches before them. They spewed wrathful taunts toward her and her brother Ice for even setting foot in any of them and encouraging the gladiators—who were more animated and stank of even more adrenaline than the spectators—to either finish them off gloriously or to die and become martyrs in the process.

As for the Hy-mun spectators in the arena, while they weren't cheering for anyone to die and become a martyr, I don't doubt they were summoning up excitement, adrenaline, wrath, and encouragement. In fact, I don't think there isn't a single major sporting event where fans wouldn't cheer for their favorites, encouraging them to do better while also slinging hateful remarks against the opposing side. Not only that, but even I could tell that the air in the arena was charged with excitement, and I don't doubt the wrestlers felt that too, an almost addictive excitement.

Virgil glanced back up at Dan-te the moment the word "addictive" crossed his mind, she also called the crimson energy of hate she felt in Nis addictive. She was easily taller and physically stronger than him; but looking into her silver eyes, pleading, trying to find some kind of answer to her questions, she never seemed so small.

"Abyssus abyssum invocat…" Virgil finally murmured.

"What," Dan-te asked.

"Abyssus abyssum invocat," Virgil repeated. "It means 'Deep calleth unto deep,' but I guess you could interpret it as meaning 'like knows like.' You told me that when you were fighting in Nis that 'an addictive frenzy of crimson wrathful energy and sharp-smelling scents of fear and excitement constantly bombarded' you. That it hit you 'as relentlessly as the physical attacks from the gladiators themselves.'"

"And that the energy, smells, and reactions from both the mob and the combatants in the sports arena were exactly the same," Dan-te agreed. "What I couldn't get was how Tempters from the Tribe of Shadows could sit side by side with the Hy-muns in the arena when back in Nis The Plan means everything to them. Just now, it was like the Tribe of Shadows' Plan meant nothing to them at all. Generations of Tempting, work, and traditions were quickly forgotten by doing nothing more than staring at a group of people fighting each other; something that can be done either on the surface or in Nis."

"And *that* is where the 'like knows like' part comes into play," Virgil pointed out. "You said that in both cases the energies, feelings, and sensations were the same, that they were addictive. I think that they literally *are* the same. It doesn't matter who's generating them; all that matters is that they are being created and that the Tempters *Know* it as being identical to what they *Know* in Nis, right up to the point where they can enjoy it as much as they do back home.

"You've already demonstrated you can *Know* me and this world. Plus, you've told me, back when we were discussing Nis's breeding practices, that members of the Tribe of Shadows have successfully fathered children with Hy-mun women. That means we are close enough as a species to be related, it shouldn't be that surprising for members of our civilizations to have the same likes and dislikes."

"I can see your point," Dan-te stuttered. "But still…"

Dan-te's mind kept flashing back to Nis, and the lessons constantly screamed throughout Envy Opal-Lo.

Know *tempting to be Good,* Dan-te remembered Envy Opal-Lo's head teacher, Solo-on, continually shouting. *The Hy-muns are evil! We, our actions, and The Plan are just! Don't listen to the words of the Rodents and the Hy-muns, they are false and full of lies! Tanas is Truth!*

I've already found out that every one of those declarations was false. I wonder how many members of the Tribe of Shadows, once put to the test and actually encounter Hy-muns, end up still believing those ideas; or are they all just performing them without even thinking? I wonder how many of the Tribe of Shadows might see themselves in the Hy-muns, and how many I might see in them?

While Virgil did not say it, electing to remain quiet while Dan-te gathered her thoughts, he also harbored similar worries about his own world and its relation to the Tribe of Shadows. From the beginning of their journey, Dan-te revealed both new and horrifying faces of his own world. They were images he either never thought about or never noticed until now; making him seriously think about himself, others, and the society he lived in.

When we started our journey together back at Spectral Academy, Virgil reflected, thinking about the start of their trip, *Dan-te said that it was dark, stressful, and filled with disbelief. As for Wanton City, she called the city a "storming torrent of lustful energy." Now, between the Hotel Avery's mud bath, gym, and sports arena she's encountered dens of gluttony, greed, and wrath; all relished by their Hy-mun patrons. The last of which, the sport's arena, turned out to be a pleasure that even members of the Tribe of Shadows could enjoy right alongside their self-proclaimed enemies. What does this mean for both of our societies?* Virgil would have thought more about it, but a sudden jolt snapped both him and Dan-te out of their thoughts.

"What was that?" Dan-te gasped, steadying herself as she felt the room move under her feet.

"Just the sand ship leaving port."

 "Sand ship?"

Dan-te started glancing around the room, noticing now that they were not in a restroom like before but a small cabin.

"We're on the sand ship? How? When? I mean, weren't we just in that arena?"

"You passed out and fell onto my back, remember?" Virgil explained, blushing at the awkwardness of it. "I carried you the rest of the way."

"You carried me?"

Dan-te did not know if she should be thankful for having Virgil by her side or angry with herself for passing out on her feet and putting them both at serious risk.

"Looks like I'm not as tough as I thought," Dan-te mumbled; ashamed, she decided to feel both thankful and angry. "I put us both in danger and made you carry a burden you shouldn't have, I'm sorry."

"Didn't I say I was going to help you?" Virgil replied, slightly annoyed by Dan-te's remarks. "We're already in danger from the Third Great Attempt, and I willingly put myself in danger the second I decided to help you. You have nothing to apologize for. If I have to carry you when you're unconscious then so be it."

Dan-te smiled at Virgil's remark. She *Knew* he meant it, the blue energy of resolve and the indigo energy of loyalty still surrounded him and pulsed with every word he spoke. However, she hoped it would not come to that.

There's enough to worry about already, we don't need to add me passing out to that list, Dan-te chided herself, thinking about what else she might witness in the Hy-mun world.

"So, how long until we reach Tri-Dominion City?"

"A day at most depending on the desert's weather conditions," Virgil answered, sitting down in the chair and stretching. "We shouldn't be disturbed down here in this cabin, so let's relax while we can until my friends come for us and bring us off the ship."

"Friends?"

"Friends," Virgil repeated, taking off his hat and tapping the pin on it. "You'll see soon enough."

"I guess I will," Dan-te replied inquisitively, remembering that Virgil claimed the pin was going to get them help, and wondering just what she missed after she passed out.

Meanwhile, back underground and just outside of Nis, a lone Tribesman from the Remnant of the Tribe was led out of the city and through the Ring of Fire-Stone; the circle of jagged volcanic rocks encircling Nis and acting as its first outer defense. The Tribesman, the only name he now called himself since killing his previous self, a member of the Remnant of the Tribe named Ice, was being led to the entrance of the Great Tunnel that connected Nis with the Keyblast Point under the Red Dominion. His new job was going to be cleaning the tunnel's rubble for the Tribe of Shadows until his death as punishment for aiding the Hy-mun girl once called the "Hy-mun Horror."

Part 2: The First Reflections

Chapter 7

"LIFT! Put your back into it," the taskmaster cried cracking his whip against the Tribesman's heavily scarred back. The Tribesman responded by merely lifting another rock upon his back and carrying it away. Elsewhere in the distance, the sound of the digging machines echoed through the Great Tunnel.

The Great Tunnel is nearing its completion, the Tribesman mulled over grimly. *This is only the start of the tunnel, but I can hear the noise from the end of it as clearly as if I was there. It will not be long now before it's completed.*

The Tribesman from the Remnant, who had once been known as Ice until his old self died while guiding the "Hy-mun Horror" in a failed attempt to kill Lord Tanas, was working near the entrance of the Great Tunnel.

I should have been killed immediately, the Tribesman reflected. *Physical death is a punishment both the Tribe of Shadows, and I Know I deserved, but for very different reasons. I deserved to die for killing my old self, Ice, and for taking Reye, a grieving and suffering Hy-mun girl, and using her as the Hy-mun Horror in a fruitless attempt to kill Lord Tanas. A struggle that cost the Tribe of Shadows an unknown number of citizens and caused massive damage to Nis. But for the*

Tribe of Shadows, they did not care about what I did to Ice and Reye, only what I did to them. But am I really that much different?

From the moment that the first stone was placed upon his back, the Tribesman had been in a state of introspection about the events that led him to this particular time and place. Each crack from the taskmaster's whip, new burn from a magma splash when he threw away a piece of rubble, every new pain, and part of his *new* life forced him to come to terms with how he arrived in this situation, and what he could do now.

The death of my old "self" really started back when me and Ice's sister, Dan-te, volunteered to become gladiators. Actually, it was even before that, it was back when they first began making their plans in Rem, the Tribesman recalled as he started carrying another stone.

***

"According to the Council, the Third Great Attempt *will* destroy us all," the Tribesman, then still known as Ice, whispered.

"But you don't think this mission to Nis is going to work, do you?" Dan-te asked, concerned about what her brother might be thinking.

"Not a chance, before they even try to listen to us we'll probably either be killed, thrown into Maestri, or made into gladiators and breeders for their enjoyment."

"Well, we have to do something," Dan-te snapped. "We need help to stop the Third Great Attempt. I'll even accept help from the Hy-muns if we can get it."

"I'm glad you feel that way. I want to share an idea with you."

***

That was when Ice first told Dan-te about the idea to join the party going to Nis, the Tribesman remembered. *Once we were predictably captured, we would volunteer to become gladiators, fight our way to the Grand Coliseum, steal the First Envy's Veil of Shadows, and use it to reach the surface to get help from the Hy-muns. And if that didn't work, there was the backup plan, fighting our way to Yam-Preen and assassinate Lord Tanas. I still remember Dan-te's answer.*

"That idea is crazy, suicidal, and is going to get us both killed long before the Third Great Attempt is even started. But it's *proactive*, let's do it!"

Reunions, Reflections, and Reconciliations

Dan-te couldn't say yes to joining up with the idea quicker, she was always a Tribeswoman of action and this plan suited her. If there was one thing my old self Knew, it's that his sister would rather be doing something instead of just sitting around Rem waiting for it to happen. Ice was sure, one way or the other, that his plan would work. Either he and Dan-te would get their hands on the Veil of Shadows and use it to contact the Hy-muns—resulting in help being sent to stop the Third Great Attempt, or they would kill Lord Tanas. Looking back, that pride was the first step toward my birth and the death, the killing, of my old self.

The Tribesman, just like every member of the Remnant of the Tribe, knew that pride was a vice that caused problems for everyone.

Throughout Nis, children were always told to take pride in both who they were and what they were doing because of what their people endured. The Stories of Rill talk about when the First Pride of Nis approached Lord Tanas that he "generated so much prideful teal energy it looked like it could lift him off the ground on a wave." The highest of Nis's ruling circles even bears his name, Pride *Aster. Even in the tales about "The Coming," the Light Bringer is described as, among other things, the personification of pride.*

Stumbling for a second, the Tribesman looked at the ground, noticing the scratches he—and other workers—made from discarding countless pieces of debris from the Great Tunnel into the nearby magma pools.

My mind must be playing tricks on me, the Tribesman thought, as the marks on the ground—illuminated by the orange glow from the magma pools—took on new images before his eyes. *That one looks like it could be one of the escaped Tribe of Shadows/Remnant children, except the features are different, there's no horn, and he seems puffed up with pride. That one next to it though does look like a member of the Remnant, but his face is also bulging with pride. I wonder if that might be what the Light Bringer and the First Pride would have looked like?*

"Quit your daydreaming and move," the taskmaster shouted, striking him with a rod. "Lord Tanas ordered you to clean *all* this debris, and that is exactly what you are going to do. After all, you were *so* helpful in creating it with the Hy-mun Horror. No reason you can't *clean it up.*"

The Tribesman would have sneered at the taskmaster's condescending tone and attitude, but he did not want to give him the pleasure. Looking again at the scratches, two new faces appeared before him; the Hy-mun girl Reye who became known as the "Hy-mun Horror," and his old image, back before he let himself die when he was still Ice. Seeing, *Knowing* his old self, bloated with the same pride and arrogant self-confidence that also characterized the Light Bringer, the First Pride, and Reye, the Tribesman realized something as he continued carrying the debris.

We were guilty of the same vices that they were, the Tribesman mused, pitching another block of rubble into the magma. *Ice, just like Reye when she was rampaging through Nis, the First Pride when he stepped before Tanas, and the Light Bringer when he led "The Coming," was so confident that his plan would work—or was working—that he became overinflated with pride in himself. Ice knew that his idea was both crazy and a longshot to begin with, but it was working. Despite the odds, he and Dan-te were making it to the Grand Coliseum, and then he was handed the best thing he could have asked for, Reye.*

At the thought of Reye, the Tribesman gazed back at the scratches that looked like Reye's face. It was still there, the same joyfully satisfied look painted on her face after she destroyed the E-gle Building staring up at him from the ground. The look only became more joyful the closer they came to Lord Tanas. But now, her face was filled with pride—pride Ice had never noticed or just did not want to notice—over the fact that she was doing exactly what she believed her dead brother had told her to do.

"My brother's final words were to fight and run," the Tribesman remembered Reye saying when she was racing through Greed U-Sez with Ice by her side.

Reye had been severely hurt by the Tribe of Shadows: physically, emotionally, and psychologically, the Tribesman recalled. Even though the Tribesman was no longer Ice, he still could not forget that first week of watching her sleep. Chained in a cell in Wrath Eras, screaming Raymond's name, as well as the names of her friends, Stella and Ann, pulsing an erratic red energy that screamed hurt and loss, and stinking of the blood from the Tribe of Shadows' warriors she killed in madness.

Her brother, almost all the Hy-muns with her, was killed before her eyes in the raid that made her a prisoner. Any remaining survivors, Ice believed were either killed or sent to Lust Atrophied to be used for breeding. Not only that, but Reye was also fed food made from the dead Hy-muns that were a part of her group. The pain and shock turned her into a monster of wrath, anger, and vengeance that needed only a little prodding to be directed toward the Tribe of Shadows like a falling piece of rock. No one would stop her, and I see now she was proud to be doing it. Ice realized soon after he and Dan-te started their plan that killing Lord Tanas would probably be what they would end up doing— coming up with plenty of ideas on how to do it—instead of what they would do after stealing the Veil of Shadows. It was an option that quickly became his main one, especially following the loss of both Dan-te and the Veil of Shadows in the Grand Coliseum. But with Reye, he was sure the plan could work. He Knew it could work. Or at least, that's what Ice wanted to believe. He Knew any other member of the Remnant would have tried to help her past her anger; but instead, he used her as a weapon. Overly confident that she could kill Lord Tanas for him, he pointed her like an arrow and let her fly through Nis, blowing up anything in their path. And that puffed up confidence and pride led to all of our downfalls.

"Come on!" The taskmaster shouted again as he came right up to the Tribesman's side this time, striking his legs with the rod, and bringing him to his knees.

"Put your back into it and toss that rock into the magma."

BOOM... RUMBLE...

The sound of another explosion, followed by rumbling from down the Great Tunnel caught both the Tribesman and the taskmaster off guard as the Tribesman further braced himself on the ground.

The diggers, the Tribesman, guessed.

"Burn those fools," the taskmaster shouted, staggering to regain his balance. "They know explosions magnify as they travel through the Great Tunnel. They are supposed to…"

Those were the last words the Tribesman heard the taskmaster say as an even louder explosion, followed by a stronger tremor, shook the entire area of the cavern. The Tribesman looked on silently as a stone spear broke from the ceiling and began plummeting towards him.

"I guess this is it," the Tribesman lamented, watching as the spear. "Humph, so much for making it down the Great Tunnel to the Keyblast Point to stop the Third Great Attempt."

The spear crashed right between the taskmaster and himself. The taskmaster, already unbalanced from the shaking did not even notice the spear until it landed between them; blowing him away from the Tribesman and headfirst into the magma pool they were using to melt rubble. Thankfully, the rock that landed between them acted as a shield for the magma that splashed up when the taskmaster fell into the magma. After the rumbling stopped the Tribesman stood up and looked around. He realized he was all alone at the entrance of the Great Tunnel.

Maybe I haven't lost my chance yet, the Tribesman beamed, realizing he had been handed the chance he was hoping for when the guards led him out of Maestri. *The Great Tunnel is going to be completed soon, it's radiating so much fearful pink energy that the whole tunnel could be colored pink. There's not much time left; but there is something I can do, that I need to do.*

The Tribesman began walking down the Great Tunnel.

Chapter 8

The Great Tunnel's initial construction began shortly after Lord Tanas and the Legion of Shadows fully integrated themselves with the Greater Tribe to become the Tribe of Shadows. Yet despite the advances made by Hy-mun machinery and the radiant pink fear energy, the Tribesman could still see marks indicating its progress.

"Reached, 10 Generations After Lord Tanas (ALT)," the Tribesman read to himself, the words carved into the wall glowed only slightly brighter than the rest of the tunnel itself. A couple of feet further was another marker, only this one read that it was made "50 Generations ALT."

"All this work and fear, for what?" the Tribesman asked himself sarcastically. He knew, as did every other member of both the Remnant and the Tribe of Shadows, why the members of the Tribe of Shadows had labored for thousands of generations to dig the tunnel that would connect Nis with the volcanoes of the Red Dominion.

Just to gain one long dead generation's desperate vengeance and reclaim a surface that doesn't even resemble the Land of our ancestors anymore. All this so the Tribe of Shadows can detonate one of the volcanoes, using Hy-mun weapons no less, to create a cloud of ash to darken the sky and block out Light. Just to make it possible for them to return to the surface and retake it. Not that I can really call them on it.

The Tribesman remembered how Ice, when he was still Ice, blindly used Reye in his own plan to kill Lord Tanas.

"What Ice did to Reye; he used her without thinking about what she would become in the process, or what he would become in the process and what would happen to both of them afterward. Is it really that different from the Tribe of Shadows pursuing their vengeance? Chasing it blindly without a care as to what they would turn into, how their world would change, and what would happen afterward if they even achieved their vengeance. No, it wasn't. Reye became like the Tribe of Shadows, and Ice became me—both of whom could be akin to Lord Tanas."

At any other time, the Tribesman might have fallen to his knees, sobbing over how far he had fallen; but he knew could not. He needed to do something far more important than fall into a pit of self-pity. Continuing down the Great Tunnel, the Tribesman marched toward the Keyblast Point where the Third Great Attempt would be activated.

After the suffering Ice caused Reye brought on by his own pride, which in turn gave birth to me, it's time I make amends for my dead life and find a way to stop the Third Great Attempt on my own.

The Tribesman collapsed under his own weight immediately afterward; his legs racked with pain from his initial charge through Nis alongside Reye, followed by the beating he received from the taskmaster while lifting and throwing away rocks at the Great Tunnel's entrance. "This is not going to be easy," the Tribesman muttered to himself, picking himself back up and trying to stare further down the tunnel. "Mostly since this is *a tunnel*, that means there's only one way in and out for whoever is in it.

"It's only a question of when I encounter more members of the Tribe of Shadows. The noise and tremors from earlier, combined with all this fearful pink energy throughout the tunnel, are more than enough indications that they are making their final preparations on the Great Tunnel."

The Tribesman soon learned that the fearful pink energy, the noise, and tremors would not be the only signs of the Tribe of Shadows' presence in the

Great Tunnel. As the Tribesman moved down the tunnel, he soon found crates left over by work crews from the Nis.

"Now these could be useful," the Tribesman mused, hobbling over to the first crate. Since the Second Great Attempt, the Tribe of Shadows had often discovered boxes, vaults, and time capsules filled with technology and artifacts created by the Hy-muns. It was because of those discoveries that the Tribe of Shadows had even managed to further the Great Tunnel to its present point. Opening the first box, the Tribesman found it empty.

"Nothing," the Tribesman spit, moving onto the next crate and also finding it and the others empty. Yet opening the last one, the Tribesman smiled.

"Now this I can use," the Tribesman whispered eagerly. Inside the crate were a bunch of yellow suits made from fake haircloth, the same kind he saw other members of the Tribe of Shadows wearing when they left the Great Tunnel while he was still clearing debris. The Tribesman realized that if he was dressed in the same suits as the diggers there would be less of a chance that he would be immediately identified as a member of the Remnant of the Tribe. There was also a smaller box inside the crate, the words "MEDICAL SUPPLIES" were written on top of it.

"Thank the Ancestors the Tribe of Shadows believes in survival of the fittest," the Tribesman prayed, opening up the supplies and finding bandages and a series of pills marked "PAIN NEUTRALIZERS." The Tribesman knew, first hand, that the Tribe of Shadows did not nurse their injured back to health. Survival of the fittest had been the law in Nis since before Lord Tanas first arrived. Taking out the bandages first, the Tribesman quickly dressed the injuries he accumulated from the taskmaster. As for the pills, he eyed them cautiously.

This medicine was made for Hy-muns, the Tribesman thought, rolling one of the pills in his hand. *How are they going to work on me?*

Carefully, the Tribesman licked one of the pills. The effect was incredible. He was dumbstruck as a wave of numbing calm washed over his body dulling all the pain in it. The results, however, were only temporary as the sensation quickly passed, and the pain soon returned to his body. But he already *Knew* all he needed.

"Those Hy-muns make *excellent* medicine," the Tribesman laughed, swallowing a pill whole, and feeling the numbing sensation again; only this time, the feeling did not go away. Wounds dressed and his body no longer in pain, the Tribesman quickly outfitted himself in the same clothing the Tribe of Shadows were using, hiding the pills on his body for the next time when he would need one.

I'll be able to move better now, the Tribesman mused, quickly making his way down the Great Tunnel. *And it's all thanks to the medical supplies and this suit I found. If I ever see another Hy-mun again, I am going to have to thank him or her for developing these, as long as I have them.*

The Tribesman stopped himself mid-thought, realizing that the way he was promoting himself was no different than someone else he recently knew from a now dead past life.

I'm acting the same way that Reye did, the Tribesman recognized. *Burn it all, Tribesman, take a lesson from what happened to Reye and yourself when you were still Ice. Do you want to suffer the Death of the Self again because of the same pride Reye displayed?*

The Tribesman remembered when Ice looked at Reye while they were traveling through Sloth Cur-Nos, Reye projected a belief that as long as she had her tools, she could do anything. Now, he realized he was giving off that same image, and he hated himself for it.

Ice stood back and watched Reye take on Nis as the Hy-mun Horror. Now, are you going to walk down a path that will turn you into a Remnant Horror? Are you really so envious and greedy for their strength that you want to become like them yourself?

The Tribesman knew the answer as soon as he asked himself the question.

Of course, I'm envious.

The Tribesman spit in contempt, slightly dirtying the suit's mask covering his face. Not that he minded, simply doing something to punish himself for finding another vice in himself—one he did not doubt also led to Ice's "death"— was worth it.

The emotion of envy and the jealousy that grows from it has always been one of the driving forces behind the Tribe of Shadows, the Tribesman reflected as he walked down the Great Tunnel, realizing he had fallen victim to envy also. *The Tribe of Shadows, whether they admit it or not, were always envious of the Beings of Light's power which drove the Ancient Tribe underground. The Stories of Rill tell how the First Envy took envious pleasure with every act he committed against both the Beings of Light and the Hy-muns afterward because they now had the power to do it and that they were doing to the Beings of Light what they did to them. After the Second Great Attempt, when the Tribe of Shadows began incorporating Hy-mun devices, the emissaries often reported an envious pleasure they experienced over using Hy-mun technology both for their own purposes and to eventually conquer the surface. While Ice led Reye through Nis, he also envied her for the level of destruction she could do, plowing through both the Tribe of Shadows and Nis, where he wouldn't; no,* couldn't. *He* Knew *full well that without either Dan-te or Reye, his plan was going to end long before the Grand Coliseum. He envied both of their strengths and used them, secretly feeling proud of himself every step of the way.*

BOOM!

The sudden exploding sound reaching throughout the Great Tunnel, quickly broke the Tribesman out of his reflecting. Turning a slight corner, he came to a section of the tunnel now filling up with smoke; the smoke collecting into pockets in the tunnel's ceiling so it would stretch throughout it.

This is one of the sections of the tunnel that is still being worked on, the Tribesman realized. All along the walls were other members of the Tribe of Shadows, all dressed in the same Hy-mun cloths that the Tribesman was wearing and working on different machines.

Some of those machines look like they support the roof of the tunnel, the Tribesman guessed. *Others seem to be digging holes in the smoke pockets, probably to ventilate the tunnel.*

As more rock rained down from the drilling, the Tribesman dived behind a pile of rubble already cleared by the Tribe of Shadows.

This tunnel might be illuminated with fearful pink energy, but that doesn't make the rest of our energies any less concealed, the Tribesman worried as he watched the other members of the Tribe of Shadows clear rocks from the tunnel. *They are alight with a joyful jam-colored radiance, tainted with grey stress, that sticks out in sharp contrast to the fearful pink energy of the tunnel.*

Between the sounds from the machines, the rocks, and smoke I should be hidden enough from the Tribe of Shadows, the Tribesman guessed as he made his way silently through the rocks and debris being piled up along the Great Tunnel's side. As he moved past the diggers, he could hear some of their voices, and those voices gave him even more to think about.

"Ma-co! Ma-co!" a voice called.

"Yes, Lom-ardo what do you want?" another voice replied.

"Ma-co, what's our current drilling status?" the one called Lom-ardo asked.

"Well, we should break through to the next cave system to vent this smoke just before the execution of the Third Great Attempt," the one called Ma-co answered.

"Good, very good."

"There has only been one problem, Lom-ardo."

"Problem, and what problem would that be?"

"The workers have been grumbling lately about working in the smoke. It's affecting their productivity slightly."

Well, that explains the grey stressful energy, the Tribesman realized, thinking about the workers. *I guess no matter how much The Plan and the Third Great Attempt mean to them, anyone can be turned back by poor conditions.*

"Then tell them to stop grumbling," Lom-ardo shouted, the wrath in his words even more evident than the fearful pink energy in the Great Tunnel. The Tribesman *Knew* he wanted his words to be heard and felt by everyone present.

"Need I again remind them the work in the Great Tunnel is a 'volunteer service?'"

The Tribesman noticed how Lom-ardo put extra emphasis on the words "volunteer service."

"Everyone here chose to work here in the Great Tunnel to forward the completion of the Plan over pursuing the life of a tempter, a gladiator, soldier, office worker, or working one of the clean up jobs around Nis. They have no right to grumble about the conditions of the job, especially now when the tunnel is near completion. They either chose to work here, or they didn't; we all have free will."

"Right as always, Lom-ardo. I will remind the workers and get them working harder than before."

The way Lom-ardo is talking, he makes it sound like the workers actually had a real choice about how they were going to serve Lord Tanas and the Tribe of Shadows; or if they did have another option, then it wasn't one worth taking at all. Still, even if a member of the Tribe of Shadows can boast about free will and choices, and how those choices led them here, what does that say for mine; for Ice's choices?

From the moment Ice first came up with his plan, the Tribesman started to realize, *every choice he made only led Reye further down a path of wrath and anger that not only killed his old self, but nearly killed her, and went against everything that he was taught.*

The Tribesman did not know if it might have been guilt from his previous life, the fearful pink energy throughout the tunnel, the jam and grey-colored energy from the workers, the smoke, or perhaps a side effect of using Hy-mun medication on himself. But he could see his old self, Reye, and the choices he made concerning her in the smoke. He did not like it.

When Reye first asked Ice about where she was, and where her friends were, he didn't have to answer her as truthfully as he did, the Tribesman reflected, seeing his old self's past in the smoke. *He* Knew *that she was hurt and that the truth would only hurt her more, but he did it anyway. Ice could have lied, especially since Reye wouldn't have Known it the way his sister would have, but he still chose not to because he Knew lying was wrong.*

"But what about a third option?" The Tribesman whispered.

Ice was only aware of other Hy-muns having been killed; he didn't know anything about Reye's friends, Ann and Stella, and that's who she was genuinely concerned about. He didn't have to tell her not to count on it. All that choice did was crush her hopes and hurt her more. Then there was when they escaped, and she asked which way to go. He could have told her or tried harder to get her to go out of the city and rescue any other Hy-muns who could still be alive in Nis. I now know there was at least one in Maestri, and she was one of Reye's friends; and according to her, Reye's other friend might be alive in Lust Atrophied. Instead, Ice chose to point her toward Lord Tanas, and every choice since then only fueled her wrath.

Every choice Ice made, I made, we made. The Tribesman said to himself. Moving through the smoke, he wondered now at what part of their journey together did Ice die the Death of the Self and leave Reye alone with him. *Was it in the Grand Coliseum after Dan-te was lost, the E-gle Building, the Great Staircase, the Rodent Control Building, or maybe the confrontation with Lord*

Tanas himself. When did 'Ice' really die? Because since then, everything he did, everything I did, only created more wrath and anger in Reye instead of removing it.

Bitter tears were forming in the Tribesman's eyes now as he broke away from both the smoke and the diggers working there. Once he believed he was far enough away, the Tribesman began stripping off the Hy-mun clothes. He did not want any reminders of the envy that they invoked in him. However, he soon put them back on, remembering there were still more diggers in the Great Tunnel and he needed to blend in with them. Behind him, he could hear Lom-ardo bellowing again, but could only make out bits and pieces of what he was saying.

"Good leadership…is key…"

"You're right Lom-ardo," the Tribesman muttered, finding it slightly strange to be getting good advice from a member of the Tribe of Shadows dedicated to the completion of the Third Great Attempt. *Good leadership is key. It's what preserved Rem for as long as it did. If either I or Ice could have been better leaders or even shown any leadership beyond pointing Reye in the direction I wanted her to go, and then following behind her once a fight started, perhaps she wouldn't have suffered as much; becoming so wrathful because of the choices we made. It might have spared her from having a lot of blood on her hands and conscious.*

Despite whatever regrets the Tribesman *Knew* he was feeling, he also knew reflecting on them was not going to help Reye now, or stop the Third Great Attempt.

"All I can do now to try and make up for it is to move forward."

And that is precisely what the Tribesman continued to do, move forward down the Great Tunnel. Meanwhile back in Maestri, Reye, the "Former Horror," was facing her own demons of wrath in a cell with her friend Ann and the other members of the Remnant.

Chapter 9

"I killed them," Reye cried out, tossing in her sleep.

"Reye, wake up," Ann shouted, shaking Reye to break her out of her trance.

"I killed them, and I was *ENJOYING IT*!"

"Reye," Ann screamed again, this time succeeding in waking Reye up. Breathing a sigh of relief, Ann watched as her friend quickly blinked the sleep from her eyes and regained her wits. This was the third time this had happened, she was quickly getting used to Reye's routine.

"Ann, where…right, we're locked up together in Maestri."

Maestri was the First Circle of Nis and served as its prison facility. After her berserker-like crusade ended with a failed attempt on Lord Tanas's life that left her a husk of who she became, the "Hy-mun Horror;" she was tossed into a communal cell, no longer fit enough to kill. Beside her was her friend, Ann Branley, another survivor of the raid that resulted in their capture. Sleeping protectively around them were the members of the Remnant of the Tribe.

How they are able to sleep through Reye's fits, I'll never know, Ann mused as she waited for Reye to steady herself. *Reye has woken up with nightmares about her past actions as the Hy-mun Horror three times now, and each time I haven't seen a single sleeping body so much as twitch. Either they are very deep sleepers,* Know *they have nothing to fear from her, or they are just really good at pretending to be asleep.*

Every member of the Remnant remained motionless in the cell. Every time Ann woke up alongside Reye to calm her, seeing them perfectly still in the red-orange glow generated from the magma vents, it always made her feel eerie.

Reye's nightmares, and us in an iron-barred stone cell filled with half-starved people who seem to be able to sleep through anything. Can this place be any more like a tomb?

The cells in Maestri were usually quiet. One thing Ann learned quickly since being imprisoned in Nis is that "justice" is carried out *very* swiftly. There were only a small number of lawbreakers reported in Nis, and it was not long before they either went to the coliseums or to Tunnel Construction; so, the number of prisoners contained there for any extended period of time was usually very small. But now, after the Remnant's failed protest, Maestri had more prisoners then it had ever seen.

Not that the guards are treating *us like prisoners,* Ann thought to herself, thinking about how relaxed the guards have been treating them lately. The only recent changes in their behavior came as a result of Reye's nightmare-induced outbursts, her screams attracting the attention of two guards. Unlike the members of the Remnant, they were well-fed masses of bluish flesh and muscle with red eyes, and no horn on their heads. Walking in front of their cell, the two of them squatted down to peer through the bars in order to gaze at the spectacle.

"Humph, the Former Horror is whining like a scared Hy-mun girl again," one of the guards snickered. He had seen Reye's outbursts before and enjoyed watching them.

"Hard to believe I once wanted to join the forces sent to catch her," the other guard joked before turning to start walking away with the first one. "It's hard to believe that this cringing female was once known as the Hy-mun Horror."

At the words, "Hy-mun Horror," Reye noticeably flinched, and Ann knew why.

"I enjoyed that name," Reye mumbled, trembling as she talked. "They were cheering because I had killed them, and I *enjoyed* it."

Ann had already heard the story, both from Reye herself and from passing gladiators pulled away from Maestri to join in the pursuit of the "Hy-mun Horror."

During the raid on our camp, Reye's brother Raymond was killed, Ann remembered, thinking back to the attack. *Seeing him die right before her eyes made her completely lose it, killing every warrior from the Tribe of Shadows that came within a few feet of her. She ended up showing such a penchant for combat that they started calling her the "Hy-mun Horror." They decided to capture her, bring her back to Nis, and put her into the Grand Coliseum. But, as soon as they did, she and two members of the Remnant attempted to steal the sacred Veil of Shadows from the Grand Coliseum. The result was the apparent death of one of the Remnant members and Reye's escape alongside the other member who led her on a bloody and destructive rampage throughout Nis.*

"All of that blood, the carnage, organs hitting me as I hacked attackers up with my ax," Reye whimpered as she talked, reliving her charge through Nis, and still unnerved that she did it. "And I just brushed it off. It was fun!"

Reye ran from the Circle of Wrath Eras all the way to Yam-Preen itself in the center of the Nis, Ann mused. *Over the course of her rampage, she had caused more damage to the city than anyone ever thought a single Hy-mun could be capable of.*

"I melted whole buildings," Reye squeaked. Her story, now more of a confession, coming out even harder. "I ran up the Great Staircase, detonating and tossing the MMCs everywhere behind me like they were children's toys; creating screams, geysers of magma, melting and crumbling the Great Staircase while it was filled with soldiers. All of them were happy, chanting, Lord Tanas, while they burned. Still, I was the happiest one of all. I was smiling over what I was doing! In Circle Emporium, I blew a volcanic chasm through the entire place. How could I do that?"

Because you've always been the type of person who doesn't pay attention and often acts without really thinking about what she is doing, Ann said to herself, not wanting to voice the comment out loud and make her feel worse. *You told me that Raymond's last words were to run and fight. I highly doubt that was all he said to you, or that he wanted you to do that. More likely you weren't paying attention,* again, *took his meaning for something else and literally ran with it. As tragic and gruesome as your actions were, I honestly could see you doing it, not that I have any right to preach.*

Ann still remembered the first gladiator she killed since coming to Nis, and every one she felled after that. It made her sick to think she murdered someone, and even more sick to think about the other survivors from the mining project raid, none of whose names she could remember! One of them died every day fighting the *weakest* of the gladiators.

The worst of it all was that I actually had to eat *that horrendous stew made from each of the other survivors after they were killed just to keep myself alive.* Ann shuddered at the memory and everything she had to do in the name of survival. *All I kept thinking was that it was going to get worse, which it did, so I did whatever I had to, to survive. For a while, it worked, but it couldn't keep the memories, or the guilt, away forever.*

"And then, after blowing a volcanic canyon through Circle Emporium, I reached Yam-Preen and Tanas himself at Decca-Ju Tower," Reye muttered, still in the midst of her story. "But once I faced Tanas, I just couldn't fight him. My whole being screamed 'submit,' and I just *knew* I couldn't fight him; and then, when he touched me…"

Reye stopped talking after that and Ann knew why. Not too long ago, Reye, now known as the "Former Horror," was carried from Yam-Preen to Maestri after facing Lord Tanas. The experience had broken her. Lord Tanas's touch drained all the warmth from her body, including warm memories, and forced her to face her own past actions. Before the encounter, those actions only blurred together into one continuing moment where her revenge was all she cared about. But the experience forced her to realize the real horror of what she had both become and done in the name of her vengeance. The shock had left her a quivering, howling, Hy-mun female, who was sent to Maestri because the Tribe of Shadows believed she was no longer worth killing.

And they would have been right, Ann thought to herself. *I remember how Reye looked when she was first tossed into the cell. How she still looked after the Remnant's Seat of Kindness and I had revived her, and how she looked now. After facing Tanas, and the memories of her own actions, Reye realized she went so far against what she thought she knew about herself, and what she had been brought up to believe in, that she* needs *to talk about what she had done. If we were back at Spectral Academy, I would have sent Reye to speak with Worm; he always had good advice. Unfortunately, he's not here now. On the other hand, maybe Reye doesn't need a Hy-mun solution at all.*

Ann looked at the sleeping members of the Remnant of the Tribe, picking out one, in particular, the Seat of Kindness. He secretly came as a part of the Remnant's mission to try to persuade the Tribe of Shadows to stop the Third Great Attempt, had volunteered to go with the party and, so far, had been unnoticed by the other members of the Tribe of Shadows. The members of the Remnant Council were chosen because they each portrayed the virtue that their Seat represented better than anyone else. Because of that, even if the members of the Tribe of Shadows *Knew* the Seat of Kindness was *incredibly* kind, without another member of the Remnant identifying him *as* the Seat of Kindness there was no way to tell whether or not there was someone better back in Rem.

When the Seat of Kindness first saw Reye, he Knew *she was a broken Hy-mun,* Ann mused, remembering Reye's arrival in Maestri and forming an idea in her head. *Broken in mind, body, spirit, and heart and that the Tribesman who had accompanied her, instead of helping her to heal, did nothing but just sit back and let her injuries get worse. Together, the Seat of Kindness and I might have brought Reye out of the stupor she was in after facing Lord Tanas, but she's not past what she has done yet. Maybe the Remnant's ritual will work for her like it worked for me.*

Ann recalled that before Reye's arrival in Maestri, she had suffered her own self-crisis over what she had done to survive in Nis and had undergone a ritual performed by the Remnant to help her move past her actions.

I think it could work, Ann realized, thinking more about her own experience with the ritual. *Granted, my actions were nothing compared to Reye's rampage. That means her experience will probably be more intense than mine, but she needs it. Now, to get her to go along with it.*

Ann looked down at Reye. After finishing her story she quickly fell asleep again, muttering the phrase, "I had a choice," every few seconds. It was clear she was still haunted by her actions and that she willingly chose them of her own free will.

"You'll go along with it," Ann mumbled out loud. "The only good thing about being imprisoned in Maestri with a crowd from the Remnant is that they can help put you on the path toward healing yourself again. No doubt it will be a challenge, but you've never been one to back away from a challenge, and for the challenge alone I'm sure you'll attempt the ritual."

Elsewhere in the Third Circle of Nis, Lust Atrophied, another Hy-mun was facing her own challenges, where multiple lives now depended upon her success.

Chapter 10

What am I going to do, Stella worried as she curled up by a magma vent. Her mind jumbled with thoughts about the new life she now carried, the father of that life, the plans being drawn up against them, and the circumstances that delivered her here.

This all started when I was chosen to be part of the Demp Cavern Mining Project alongside my best friend, Reye, and her twin brother, Raymond, Stella remembered, the memories feeling like they belonged to someone else now. *At the time, we thought that it was the best thing that could have happened to us. The three of us were going together. Ann from Volcanology was also coming with us, along with my crush, Sol.*

Stella paused and giggled slightly in spite of her circumstances. She now realized it was the first time she had ever called Sol her "crush." It was actually the first time she thought about him in a while.

It took being attacked by the Tribe of Shadows, captured, brought to their home—the city of Nis—and everything that happened afterward just for me to call Sol a "crush." Spectral Academy really was a lifetime ago.

Stella could not think about Sol the same way she once did. She knew everything that had happened to her recently had changed her.

During the attack, I fell unconscious after witnessing Reye's twin brother, Raymond, get killed right in front of me. That towering mass of blue flesh and muscle—burning black in the light, those red eyes, and that hammer coming down on Raymond's head just before he spoke his last words, "Run, Fight, Live." I was certain that I was either going to die next or that everything was just a dream when I passed out. If I only knew my "nightmare" was just beginning.

Stella could not forget waking up in the room, the red-orange light from the vents on the floor, the soporific gas that made her feel hot and lethargic, and him.

The boy from the Tribe of Shadows, Met-on, he was here with me, too.

Stella looked up from where she was curled up by the vents to the bed where Met-on was sleeping peacefully. He looked different from the members of the Tribe of Shadows that she had seen in the attack; a fact he claimed was because he had "Rodent-blood," that his mother came from the Remnant of the Tribe. Met-on had ash-grey skin and two black horns that grew around his head until they joined into a small horn on his forehead. He was also shorter, and extremely feminine-looking, but that could also have been because of his age. Stella was sure he was still just a boy.

A "boy," Stella scoffed, the slight absurdity of her own thought almost making her laugh. *What that "boy" did to me while I was under the effects of the gas and continued to do to me every chance he came here goes against everything I was ever taught.*

Stella still shivered at the memory of their first encounter. Waking up, not knowing where she was, and then suddenly realizing she was naked as a then unknown assailant began examining her before having his way with her.

But the scariest thing about that encounter wasn't that it happened, that Met-on was who he was, or that he even said he would try to reserve me for himself, Stella thought to herself, the experience still haunting her mind. *The chilling thing was that he believes, even now, that he is entirely innocent of any wrongdoing.*

Met-on did look innocent, from the first time he came to her—and upon her, every time after that, and each instance where he stayed in the room to sleep off the encounter. He had a happy innocent look on his face and conducted himself like he was up to joyful work.

Is it any wonder I thought this was all a dream, Stella lamented. *Met-on's attitude, the complete impossibility of this against what I had been taught, how could I have not doubted my own eyes? Humph, I was a delusional fool acting out my own fantasies.*

Stella remembered all the different ways she tried to convince herself that everything happening to her was just a dream; including calling Met-on "her desires," and believing that if she could escape the city, she would "wake-up" and find herself back in the mining camp as if none of this ever happened. The belief led her to begin talking with Met-on, something he was thrilled to do, and learn as much about her "dream world" as possible.

Okay, let's review what I know, Stella encouraged, shaking off her sorrows and deciding instead to focus on the crucial thing—escape. *I know I am in the city of Nis, home to the Tribe of Shadows and its ruler Tanas; the same Tanas who, by all indications was once the closest friend to the Great Master Ash Addiel until he betrayed him and was then banished underground by him.*

Stella fearfully shivered at the knowledge that the *real* Tanas was alive somewhere in this city. Turns out just believing he exists trapped beneath the surface, even having faith that he was there, was nowhere near as frightening and strangely comforting, as to know *the truth* with absolute certainty. It was frightening to think he had been imprisoned underground all this time, but also comforting to know that he *was* there.

I know I am in the Third Circle of the city of Nis, Lust Atrophied, which is where women of the Tribe of Shadows are kept solely to provide future generations for the Tribe of Shadows. I also know some of the Tribe of Shadows' history.

That history Stella learned from Met-on also sent another tremor up her back. It is true that she felt comforted to know that Tanas was imprisoned underground, but she realized that imprisonment forced him into another group; one that had already suffered too much because of both Tanas and the Nag-el.

I know that the Tribe of Shadows once lived on the surface long before the Hy-mun were ever created. Back then they were just called the Tribe, and if I take what Met-on told me to be accurate, there was also no sunlight on the surface. Something must have been blocking it. Until the Nag-el, the "Beings of Light," invaded in a near genocidal attack Met-on referred to as "The Coming," an attack in which sunlight first shined on Prism. Afterward, the survivors escaped underground where sunlight, lethal to the Tribe, couldn't touch them. After that, the Tribe split into two groups; the Greater Tribe and the Remnant of the Tribe.

At the thought of the Remnant of the Tribe, Stella found herself gazing over to Met-on's sleeping form. He had already told her that his mother was a member of the Remnant of the Tribe and it was also the reason for his ash-grey skin and black horn. He also mentioned that the Tribe of Shadows considers members of the Remnant to be "Rodents." Yet since the discovery of her pregnancy, and with it the realization that she could not return to the surface until the baby was born, the Remnant seemed her best chance for survival, especially considering the rest of Met-on's story.

Met-on told me that after the Greater Tribe and the Remnant split, the Greater Tribe started looking for ways to fight the "Beings of Light." It was during that time that they were first contacted by Tanas and his Legion of Shadows—more betrayers that were exiled underground by the Great Master Ash Addiel. Joining them and becoming the Tribe of Shadows in the process. Afterwards letting Tanas restructure their whole civilization into what it is now and giving the Tribe of Shadows the tools they needed to begin attacking the surface.

That battle, the Remnant apparently wanted nothing to do with, Stella figured, trying to read into Met-on's story. *When the two factions split up, Met-on said that the Greater Tribe, later the Tribe of Shadows, worked to rebuild their society and make a plan for vengeance. A "Plan" that would later be improved upon by Tanas into what would later be called the Three Great Attempts. Each designed to make it possible for the Tribe of Shadows to regain the surface from the "Beings of Light," also known as the Nag-el, and their successors, the Hymuns. Meanwhile, the Remnant distanced themselves from the Tribe of Shadows and went to live beyond their borders. If they still don't want anything to do with the Tribe of Shadows' fight for the surface, then they might be the only ones I can go to. Of course, first I have to get out of here.*

From her talks with Met-on, she knew that Lust Atrophied was the third circle from the edge of the city. Originally, Stella had planned to slip out of her room while Met-on was asleep and attempt to escape while the city was distracted by the chaos of the "Hy-mun Horror." But as soon as Stella cracked open the door of her cell, she found that running was far more difficult than she had ever planned.

Those guards outside are the immediate problem, Stella fumed, gazing at the door and imagining the guards bursting in on them right now to kill them. *From what I overheard, if they discover my pregnancy, I'm dead. But if I wait and do nothing, I'm still dead. They have orders to kill me after killing Met-on and everyone else in the city like him. That just leaves me one real option, getting Met-on himself to help me.*

After discovering both the guards and their agenda, Stella realized that she would not even be able to leave her room alone, to say nothing of the city, especially considering she overheard one of the guards mention that the Hy-mun Horror had been captured. Stella knew that her best chance for escape and survival rested in convincing Met-on that both of their lives were in danger. Getting him to take her out of the city.

But I can't just tell *Met-on we're in danger,* Stella realized, casting a worried glance back at Met-on. *He'll never believe me. Regardless of everything that the Tribe of Shadows has done to him over his life, Met-on still considers himself one of them and believes they won't betray him.*

Over the course of their dialogue, Met-on not only talked about the history of the Tribe of Shadows and the workings of the Nis, but he also talked about some of the treatment he, and others like him, endured since half of his parentage came from the Remnant.

"Members of the Tribe of Shadows like me are taught by others like me. Teachers often told me that unless I found somewhere really *safe that I shouldn't sleep in the same place all the time,"* Stella remembered Met-on telling her. *"When I did, I found myself being rudely awakened by gladiators using me as a practice dummy. Not that they would kill me, I'm unworthy of the honor of martyrdom. They were just toughening me up for when I am given a branding mission. But recently, I have found a safe place to sleep."*

Yeah, here, Stella wanted to spit after hearing that, yet instead, she wisely held her tongue. She had already learned about brandings and the missions needed to earn them. Each branding was obtained after a member of the Tribe of Shadows completed a specific task for both the city of Nis and the Tribe of

Shadows. Receiving all of the brandings meant being welcomed into the Tribe of Shadows as an equal with unrestricted access to any part of the city. During her first escape attempt, Stella not only discovered the guards and their plans for her and Met-on, but also the details of Met-on's first branding mission.

"Get this," a voice Stella remembered snickering as its owner talked from just beyond her door. *"The Warden told the half-Rodent, if he could get the Hy-mun pregnant, or just make the Hy-mun fall for him and admit that she loved him, he would get his first branding."*

But the moment that happens, instead of giving Met-on the branding he wants you and your partner are going to storm in here and kill all of us, Stella shivered, remembering the rest of the guards' conversation. *And even if I don't do anything and manage to hide the pregnancy, you're just going to kill us all eventually anyway. So, what am I going to do?*

Stella looked again at Met-on, sleeping innocently in the bed. As much as it disgusted her, he was the only one she could count on for *any* help whatsoever; and from what she had learned, the only one she might be able to coax into helping her.

According to the guards, you need to get me pregnant, fall in love with you, or just confess to being in love with you for you to get your first branding, Stella thought, reviewing what she knew, piecing together a plan. *And you've already told me you would do anything for a branding, so just what counts as "anything?"*

A somewhat amused smile began creeping its way onto Stella's face. She knew that if she had not spent so much time trying to convince herself that her imprisonment was some kind of dream, she might have come up with this idea a whole lot sooner. Still, there was no guarantee that she would not have become pregnant by then so there was also no point in crying over it. All she could do was try it and hope it worked.

You already succeeded in getting me pregnant, and for all our sakes that cannot be discovered, Stella realized, knowing that her pregnancy would literally mean the death of all of them. *So, if I asked you to take me beyond the city, promising a profession of love for it, would you do it?*

Stella's smile grew the more she thought about it.

Of course, you will. It's to get your first branding after all, and you did say that you, or any member of the Tribe of Shadows like yourself with "Rodent-blood," would do anything for a branding. I imagine it will take a lot just to keep you from doing it. Now, I just have to ask you.

Stella walked over to the bed and began shaking Met-on. Positive her plan would work, she wanted to get out of Nis as quickly as possible.

"Met-on, get up, you have to get up."

Met-on rolled over where he slept, content where he was.

"Met-on," Stella pleaded, shaking him even harder. "You *have* to get up *right now!*"

"Okay, Big Sis," Met-on slurred, slowly waking up. "Do you want to…"

Met-on's eyes suddenly popped open as he jumped out of bed, quickly grabbed his clothes, and made for the door.

"Sorry I have to run, Big Sis Stella," Met-on apologized, both panic and urgency clear in his voice. "I just remembered there is something I have to do in regards to my duties, and it can't be put off. I'll see you later."

Stella, stunned silent by Met-on's sudden departure realized only after the door closed behind him that she had not asked him to take her outside the city. Instead, more questions began filling her head.

What could be so crucial that Met-on, who spends almost all of his time here, would need to rush for the door?

Suddenly, Stella remembered the guards' conversation and realized her death might be coming much sooner than she thought. Flattening herself against the wall, she tensed herself, waiting for whatever was going to happen next.

At least I know they're coming, Stella panicked, fearful for what was going to happen next. *When that door opens, and the guards come in, I'll run, and may the Great Master show mercy on both of us.*

Part 3: Reunions and Revelations

Chapter 11

"Sir Woody," a female voice called as its owner knocked on the cabin door, the knocking sound reverberating throughout the small cabin. "The ship will be docking into Tri-Dominion City's port soon."

"Please wait for me at the end of the hall," Virgil said through the door to who he guessed was Leslie's wife, Lucy. He knew they never traveled without each other and if she were picking him up, then Leslie must have been occupied on deck. "I'll meet you once I am in costume, and please drop the 'Sir.'"

"As you wish, Mr. Woody," Lucy acknowledged before making her way back down the hallway.

Virgil staggered to his feet, moaning as he stretched out. He did not sleep well on the metal floor of the SS Phlegyas, while Dan-te slept like a stone in the bed. After walking through Wanton City and the entire Hotel Avery Resort Complex leading to the port, Dan-te was emotionally and spiritually shocked; especially after seeing other members of the Tribe of Shadows enjoying themselves alongside Hy-muns while watching a wrestling match. That shock knocked her out and forced Virgil to carry her the rest of the way to the sand ship's cabin where he was able to revive her. But soon after that, she fell back asleep. Looking over at the bed, Dan-te was still fast asleep, the noise from Lucy not even stirring her.

"Dan-te, wake up," Virgil whispered into her ear, expecting she would hear him, but receiving no reply. Changing tactics, he started shaking her shoulder. It only took the slightest jolt of her shoulder for Dan-te to bolt upright, fully awake, so quickly Virgil jumped back.

"I'm up!" she shouted, a lifetime of evacuation drills making her used to rising to full wakefulness. "How long was I out?"

"Almost the whole trip," Virgil answered, getting dressed into costume. "Soon after the ship left port, you laid down on the bed, closed your eyes, and you were out. I didn't want to wake you since I figured you needed the rest."

"Burn it all again," Dan-te grumbled, she did not mean to fall asleep. Pulling the Veil of Shadows back over her and vanishing from Virgil's sight she walked over to him, into his shadow, and took his hand to establish the connection between them.

"Thanks for letting me sleep," Dan-te whispered through their connection. "But let's get going."

Virgil did not need more encouragement than that. Feeling Dan-te's veiled hand in his own, he became a blind man again and opened the door of their cabin, slowly walking down the hall tapping his cane with every step—getting into character—until they came to Lucy at the end of it.

"The ship is docking in Tri-Dominion City's port. Leslie is out on the deck. I'll guide you to the departure area, things have become somewhat crazy topside."

"Did something happen?" Virgil asked.

"Four of *them* decided to pay a surprise visit to Tri-Dominion City today for a retreat."

Dan-te almost flinched from Virgil's reaction.

"Virgil," Dan-te whispered, trying to get his attention. "What's going on? Who are *them*?"

Virgil merely stood there radiating the same golden energy of shock and awe that he generated the first time they met. Only this time, the energy was more intense and mixed with white mental energy and fearful pink energy.

"Mr. Woody," Lucy beckoned again, this time taking Virgil's shoulder, "we have to get going."

"Yes, of course, ma'am," Virgil stuttered, still in shock. "Could you please lead me to the deck and off the ship? With four of *them* in the city for a retreat I can imagine the port must be crazy."

"I would be glad too, right this way, sir."

Lucy led Virgil, still shaken, and the veiled Dan-te, still wondering who the mysterious *"them"* were, up through the ship. Lucy knew that Virgil did not need a guide, but to keep Virgil's cover intact she took him up to the main deck of the ship where Leslie was waiting. From there, the four of them were able to look out over the sand ship port and up Tri-Dominion City.

Tri-Dominion City got its name from its location. It sat on the intersections of the Yellow, Green, and Violet Dominions' three borders and shared some of the physical traits of all three dominions. The city contained the desert sands from the Yellow Dominion, grass plains from the Green Dominion—both joining together at the city's sand ship port, and the plateau of the Violet Dominion. The bulk of the entire city was built inside and up a massive split in the plateau that ran from the surface all the way to the summit where the border of the Violet Dominion was located. Because of its location Tri-Dominion City was a neutral city that did not fall under the jurisdiction of any Dominion and was often visited by all walks of Hy-mun life; and as Virgil and Dan-te witnessed on deck, it was getting ready for the "highest" level of Hy-mun life.

And I thought Virgil was shocked, Dan-te thought to herself. *Every Hy-mun on the ship is a golden ball of shock, awe, and more.*

Everywhere Dan-te looked, Hy-mun crew and passengers were struck silent. Each one was alight with the same golden radiance of shock and awe Virgil was generating. However, they lacked the white mental energy and fearful pink energy that Virgil produced, creating only the golden energy. Only their energies seemed more intense as they shouted and pointed toward a series of sand ships bearing a flag with a different colored ouroboros, a snake curled into a circle and eating its own tail, printed on it.

"What's going on," Virgil asked Lucy and Leslie, acting like he was blind and unable to see the commotion before him.

"Four of the seven Virt Princes have come to Tri-Dominion City for a retreat," Leslie answered. "As you know, the Virt Princes are the rulers of the Seven Dominions of Prism. Alongside us now are the personal ships belonging to Virt Prince Noah Virt Red-Scipian of the Red Dominion, Lucan Virt Orange-Licht of the Orange Dominion, and Moses Virt Yellow-Lien of the Yellow Dominion. The fourth Virt Prince to arrive, Ovid Virt Violet-Esprit from the Violet Dominion, came to the city via his own personal caravan across the Violet Dominion."

No wonder everyone's so shocked, Dan-te thought to herself, understanding now why Virgil and the rest of the Hy-muns on the sand ship were radiating golden shock and awe. *I remember Virgil telling me about the Virt Princes back at Spectral Academy when we were talking about the surface and how the Hy-muns ruled it. He said that when Hy-muns first spread across the Cherubi Continent that it was divided into the Seven Dominions; each named for one of the seven colors of light that radiated from the Seven Ziggurats that dotted the continent that, on the Day of Rainbow Light, created the boundaries for each Dominion. The Dominions were then divided further into divisions called Palaces, each ruled over by a Prince or Princess. But the Dominions themselves where ruled over by the Virt Prince, or Virt Princess, from one of the Seven Ziggurats. The Virt Prince or Virt Princess was a descendant of the ones who first found the Ziggurats and continued to pass the title and responsibilities on to their children once they died. And the Hy-mun people held the Virt Princes in very high regard.*

So high in fact that Dan-te was a little uncomfortable. Looking at Virgil and the other Hy-muns, *Knowing* how much they were in awe of being in the presence of a Virt Prince, reminded her slightly of the Tribe of Shadows and their devotion to Lord Tanas. Granted, the Hy-muns' awe was not the same as the Tribe of Shadows' devotion; but it was close enough to make her a little uncomfortable.

"Are the other Virt Princes going to come to Tri-Dominion City, too?" Virgil asked, his question snapping Dan-te back into the moment and making her realize something. Virgil was the *only one* generating mental white and fearful pink energy.

Why is that, Dan-te asked herself as Virgil focused on Lucy and Leslie, waiting for their answers.

"No. Archimedes Virt Green-Gander from our own Green Dominion isn't going to be in Tri-Dominion City today," Leslie answered. "Neither will Aeneas Virt Blue-Canoe from the Blue Dominion, or Hesiod Virt Indigo-Castitas from the Indigo Dominion."

The change in Virgil was immediate. As soon as he heard that Hesiod Virt Indigo-Castitas was not going to be in Tri-Dominion City, Dan-te noticed the fearful pink energy begin to dissipate.

Hesiod Virt Indigo-Castitas is the Virt Prince from Virgil's home, Dan-te quickly realized. *I can understand why Virgil would be in awe of him, but why is he afraid of him? And why is he still generating white mental energy? Has Virgil somehow met him before?*

Dan-te already knew that Virgil kept much of his personal past a secret. The little she did know, his involvement with the Alien Astronaut Movement, a group many deemed heretics, and his near-death encounter with the Hammers of the Orange Light, an extremist group that publicly did not exist was dangerous enough. Adding to it, some kind of family situation resulting in him having to travel in disguise told her that if he publicly exposed himself, he knew he would be risking not only his own life but also his family's.

But if Virgil, or his family, has some kind of connection to the Indigo Dominion's Virt Prince, then his family situation could be more complicated than I thought.

"Anyway, we need to get you off the ship," Lucy insisted, hurrying Virgil and the veiled Dan-te across the ship's deck. "You *did* risk coming all this way just to get to the Tri-Dominion Caverns, right?"

"Right," Virgil acknowledged, peering upwards towards the top of the plateau.

"Just this way then," Lucy continued, leading Virgil and Dan-te carefully from the deck of the sand ship to the dock. "Please be careful and stay close to me, with four Virt Princes visiting today the outer city is going to be filled with onlookers, fans, and every other type of person imaginable hoping to meet a Virt Prince. Also, security is going to be that much tighter, so I hope you're ready for *surprise inspections.*"

Dan-te noticed the peculiar way Lucy said the words "surprise inspections;" plus the flash of white mental energy and fearful pink energy from Virgil after the words had left her lips.

There are more to these inspections then they are letting on, Dan-te figured. *But the fear Virgil felt now only flashed through him. It wasn't something steady like when he thought the Virt Prince of his homeland could be here. Virgil must have set something up for the inspections thanks to his family circumstances. Whether or not it works, or if it is even needed, that must be what he's nervous about. Humph, when I get the chance, I am going to have to ask him more about what those* situations *surrounding him and his family actually are. I'll bet they're the reason why Lucy and Leslie are so eager to help us.*

Dan-te remembered the story Virgil told her about when he was a part of the Alien Astronaut Movement. He had to join under the alias "Uni," wearing a mask everywhere he went so that only a few people knew who he really was. Virgil claimed the reason for the anonymity was a "certain situation" involving both him and his family, and that situation was also the reason he was the only survivor of the Hammers' raid.

Virgil never mentioned those "situations" again after that, Dan-te mused, thinking back on all of their conversations since then. *But I* Know *it's something* extremely *private to Virgil and has left him with mixed feelings. At times, like right now, he's glad to have them. From the moment Lucy put his hand on his shoulder to lead him, his energy calmed; and if she and Leslie are here because of Virgil's family situation, and I bet they are, then he's glad for it. But at other times, like when he talked about needing to hide his identity and how his "situation" ensured he would survive the Hammer's attack, that told me he would rather have been rid of them altogether. But right now, whatever those situations are, they're working in our favor. I just wish he could tell me what was still bothering him.*

Dan-te would soon learn what was bothering Virgil, and more, as their party slowly made its way off the SS Phlegyas and onto the sand ship port to the outer portion and Stone Gate of Tri-Dominion City. But getting through that gate would prove to be more difficult than any of them thought.

Chapter 12

"Is it always this crowded and noisy?" Virgil and Dan-te asked in unison; Virgil playing the part of a tourist and Dan-te whispering in genuine curiosity.

"It's usually not *this* bad," Leslie answered among the din of tourists, passersby, and normal residents. "The Virt Princes' arrival has stirred everyone up. I would recommend just ignoring them and focus on where you need to go."

Easy for you to say, Virgil thought to himself, a phrase Dan-te *Knew* he wanted to shout to Leslie. Yet what was even more surprising was how everyone else in the city could just ignore everything else around them because of the Virt Princes' arrival.

Is it the awe of being near the Virt Princes, Dan-te wondered, noticing dozens of Hy-muns gathered near the Virt Princes' ships, each one glowing fiercely with golden energy that concealed all the others. *Or is it the awe of the city itself and how it is built inside the plateau? But almost every Hy-mun present in this city seems to be amazed by one thing or another and can't stop talking about it, and those feelings of awe are blinding them to anything else they could be feeling or what could be going on around them.*

Thinking back to her encounter in Wanton City, Dan-te realized that the Hy-muns there were as blind as the ones in Tri-Dominion City. The only difference was that before they were consumed by lust, now the blinding emotion was awe. Virgil, Lucy, and Leslie were the only ones who seemed different, for varying reasons.

Both Leslie and Lucy are muting themselves to everyone except themselves and Virgil. Their energies are so withdrawn that I can barely see any color in them at all. The only thing I can tell is that they are projecting a blue resolve energy and focusing it directly on the road ahead of us. They want to get Virgil to wherever it is they need to take him as quickly as possible, and they are determined not to let anyone or anything distract them from that. I wonder why he's so different from them?

The mystery of Virgil's past was becoming more profound by the second. But if Dan-te thought Virgil would give her some clue through his energy and reactions, she was wrong.

Virgil's not concealing his energy, even the fearful pink energy I noticed him generate the moment he learned about the Virt Princes; he's spreading it out, changing his focus all the time, looking everywhere, even though his head is still pointed forward. I'll bet if I looked under his glasses I would find that his eyes are searching the area. But that's something I've seen him do before. He did that back in Wanton City, and he could just be doing it again right now. It's not like it means anything about his past. The only places that he does seem to be paying particular attention to are the big stone gate and gatehouse in front of us and the top of the plateau, the latter of the two I understand his interest in completely.

Before leaving Spectral Academy, Virgil told Dan-te that the Tri-Dominion Caverns they needed to reach started inside a crevasse outside the city at its highest point, where it entered the Plateau. Dan-te easily realized that Virgil's interest in the top of the plateau was because the Tri-Dominion Caverns were there, and she had the same interest. But Virgil's interest in the city's large stone main gate built at the base of the plateau where the crack in it began—as well as the gatehouse in front of it—was entirely unknown to her. Even more curious was how Virgil's pink fear energy seemed to build the closer they came to the gatehouse—and even more so once they walked inside.

"I hope you are prepared for what you are going to find in there," Leslie whispered, patting Virgil on the back in a sign of departure before turning to walk away with Lucy.

"I am," Virgil replied, a flash of understanding passing between the two of them Dan-te did not fail to miss. Before leaving, while Dan-te slept and regained her strength, Virgil had set up two plans to get them through Tri-Dominion City's main gate in the event of trouble. Now he knew those plans were going to be tested.

I just wonder what we need to be ready for, Dan-te mused, mentally trying to prepare herself for whatever she might experience.

Also, just what *preparations did Virgil make?*

"This is as far as we can take you," Lucy sighed, depositing Virgil and Dan-te into a line of Hy-muns heading toward a door marked "Entry." "Enjoy your stay in Tri-Dominion City," Lucy called back, "and *good luck to you.*"

Lucy and Leslie's send-off was as customary as it could be for any traveler, but neither Virgil nor Dan-te could not help overhearing how they phrased their words. They both knew that they wished them exceptional luck based partially on who Virgil really was but more for what they still had to face.

Inside the gatehouse, while Dan-te waited with Virgil in the line leading to the city's main gate, Dan-te was able to get a better look at it through a window in the roof of the building. The stone gate radiated slightly with the various energies coming from the city, but its design and overall look cast an eerie shadow in her mind.

Whoever carved and built this must have had the same idea as the builders of the main gate of the city of Nis, Dan-te reflected. *The design and the way that it looks are almost identical. I wonder if a Hy-mun was once snatched by the Tribe of Shadows, saw the gate, escaped, and then rebuilt what he saw here—or maybe the opposite.*

Dan-te already knew the Tribe of Shadows were no strangers to taking things created by the Hy-muns and incorporating them throughout Nis. While the most significant period of this incorporation began at the ending of the Second Great Attempt, there was no reason to believe it did not happen before that.

Maybe Tempters watched the gate as it was being built and then went back to Nis and copied it. In fact, if Virgil's maps were correct, we should be over Nis now.

Dan-te gazed slightly at the ground, realizing that now she was standing over Nis, the very place she escaped from. Thinking about Tempters also brought another realization forward. Despite all the Hy-muns, she had not seen a single Tempter yet.

They must be getting ready to start the Third Great Attempt, Dan-te guessed. *We need to hurry. At least this line is moving smoothly.*

The line of Hy-muns did move smoothly, but every so often it would stop for some reason before quickly resuming. It was not long, though, until both Dan-te and Virgil were almost outside of the gatehouse and in sight of both the stone gate itself and the central part of Tri-Dominion City beyond it.

The city starts at ground level, Dan-te thought to herself, taking her first good look at it. *From there, it builds upwards on the ledges and cliffs in the crack running up to the top of the plateau. Some of those ledges even lead out to other areas alongside the plateau. But the different levels, they seem like...*

Dan-te did not finish her thought, she let it hang in her mind. She did not want to say to herself that what she *Knew* about Tri-Dominion City from her first real glance of it genuinely reminded her of Nis. Perhaps the most similar resemblance to Nis was how each section of the city seemed to be reserved for a specific city function. Just like Nis, with all its different circles, Tri-Dominion City's multiple ledges and levels were devoted to various functions. She *Knew* that was the case from the energy each ledge radiated just as quickly as she *Knew* the purposes of each of the Circles of Nis from the moment she entered them. Dan-te was losing herself over this eerie resemblance so much that she almost lost contact with Virgil until a voice suddenly stopped both of them.

"Papers?" the voice asked.

Since Virgil played the role of a blind Hy-mun he acted surprised at being stopped by a checkpoint guard who suddenly put his arm across Virgil's chest. Dan-te quickly looked at the guard, who radiated sable colored monotony. She *Knew* he was not paying attention to see if Virgil was blind or not, he was simply repeating the same motions again and again with no ambition beyond repeating them. After looking up and noticing Virgil's disguise the guard ignored it asked the question again.

"Papers?"

Virgil, regaining his composure, produced a booklet which he presented to the checkpoint guard. The guard, after looking over the papers in it, quickly stamped them before handing them back to Virgil and pushing him on his way.

"Get going," the guard said, turning away from Virgil and the veiled Dan-te and moving onto the next Hy-mun waiting in line.

"Glad that's over and done with," Dan-te whispered. Virgil nodded slightly in both acknowledgment and agreement, relief washing over him as he exhaled a long-held breath as the two of them began walking toward the stone gate and the city beyond it. But no sooner than they started, an alarm began ringing throughout the area.

Chapter 13

"All entries, stay where you are," a voice boomed across the arena. "Prepare for a Fury Spot Check!"

"Just what I was afraid of," Virgil whispered, and Dan-te *Knew* it. The moment the alarm sounded Virgil pulsed fearful pink energy. Whatever this "Fury Spot Check" was, it was making Virgil scared, and not only for himself but also for *her* as well; and he was not the only one. Across the arena leading to the stone gate, multiple Hy-muns were flashing in the same fearful pink energy as Virgil. Dan-te was about to ask Virgil what was going on when a new sound quickly drew her attention, an onrushing mob of women coming from the building between them and the stone gate. Each one extruded ferocious scarlet energy as they struck like rabid hunters, taking random people into custody, and bringing them back into the building that they emerged from.

"Take that one," a group leader bellowed, "and take the blind man, too!"

Dan-te could tell Virgil was *really* scared, his fearful pink energy flowing out of him now. However, he kept his disguise up. Anyone else would have thought he was only a trembling blind man until three women came up to him and spirited him away into the building with the other Hy-muns. Virgil started acting more scared after that, but Dan-te *Knew* better.

Virgil's terrified, Dan-te realized, the fearful pink energy now pouring out of him in waves around them. *I've never seen Virgil this scared, even when he figured out the super volcano, but from the moment that alarm went off he has not stopped being afraid. Just who, or what, are these Furies?*

Now that they were all in the building, Dan-te shifted her gaze to the nearest Fury to see what she might find out about her from her energy. It did not take long for her to *Know* that it was the Furies' job to uncover secrets. When they first exploded into the area, they gave off ferocious scarlet energy, the energy of a hunter. Dan-te could also see they were generating a focused white mental energy. That energy followed each of their gazes, piercing each Hy-mun in the room. As it did the energy in their minds pulsed bigger and brighter. They were looking for disguises, masks, concealments—everything that both Virgil and Dan-te represented.

No wonder Virgil is so scared, Dan-te thought to herself. *Virgil told me that it would have been a bad idea to go public with the danger presented by the Third Great Attempt because no one would have listened to me. If I tried, I most likely would have been killed before I could make my case to prevent my story from causing any kind of conflict with the mainstream religious and social structures of the Hy-mun world; killed by Hy-muns like the Hammers and these Furies.*

The Furies, they live *to expose secrets, and I already know Virgil is keeping plenty of them, not just my secrets, but his own as well.* Dan-te *Knew* Virgil was thinking. Deep inside all that fearful pink energy shined a mixture of mental white and stressful grey energies. Dan-te could guess he was thinking about the secrets he was carrying, and how to get out with those secrets secure. But she could also tell that a part of him was reliving his past.

Virgil's white mental energy is drifting slightly, Dan-te noted, watching as the Furies sorted each of the Hy-muns in the room. *I'll bet a part of him is reliving the attack on the AAM camp right now when he faced the Hammers of the Orange Light. These Furies with their ferocious scarlet energy definitely seem to come from the same extremist stock that the Hammers come from. And like the Hammers, encountering them might cost us both a lot more than just time.*

"Come along now, move," one of the three Furies screamed, pulling Virgil, the veiled Dan-te, and another Hy-mun into another room in the building. As they entered the building, Dan-te noticed someone else joining the other Hy-mun.

"A Tempter," Dan-te whispered to Virgil. "A Tempter just appeared next to that other Hy-mun."

It was a Tempter from the Tribe of Shadows, the first one Dan-te had seen in a while. Thankfully, the Tempter seemed too busy with the Hy-mun he was with to notice Dan-te and Virgil, and Virgil was too busy acting less scared then he really was to fake anything for the Tempter's benefit. As for the Furies, they had their hands full with the other Hy-mun.

The Furies led the other Hy-mun in front of a strange silver machine built into the form of a female Hy-mun's head. The Lead Fury fixed him into a chair in front of the device while three more Furies walked behind it.

I wonder what all this is for, Dan-te thought to herself, receiving her answer sooner than she would have liked.

The three Furies pressed a series of buttons behind the head-shaped machine causing its eyes to open and cast a white light upon the man on the chair. But what took Dan-te's breath away was the shadow being cast. It was not only the Hy-mun's shadow but also the *Tempter's.* Quickly looking to the Furies, she saw that each of them radiated the same grim recognition.

"They've *seen* Tempters before," Dan-te whispered.

Virgil did not answer, but Dan-te noticed him nodding slightly in agreement. The Tempter also seemed to realize that his cover was blown. He reached for his hand to try and press the stone that would send him back to Nis but found that it did not work. He tried shadow walking next but quickly realized that he could not do that either; he was trapped and bound to the Hy-mun.

"Where is the nearest purification chamber," the Lead Fury asked with a grin.

"Purification?" the Hy-mun in the chair asked. "Why do I need purification?"

The Hy-mun in the chair had been strapped so he could not see behind to the Tempter's shadow trying to break free of him.

"Tri-Dominion City Hospital," a Fury answered.

"Take this one there and purify him; now, onto you."

The other Furies unstrapped the Hy-mun, still asking what he needed to be purified from, while the Lead Fury approached Virgil and the veiled Dan-te.

"Since you can't see this machine, or what it just accomplished, let me give you a brief explanation of what it is and what it's going to do to you."

Dan-te easily noticed the teal pride seeping out of the Lead Fury as she talked. She was not helping by explaining the machine. She just wanted to boast about it.

"This is the Medusa Machine. It's a divine tool originally crafted by the Nag-el and gifted to Tri-Dominion City by the Violet Dominion after the Great Rainbow War."

The Medusa Machine is a relic left behind by the Beings of Light, Virgil's "Nag-el," Dan-te whiffed, now as scared as Virgil and tightening her grip on Virgil's hand; a hand that was also shaking. *Worse, it looks like it can reveal anyone hidden by the Veil of Shadows and bind them to whomever they are attached to.*

"After the Great Rainbow War, we discovered how to make the Medusa Machine's eyes open," the Lead Fury further explained. "And when the eyes of the Medusa Machine opened, we discovered spies of Tanas, criminals against the nature and the order of the Great Master Ash Addiel hiding in the shadows of our own people. But the Medusa Machine petrifies them like stone in the shadow of whatever Hy-mun they've attached themselves to until they can be purified. So just relax, you have nothing to worry about."

Dan-te and Virgil had *plenty* to worry about, and they *knew* it. They already witnessed the Medusa Machine reveal and bind a Tempter to a Hy-mun. Once its eyes opened, Dan-te would be exposed to the Furies, and both Virgil and Dan-te would be sent to be "Purified." Neither one of them had any idea what that meant, but neither one wanted to find out.

"Now let's get you into the chair," the Lead Fury chuckled gleefully.

"Ah, do I really need to go through with this," Virgil asked skeptically, his voice trembling as he talked. "Do you really think Tanas would want to use someone like me as a spy?"

"What better person?" the Lead Fury countered. "Now stop fidgeting. Furies, get this one into the chair."

Dan-te *Knew* Virgil was trying to buy time, but she could not tell for what.

Every door is guarded, there aren't any windows, what are you doing? Dan-te wondered as Virgil was dragged to the chair and strapped in place.

"If you have a plan, Virgil, tell me now," Dan-te whispered; but Virgil remained silent. Remembering the other Tempter, Dan-te ducked behind the chair hoping her own shadow would be masked by Virgil's shadow.

"I'm already stuck with you," Dan-te said, knowing that the damage to the Veil of Shadows made it impossible for her to shadow walk. "The worse this machine can do is reveal me. Let's just hope I can keep that from happening on my own."

Chapter 14

"All right, open the eyes and…"

The Lead Fury was interrupted when the door burst open and another Fury entered the room carrying a letter that she gave to the Lead Fury. Dan-te quickly noticed the new Fury's face, and the Lead Fury's face after she read the letter.

They're shining with the same golden energy of shock and awe that the Hymuns at the harbor were alight with, but it's also mixed with fearful pink energy. What's more, that energy is being directed toward Virgil.

Virgil, however, was holding his breath in anticipation, expectation, and hope. He knew this was the moment they would either be caught or be set free.

"Shut down the Medusa Machine and take this one out now," the lead Fury screamed, surprising everyone in the room; no one ever left a Fury Investigation. "Did you not hear me, shut down the Medusa Machine and take this one out of here *now*! Furthermore, this incident *never happened*, understood?"

Dan-te *Knew* that none of the Furies understood what was going on, their white mental energy had become erratic and confused the moment the Lead Fury ordered the Medusa Machine to be turned off. However, she was not going to argue. Nor was Virgil. Dan-te could not begin to describe the relief she felt from him; the fearful pink energy falling away from him as the Furies unstrapped him and took him away from the Medusa Machine. Still, something troubled her.

Why hasn't the fearful pink energy completely dissipated from him?

While most of the fearful pink energy was gone, a steady pulse of it continued coming from inside Virgil, meaning there was still *something* for him to be afraid of.

Also, why did the new Fury and Lead Fury suddenly emit fearful pink energy and the golden energy of shock and awe and direct it toward Virgil? What's so special about him?

"Lead Fury! I don't understand," one of the other Furies shouted, clearly sharing the same questions as Dan-te and many of the other Furies in the room. "Why are we letting this one go before being examined by the Medusa Machine? He could have one of Tanas's minions attached to him, he could need purification, he could…"

"Enough!" the Lead Fury shouted, silencing the other Furies and moving to personally take charge of Virgil and the veiled Dan-te. "The powers that be have spoken on the matter so forget it and move on."

That one sentence seemed to quiet the other Furies, but Dan-te *Knew* otherwise.

They are not *going to forget this and move on. Each one of the Furies is a frazzle of white mental energy. They want answers about what was in that letter and why it made Virgil exempt from the examination. Not only that, their frazzled energy is being directed toward that new Fury who delivered it. I bet as soon as we walk out of this room they are going to start grilling her for information.*

Dan-te was right, as soon as the door closed behind them she could hear a muffled commotion from the room with the Medusa Machine; the other Furies were *very curious* about why Virgil was being escorted from the building by the Lead Fury herself. As for the Lead Fury, once they left the building, her entire energy and demeanor changed.

If her eyes weren't still shining with the same scarlet energy that the rest of her body had been generating, I would almost think she was about to suffer the Death of the Self, Dan-te observed, thinking about the Lead Fury's sudden change in all aspects but her eyes. *Before, she was radiating the predatorial scarlet energy of a hunter and a sharp mental white energy along with all the sharp smelling odors that I smelled from gladiators in Nis. Now, she is glowing with the golden energy of shock and awe, displaying only enough mental energy to perform the duties assigned to her, and giving off the soft scent of submissiveness. Only the eyes are unchanged.*

Dan-te knew that when someone experienced the Death of the Self, their energy, scents, character, everything that makes them a unique person is supposed to change from one form to another to the point that the "new" self essentially "kills" the old one. In the process of that change, the eyes, which held one's true nature, were the last thing to change, and if the eyes didn't turn than the Death of the Self had not happened yet.

"Now I *really* want to know about your past," Dan-te whispered to Virgil, curious how he, or a letter concerning him, could cause such a drastic change in the Lead Fury as she took them to the stone gate where a Hy-mun waited for them. The Hy-mun watched them intently and radiated the same golden energy as the Lead Fury.

"Your *ward*, sir," the Lead Fury said cautiously, delivering Virgil to the Hy-mun. "While I did take him out of examination I do recommend he is at least *seen* at Tri-Dominion City Hospital. For *security* purposes and…"

"Thank you, Lead Fury," the Hy-mun said cutting her off. "My boy and I were just going there now anyway to check on an old friend. Good day."

The Hy-mun, placing his hand on Virgil's shoulder, led him through the stone gate and into Tri-Dominion City. Dan-te, still protected by the Veil of Shadow, took a good look at this new Hy-mun whom she guessed was responsible for the letter that got them out of the Furies' investigation.

This Hy-mun is like Leslie and Lucy. He's met Virgil before, Dan-te realized. Now closer, she could tell that beneath his golden energy there was also a pulse of white mental energy that was now directed at Virgil.

But he's also afraid. Dan-te could see that besides white mental energy, fearful pink energy mixed with it also. *Besides holding Virgil in great awe, he's also afraid for what could happen to him. This Hy-mun must have been keeping watch for Virgil since we first approached the stone gate, ready to act in case we were taken by the Furies.*

"Another of your *preparations,* I imagine?" Dan-te whispered.

Virgil, however, gave no outward answer the other Hy-mun could notice beyond a slight nod of his head that could be taken for anything. But what Dan-te could feel and *Know,* told her much more.

The way I can feel your whole body is heating alone tells me you're embarrassed, Dan-te observed. *But also scared. Your hand is trembling as much as it's warming up. That spark of fearful pink energy hasn't left you, it's still there in your head mixing with the white mental energy in your head. You're actually reminding me of my brother again. During the gladiatorial fights when it was the two of us against the Tribe of Shadows' gladiators, he would have a spark of pink fearful energy in his head, too; always afraid of where the next gladiator was going to attack us from.*

"You really didn't want to rely on this Hy-mun to get us out of that mess, did you?" Dan-te guessed, figuring that whatever secrets Virgil needed to reveal about his past through this other Hy-mun were things he did *not* want to be uncovered or have others talking about. Virgil again nodded slightly in reply, but beyond that maintained the persona of a blind Hy-mun being directed by another one as they continued into the lowest parts of Tri-Dominion City.

The bottom of Tri-Dominion City felt like a well bottom. Looking up, after passing through the stone gate, the city itself quickly gave Dan-te the impression that she was at the bottom of a deep well, a fact she realized was intentional in the city's design. The crack Tri-Dominion City was built into ran further into the plateau then she initially thought, and now that she was inside, she could look up and see buildings and roads of all shapes and sizes surrounding her and working their way to the top of the plateau. Another eerie reminder of how Tri-Dominion City seemed to mirror Nis was how some of the best places rested at the top of the city and the worst at the bottom.

This place might not look like Maestri, Dan-te thought to herself. *But it certainly feels like it.* On the surface level of Tri-Dominion City, Dan-te found herself confronted with not only Hy-muns moving in and out of the city, but also with more Hy-muns giving off the same scarlet energy as the Furies. Not as fierce as the Furies, but the purpose was the same—to hunt down anyone causing trouble. Dan-te also noticed another building, slightly sunk into the ground with a patrol of Hy-mun in front of it. The energy from the whole building burned with a flaming scarlet and white energy as the silver energy of life drifted slowly away from it, giving it the appearance of one large open burning grave.

Some kind of prison, Dan-te guessed, remembering Maestri and when she and the other members of the Remnant were first taken by the Tribe of Shadows into Nis. *The warriors in Maestri also burned with scarlet energy and white mental energy when they decided what should be done with us. I don't even want to imagine what might be happening in a Hy-mun prison, especially if it costs lives.*

Dan-te *Knew* that if silver life energy was drifting away from the building it meant Hy-muns were dying there. Why they were dying, she did not want to guess. Lost in her unease about the close similarity between Tri-Dominion City's lowest level and Nis's Maestri, Dan-te almost lost her hold on Virgil. Quickly realizing her mistake, she tightened her grip on him. Continuing on, the three of them soon came to another building. This one glowed with both fearful pink energy and silver life energy, the latter sometimes drifting away from it. Around the entrance, the words "Tri-Dominion City Hospital" were written.

"This is the hospital the Furies sent that other Hy-mun to for 'Purification.' The one the Hy-mun leading us said he also needed to go to so he could look in on someone," Dan-te thought to herself as the other Hy-mun led them inside, checking them in at a desk just past the doors, and taking them further into an empty room, and closing the door behind them.

"Thank you for your help, Mr. Geryon," Virgil exhaled to the Hy-mun, now identified as a Mr. Geryon. "I apologize for getting you involved like I did. I would rather you just met me on the other side of the stone gate like I wanted."

"Lord Virgil," Mr. Geryon began, using the honorific "Lord" that almost caused Dan-te to shout out in surprise. The moment the word "Lord" came out of his mouth, Mr. Geryon flared up with an even more brilliant golden energy of shock and awe and Virgil equally flared up with fearful pink energy. "I thank you for your concern, but you shouldn't worry yourself. You know we would do anything to aid you and your family."

"Please do not call me 'Lord,'" Virgil begged. "It is not safe. Just call me Woody."

"Very well, Woody, for the time being, you are my Ward who is joining me to visit a sick friend here before going to a resort near the Tri-Dominion Caverns.

However, I should let you know now that getting to the caverns may not be possible."

"What," Virgil and Dan-te said, even though only Virgil's voice could be heard. They both knew what not getting to the caverns would mean.

"Some group is setting something up there," Mr. Geryon explained. "They have the backing of the Virt Prince of the Violet Dominion, so they have been able to keep it very quiet. It started not long after that mining accident in the Red Dominion. Only certain people have been allowed to get close."

Virgil knew that the "mining accident" Mr. Geryon referred to was the attack by the Tribe of Shadows on the Demp Cavern Mining Project that Reye and the others joined. The fact that there was now something secret going on at the Tri-Dominion Caverns soon after the attack was starting to set off Virgil's skepticism and paranoia; a signal that Dan-te quickly picked up on, noting the white mental energy sparking throughout his head.

"I need to get to those caverns quickly Mr. Geryon, no questions asked. It would take me too long to try and get to the Prison Caverns, especially from here. Just get me as close as you can, and I'll do the rest. I've gotten through tougher things before."

"That I know, Woody," Mr. Geryon responded somberly. Dan-te *Knew* that both Virgil and Mr. Geryon, at that moment, were remembering how Virgil made it back home after the Alien Astronaut Movement were all wiped out except for him. Their white mental energies, both hazy as they remembered the past, were also hazy in the same way as they remembered the same event.

"So, now what do we do?" Virgil asked Mr. Geryon.

"You wait while I make some arrangements at the front desk to check up on my friend who is here," Mr. Geryon explained. "I didn't lie to the Lead Fury about knowing someone here, so we need to check up on them in case the Furies have spies lurking around the hospital. It might also be a good idea to take a small tour of this hospital just so your face is seen here."

"Just as long as it's quick," Virgil countered. "I want to get moving as soon as possible."

"It will," Mr. Geryon assured. "After the tour is over we'll head for the resort near the Tri-Dominion Caverns, a mini-airship will be meeting us here to take us there faster. I'll be right back."

Mr. Geryon left the room. Alone, Dan-te decided that now would be the best time to talk about some of the recent *happenings* that had come up.

"So, *Lord* Virgil," Dan-te began. "I think that there are quite a few things that you need to tell me about your past. Things that I now *want* to hear."

"And you would be right about that," Virgil said in reply. "It's time I told you everything about my past and why I've been keeping certain things about myself secret. Not just from you, but from everyone." Taking a deep breath, building up his resolve, he began to tell his story.

Chapter 15

"My full name is Virgil Virt Indigo-Castitas, my father is the Virt Prince of the Indigo Dominion, Hesiod Virt Indigo-Castitas."

"Oh," Dan-te whiffed, not knowing what else she could say to that. She had already witnessed how the general Hy-mun population reacted to just being potentially near a Virt Prince. If it became common knowledge that the son of one of them was standing in their midst, he would never get a moment's relief from the adoration that would be dumped on him. The Lead Fury's sudden change, radiating shock and awe, and taking Virgil out of the building suddenly made a lot more sense. She had found out who both Virgil and his father were and did not want to risk making the wrong person angry.

"Yes," Virgil continued. "My father is the current Virt Prince of the Indigo Dominion, and I am one of his two twin sons. My early years were spent mostly secluded from the outside Dominions. I only left the Dominion on rare occasions. Thankfully for me, I was a quick study. By the time I was 14, I knew just about all I could learn from the tutors my father hired."

"So, your father sent you to receive an education outside of your Dominion?" Dan-te asked.

"Not a chance," Virgil countered. "If my father had his way I would have never left the Indigo Dominion or the Tanzanite Ziggurat. It was my mother who made it possible for me to study abroad."

Dan-te remembered Virgil talking about his mother. He said her family was the one with the ties to the AAM. Those connections allowed Virgil to work with the AAM and make it safely back home after the AAM was wiped out by the Hammers of the Orange Light.

"My mother is an extremely open-minded individual, a trait I am happy to have inherited from her. She's always interested in the newest innovation, idea, or concept. A favorite saying of hers is, 'sapiens qui prospicit'; which means, 'wise is he who looks ahead.' She first heard that from her own mother and took the saying to heart when it came to projects and ways of thinking; always looking ahead to the future and what it could be. That was how her family first came in contact with the AAM and was how she later managed to make me a part of it, provided the bulk of the members didn't know who I was."

"Which was why you needed to wear the mask," Dan-te reasoned, remembering Virgil's story about the AAM. "I've already noticed how everyone reacted just from possibly being near a Virt Prince. If the son of one tried working with the AAM, I'm guessing you would have found it *inconvenient*."

"Exactly," Virgil agreed. "The public story was that I had a facial blemish that needed to be covered, and after what happened to the AAM, which only my immediate family and a few close friends knew I had joined, no one wanted me to leave the Dominion again in case I might have been identified by the Hammers, until I finally convinced them, and myself, to let me attend Spectral Academy. Being identified is probably one of the biggest fears any of us have. Besides a lot of unwanted attention, if the Hammers discover that the child of a Virt Prince was involved with a group of heretics, the political repercussions would be severe."

Dan-te did not understand Hy-mun politics, but she *Knew* Virgil did. From the moment he started talking about his real identity and his fear of being identified as the son of a Virt Prince, his pink fearful energy had been steadily rising to the surface.

Virgil is putting himself more at risk then I thought, Dan-te realized, seeing the pink energy rising from inside of him. *No, I have that wrong, it's not just himself he's risking to help me, he's risking his entire Dominion. And he Knows it. Still, one thing doesn't make sense. From all the golden energy of shock and awe I've seen projected just toward the potential residences of the Virt Princes, the Hy-muns must know everything they can about them. So, if Virgil is one of two* twin *sons, one fact still seems out of place.*

"Virgil, how have you *not* been identified before now?" Dan-te asked. "You said you have a twin brother, and if that brother has made any public appearances couldn't someone recognize you as being his twin?"

Virgil chuckled at Dan-te's question.

"What's so funny?"

"I'll be able to show you later," Virgil explained. "It is true that my brother Homer is the heir apparent to become the next Virt Prince after our father, and he is in the public view all the time. But you see, my brother and I aren't identical twins, we're *fraternal* twins. That means the two of us look nothing alike. In fact, if you saw the two of us next to each other, you might not even think we were related. Plus, outside of the Tanzanite Ziggurat, *no one* knows what I look like. All anyone knows is that I just exist and that I am studying privately."

"So, no one outside your immediate home has ever seen you and realized you were the son of the Virt Prince?"

"It's only happened once," Virgil answered.

"But doesn't that mean that person could identify you now?"

"I highly doubt it. It happened a year before I left for Spectral Academy. My father was hosting ambassadors from the Violet Dominion and I, like always, was kept away from the crowds. Feeling bored, I snuck out and went exploring through some of the older corridors in the upper levels of the Tanzanite Ziggurat, levels off-limits to anyone except the ruling family and certain staff members. Turning a corner, I found a girl in a deep violet dress holding a mask on a balcony at the end of the hallway."

"That girl is the one who saw you," Dan-te figured, listening to Virgil's reflection on the event. "But I'm guessing the girl was not supposed to be there."

"Right on both counts. The girl who saw me, or to be more precise the girl I saw first, was sneaking around in the Tanzanite Ziggurat when I spotted her. If I reported her she would have found herself in a *lot* of trouble. Not only that, she wasn't wearing her mask."

"Why would that be an issue?"

"The wearing of a mask is a style of dress that some of the more extreme conservatives of the Violet Dominion make their children practice until they come of age. The fact that she was still holding it and that I could see her face told me that she hadn't reached that point yet."

"I thought extreme conservatives only came from the Yellow Dominion," Dan-te interrupted, remembering the story Virgil had told her about the Great Rainbow War and the extremists groups in it.

"The Yellow Dominion is the best example of extreme conservatism, but in one way or another, examples of it spread throughout all the dominions. The girl was standing on the balcony with her mask off, something I knew she was not supposed to do in public until she turned 18 and went through her Unmasking Ceremony, and was just letting the sun shine on her. I could tell that she was close to my age from her looks and that by just being seen unmasked it would mean serious trouble for her, especially with her family."

"You didn't sneak up on her and surprise her?" Dan-te asked.

"No, I didn't, in fact, neither of us did anything at first. The girl just stood there in the sunlight, breathing deeply, and trying to imprint everything she was looking at into her mind so that she would never forget it. As for myself, I just watched, then decided to go back to my room. I realized if either one of us became aware of the other, it would mean trouble for both of us. Unfortunately, something happened that made the situation *really* problematic."

"What?" Dan-te asked.

"An attendant showed up and surprised me," Virgil answered.

"Oh, no."

Dan-te could picture Virgil becoming scared by an attendant, wondering why he was out instead of in his room, and at the same time alerting the girl to his own presence.

"Exactly, I can still remember what that attendant said to me. 'Lord Virgil, what are you doing here? Your father, the Virt Prince, gave explicit instructions that you are not to be seen. You are *supposed* to be receiving private schooling.'"

"And who is going to see me here," I countered, resting against the corner and noticing the girl's shocked expressions at not only being discovered, but also by being found by the son of a Virt Prince. "The only ones who should be in this part of the Ziggurat besides ourselves are the other staff."

"Still, my Lord, I must request you return to your room immediately."

"Fine, just get going, I'll catch up in a second."

"Thankfully the attendant didn't press the issue and started walking away. Turning my head to the girl, meeting her face, I mouthed 'I won't tell if you won't,' waiting until she nodded in reply before walking away myself."

"So, you did the girl a favor by not reporting her. That's why you are not worried about her identifying you. If she did, she would have to explain *how* she could identify you. But I'm guessing you saw this girl again after the incident." Dan-te noticed how Virgil's white mental energy sparkled white and fresh, meaning the memory of this girl was more recent than it seemed.

"You're right," Virgil said calmly. "Turned out she also became a student at Spectral Academy. Her name was Stella Sky."

"Stella," Dan-te gasped, recognizing that name instantly. "You don't mean who I think you mean, do you?"

"I do," Virgil confirmed. "Reye's best friend who was also a part of the Demp Cavern Mining Project. She even introduced us. The moment we first saw each other we recognized each other instantly. I reacted as if I had just met her for the first time in my life, but the moment she saw me she started cringing away from me, almost trying to mask herself with her hair; a habit Stella continued to do every time she would see me after that. Later on, she privately confronted me and told me she hadn't revealed who I was to anyone. Like you said, it would mean she would have to explain how it happened. But seeing me again freaked her out. She wondered what a member of a royal family was doing at Spectral Academy. Whether or not I knew if she was going to that school and if I was stalking her or trying to keep tabs on her to make sure she didn't talk about being in a restricted area of the Tanzanite Ziggurat. I told her 'no,' that I was here to learn like everyone else, and that I was not Virgil Virt Indigo-Castitas, I was Virgil Wood and to leave it at that."

"'Virgil Wood,' and that's why you chose the name 'Woody' when we were traveling." Dan-te injected.

"Exactly," Virgil confirmed. "As for my nickname 'Worm,' once I reached Spectral Academy I dove straight into the library, reading and checking out books like there was no tomorrow. One of the librarians claimed I was a natural bookworm, so I decided to use 'Worm' as a new nickname, regardless of what it made my classmates think of me."

"Others thought differently of you because of your nickname?" Dan-te asked.

"Yes, but it was also useful. I've always given off a weird feeling. My mother said it was because I was so open-minded, and when I started using 'Worm' as a nickname, it just increased the whispers. Mostly that I was either some kind of 'smart guy' or a 'plant guy' because a bookworm is a nickname for people who read a lot and wormwood is a type of plant."

"I never thought you projected anything weird," Dan-te said.

"Thank you, you're one of only a few people I've known who have said that. But honestly, I don't mind. There are worse things to be avoided for than just giving off a weird feeling."

"Like what?"

Virgil did not answer that question, nor did he need to. Once it left Dan-te's mouth Virgil's energy flashed fearful pink, and his white mental energy became erratic. She *Knew* she had just triggered the memories of the Hammers of the Orange Light; and Hy-muns like that, killers who slaughtered others because they weren't "proper" for Hy-mun society, were definitely ones to be avoided.

"I'm sorry," Dan-te apologized. "I wasn't thinking."

"Forget it," Virgil said. Just then, a sudden knock on the door startled both of them.

"Woody," Mr. Geryon called from the other side of the door. "Are you alone in there? I thought I heard you talking to somebody."

"Myself," Virgil answered, knowing that only he could hear Dan-te's voice while she was still veiled. "I was just talking to myself."

"Well, I'm coming in now."

"Okay. Sounds like our time is up Dan-te, we'll talk later."

"Yes, we will," Dan-te whispered, also squeezing Virgil's hand twice as Mr. Geryon entered the room to find Virgil apparently alone as he left him.

"It's time for us to begin our tour, Woody. Let's get going," Mr. Geryon said, placing his hand on Virgil's shoulder and guiding him out of the room.

"Ok, Mr. Geryon," Virgil replied as he, with Dan-te veiled behind him, walked out of the door. His thoughts drifting back to Stella for a second.

Talking about my past and my first meeting with Stella is making me worry more about what could be happening to her right now, Virgil thought to himself. *If she's alive, I hope she's all right.*

Chapter 16

Lying alone in her cell in Lust Atrophied, Stella was anything but all right. She was pregnant, stuck in a guarded room, had only a short amount of time left before being killed by the guards outside of the room, and every second until either that moment or until she figured out a way to escape was devoted to thinking about it.

Met-on left immediately after he woke up before I could try and get him to take me out of Nis, Stella thought to herself. *I'll bet he's reporting to the Warden that I haven't confessed my love for him yet or showed any signs that I'm pregnant.*

Stella learned from Met-on, while he was sleep talking, that before he first came to her, he was given the task of making her fall in love with him to receive his first branding. She learned earlier that all members of the Tribe of Shadows needed to earn four brands to be fully recognized as belonging to the Tribe of Shadows. Since Met-on possessed "Rodent-blood" because his mother came from the Remnant of the Tribe, he had not received any brands, nor would he probably get one. However, someone called the Warden gave him this task to gain his first one. Yet things had quickly become far more complicated, and Stella could not stop thinking about them.

The longer I stay here, the more likely I'm going to die here. As soon as the pregnancy is discovered, I die. When this purging event happens, I'll also die. If I just try to walk out of the room, the guards will kill me. I need help if I am going to escape this city and make it to the Remnant. I need Met-on.

Not long ago, Stella would have shivered at the thought of needing Met-on for anything. He was just a fantasy she created while she still deluded herself into thinking that Nis, the Tribe of Shadows, and everything happening to her, was nothing more than a dream. But in the time since she accepted the reality of her situation. She also realized that Met-on was the only potential ally and chance she had.

When is he going to get back? Stella wondered. *If he doesn't get back, how am I going to try and get him to take me out of the city? But even if I do get him to take me out of Nis, where do I find the Remnant, and will they also accept me; or would it just be safer to live alone somewhere until the child comes to term?*

Ever since Met-on left abruptly the same questions had been haunting her. Stella already knew that even if she did escape she could not return to the surface because the sunlight would kill her child when he/she was born; possibly herself, too, in the process. Even if it did not, she knew her family would never accept her again after this.

I can still hear my parents when they banished my older sister: "Touch filth, become filth," they chanted. She paid them no mind. I was almost shouting with them, but now I'm in an even worse situation then she could ever be in. And my options are far fewer than hers could ever be.

If she could escape, Stella knew her best option would be to go to the Remnant of the Tribe, but she still did not know if they would be any better than the Tribe of Shadows.

How did I ever wind up in this situation in the first place? Stella already knew a partial answer to *that* question. *I ended up in this mess because the Tribe of Shadows attacked the Demp Cavern Mining Project; but that would have happened whether I was a member of the project or not, wouldn't it? Why did I even sign up for it in the first place? Why did I go to* Spectral Academy *in the first place?*

With few other options besides wondering about Met-on and if she could convince him to help her contact the Remnant, and what could happen if that goes wrong, Stella found herself reflecting on her life and the choices that led her here. She was looking for that one mistake that led her here.

I wanted to join the Demp Cavern Mining Project because I wanted to study deep earth soil deposits. That was also the reason why I applied to Spectral Academy in the first place. Back home in the Violet Dominion, there is only so much farmable ground on the surface of the plateau. Spelunkers and farmers study the soil and water deposits in the cave systems and establish underground farms there. I was studying to become a farm technician and work on one of the subterranean farms. I applied for the project to get a taste of what living underground and studying there would be like. Or at least, that's what I told myself, because those weren't my real reasons. Even now, thinking about why I joined the project, the same two faces keep appearing in my mind.

"Reye and Sol," Stella whispered, immediately hushing herself the second she thought she heard a noise from the door behind her. She knew she could not be too careful. If the guards overheard her and figured out what she wanted to do, they might just kill her right there. Still, whispering Sol and Reye's names only made their faces appear more vibrantly in her mind.

I still remember when Reye first brought up the project, Stella remembered. *Reye wouldn't stop going on about it. We were with Raymond at AB's when she pulled the flyer out in front of all our faces. "This is the chance of a lifetime," she said, "Raymond, you'll get to explore a true unexplored region, and I'll get the underground dive prerequisite I need for terranaut projects. Plus we'll both get the chance to make some real contacts. Stella, you'll also get some firsthand experience at some of the soil work you want to do. I also spotted this same flyer during the last martial arts club meeting. It was inside a 'certain someone's' bag. Someone I know you need to start talking with."*

I knew she was talking about Sol and barked at her to not push that, mainly since we were in public and I didn't know if he was around. But I didn't tell Reye the fact that he could possibly be going on the trip, and that both of them were definitely signing up, all but made me decide to sign up too. I did not want to be left out if they went, nor did I want to miss a chance at being near Sol. It feels like a lifetime ago looking back on it now, one where I was much more simpleminded. The only thing that attracted me to him in the first place was my curiosity about him.

Stella had never had any form of romantic relationship with anyone before. The most she knew of it came from watching others and reading books. Her favorites were the ones about mystery men who walked into a woman's life.

Yeah, it was that air of mystery he carried about him that attracted me to him. He seemed full of secrets, and I wanted to find out more about him. But I still didn't want to get close to him because I was afraid of being banished like my sister.

Stella remembered what her sister used to say to her before she decided to break tradition, marry outside the Violet Dominion, and be banished from her family. She described the moment of falling in love as being similar to the Unmasking Ceremony, "When you take off your mask to a complete stranger and reveal to them *exactly* who you are."

"The Unmasking Ceremony," Stella whispered, remembering both the ceremony and the Tradition of the Masks practiced in the Violet Dominion.

Before turning 18, whenever boys and girls went out in public they were required to wear a unique mask meant to teach children "modesty, and to value yourself for who you are"; according to the Violet Dominion's Book of Sayings. That same book also treated the moment of the Unmasking Ceremony, when children entered the adult world and entered society unmasked as a time when "the beauty of oneself emerges as a glorious sight, shining onto the face of civilization. A sight that should always be hidden until the proper moment."

Well, as shy as I might have been around Sol, I was never shy about keeping that mask on. Whenever I was outside and masked, I just wanted to get away from everyone and take it off, and I did, every chance I got. In fact, it was the mistake that eventually led me here in the first place.

Stella's mind clicked. Reflecting on her life, she identified the critical mistake she made that eventually sent her to Nis, a decision that was no one's fault except her own, and one that she had been unjustly treating another for because of it.

My family joined a delegation from the Violet Dominion, including the entire royal family, to visit the Tanzanite Ziggurat in the Indigo Dominion. The whole party was a complete bore, nothing but politicians trying to impress and work their way into the Virt Indigo-Castitas's good graces. Even I and several other girls were just invited to try and impress Virt Prince Hesiod Virt Indigo-

Castitas's son Homer—the absolute biggest meathead flirt I had ever seen. All I wanted to do was get away and rip off my mask, and I did. I ditched that party and snuck into a restricted part of the Ziggurat, finding a balcony overlooking an interior garden where I could take off my mask and find some peace, at least, until I was discovered by Homer's brother, Virgil.

We all knew Homer Virt Indigo-Castitas had a twin brother, but when I saw him, almost the exact physical opposite of him, I couldn't believe it. If it weren't for the attendant's voice around the corner identifying him, I wouldn't have known who he was, or that he was there. All he mouthed to me after the attendant left was, "I won't tell if you won't," and walked away. If I had been caught unmasked, it would have been an embarrassment to my family. Unmasked and caught with someone else, I would eventually have to marry him just to avoid the shame, precisely what the politicians from home would have wanted. That was why once I made it home I decided to work to get into Spectral Academy. I had to be as far away from my mistake, Virgil, and scheming politicians as possible. Yet as soon as I am settled there with friends and a life, Reye introduces me to her friend Worm, a.k.a. Virgil Wood, who I recognized immediately as Virgil Virt Indigo-Castitas.

"What is he doing here?" I asked myself. "The son of a Virt Prince would never come here, associating as freely as he is doing with Reye. Is he checking up on me? Is he pursuing me?" Virgil assured me privately that he didn't know I was going to be here and that he was just here to learn. But I never believed him and acted nervous every time I so much as heard his name afterward. I said it was because he seemed "odd," but it was because I didn't want anyone to know who he was, or worse how I knew he was the son of a Virt Prince. I treated him poorly because I was hiding my own mistake; a mistake only he could forgive.

Since being captured and brought to Nis, Stella knew what had been done to her and what she had chosen to do would make her an outcast not only in her home Dominion but in most of the other Dominions as well. The only ones on the surface that could forgive a transgression like hers and allow her to return to Hy-mun society were the members of the Seven Royal Families of Prism like Virgil. Of course, just *approaching* any of those families was never easy, which was another reason why Virgil made her nervous whenever he was around her.

Reunions, Reflections, and Reconciliations

The Royal Families were all blessed by Ash Addiel, Stella remembered, the stories all but ingrained into her head. *The Rainbow Ouroboros, a physical manifestation of both Ash Addiel and the rainbow, led each of the different groups of Hy-muns to the Seven Ziggurats on the Day of the Rainbow Light. The day when the Sun struck the Platinum Throne and created seven different rays of light which lead to them to the Seven Ziggurats. When each group reached a Ziggurat, a beam of light shone down onto a family of Hy-muns from that group. Those families, chosen and blessed by the Light of Ash Addiel, became the Royal Families. Each one took a different colored Ouroboros, an Ouroboros formed from the ray of light cast from their Ziggurat, as the standard for their family and Dominion. The Colored Ouroboros protects the Royal Families, their actions, and gives them the freedom to forgive the highest transgressions; all because they were blessed by Ash Addiel.*

Aside from the attendant's remarks, the Indigo Ouroboros was another way Stella recognized Virgil as a member of the Royal Family. He was wearing the Indigo Ouroboros around his neck when she spotted him.

But I doubt I am going to see Virgil, or a member of any of the Royal Families anytime soon. Even if I did see Virgil again, between how I treated him, and this child I am carrying, there is no way I could just ask for forgiveness and re-entry into society as if nothing happened. Besides, the real problem I have to face is Met-on. I have to somehow convince him to take me outside the city if any of us hope to live at all.

"Hope," Stella murmured, almost in prayer to whoever could be listening.

Met-on told me that the Tribe of Shadows rejects hope, that it's a distraction. I wonder if any of them ever realized what they lost when they decided to give up hope. How could I give it up, especially now when it's the only real light I can still look to.

Stella's thoughts were interrupted by the sudden urge to regurgitate, causing her to jump toward the magma vent. She knew she had been fortunate with keeping the signs of her pregnancy hidden, but it was still a matter of time before they would notice she was with child.

The child, Stella thought again, the reality of the pregnancy still seeming as unbelievable as both the Tribe of Shadows and the city of Nis itself.

My child, mine and Met-on's; I may be ostracized because of this and Met-on might be the lowest of citizens in the city of Nis, which would make this child even lower than that, but that doesn't change the fact that the child is still an innocent being.

Stella remembered a translated saying that her mother, and even Virgil, used to quote from the Tome of the Ouroboros about the creation of children.

"The Great Lord fashions all children from earth and light, filling their hearts with his own light and revealing the world and its wonders to their pure sight."

Stella knew the child she was carrying was forced upon her, a child of two worlds: the Hy-mun and the Tribe of Shadows; but still believed the child should not be held accountable for that and should be granted the same respect as any other child. Stella's thoughts about the child came to an abrupt halt as the door to her room creaked open, and Met-on walked in.

"Hello Met-on," Stella greeted him, trying to sound friendlier. Since Met-on stopped using the gas, she had been able to react quickly to his presence, and she intended to make every possible appeal to him to get him to help her.

"Hello Stella, you seem different."

"*Different*," Stella wondered, fear starting to choke her.

"What do you mean I am different today?" Stella asked, now on guard, fearful that he might know she is carrying their child. If Met-on did make that realization, then they were all dead.

"You seem to be glowing differently today," Met-on explained. "You've always radiated a frazzle of fearful pink energy since I first started coming here, but now it's become more intense, solidifying around you so I can't see any other energies. I've never *Known* you like this before."

"Well, I do have a lot that I'm scared about," Stella answered. She did not have to try lying about it, she did have a lot to be scared about.

"Like what?" Met-on said, suddenly interested.

"Like what would happen to me if you didn't come back, for starters?" Stella replied, still being honest about it. She knew that as long as Met-on came back, she still had a chance to convince him to help her. If he did not come back, then her own death was all but upon her.

"You're scared I might not come back to you," Met-on asked, walking toward her cautiously.

"Yes."

"Don't be," Met-on exclaimed, hugging Stella and lifting her off the ground in the process. "I'll prove to you that you have nothing to fear from me and that I can be someone you can count on."

"I hope so," Stella stuttered, surprised by him being able to lift her off the ground.

He probably thinks that if I'm afraid he won't come back, then I must be falling in love with him, Stella thought to herself as Met-on swung her around the room. *That can work for me, especially if he feels he needs to prove himself to me. I might be able to convince him to help me yet.*

Part 4: Deadly Light in a House of Healing

Chapter 17

"Right this way Mr. Geryon."

"Thank you, Dr. Ness, keep up Young Wood."

"Right behind you Mr. Geryon," Virgil replied, following Mr. Geryon through the halls of Tri-Dominion City Hospital.

Virgil, in his blind man disguise with Dan-te cloaked in the Veil of Shadows, was being led by a Dr. Ness to a different section of the hospital where an acquaintance of Mr. Geryon was resting. The "official story" to explain Virgil's presence was that he was Mr. Geryon's ward, Young Wood, and despite being blind had a perfect memory and could recite anything that he had heard. The group was currently walking through a muscle therapy room.

"As you can see Mr. Geryon," Dr. Ness explained, "we have made numerous improvements to our muscle therapy division. Once your acquaintance is among us again, he will be transferred here to begin the next phase of his recovery."

Dr. Ness led Mr. Geryon, Virgil, and the veiled Dan-te down a row of large metal containers, each one containing bubbling water. Behind him, Virgil felt Dan-te's hand beginning to shiver.

I hope nothing in here causes her to faint again, Virgil worried. They both knew that they needed to keep moving and could not afford any holdups; if not for the problem with the Furies then they might have been able to skip this detour entirely. But now that they were here, they knew the best thing would be to get through it as quickly as possible.

"These containers provide hot water baths for some of our more elderly patients as well as those suffering and recovering from physical injuries," Dr. Ness further explained proudly. "As you can see, some of the baths are already being used by our clients to relax and ease their muscles before undergoing physical therapy."

"The bath occupants on your right are waving at you, Young Wood," Mr. Geryon whispered. "Be polite and wave back."

At Mr. Geryon's word, Virgil lifted up the hand holding his cane and waved to the bath occupants. Usually, Virgil would have looked over to the baths and waved, but since he was playing the role of a blind man he had to act as if he could not see them. Virgil, however, was more occupied with what Dan-te was feeling at the moment.

Dan-te hasn't stopped shivering since we walked in here, Virgil worried. *I already know the way Dan-te* Knows *something is entirely different from the way I do. Considering what we've seen so far, it wouldn't surprise me if she* Knows *the muscle therapy division as something else entirely. When she first told me about the city of Nis and the Tribe of Shadows, she mentioned they devour the dead as food. I wonder if seeing Hy-muns sitting in bubbling water must appear to her as Hy-muns being cooked.*

"Are you alright?" Virgil whispered, as softly as he could and squeezing Dan-te's hand so she would know he was trying to talk to her.

"What was that, Young Wood?" Mr. Geryon asked Virgil, having heard him whispering.

"I'm just wondering if the patients are going to be alright, Mr. Geryon," Virgil answered quickly, altering his question. "Does this therapy really work?"

"It does, Young Wood," Dr. Ness interjected. "The hot water baths use heated water to stimulate blood flow throughout our patients' bodies, and at the same time it relaxes and loosens the damaged parts of their bodies. By doing that we increase the speed that the body naturally repairs itself."

"And that works?" Virgil queried, acting like he wanted to know more.

"It does," Dr. Ness assured him. "In fact, most of our patients here are professional athletes, and all of them are familiar with hot water bath treatments to loosen and relax their muscles."

"Interesting," Virgil replied, trying to act like someone who just learned something new.

"All right then, Young Wood," Mr. Geryon added, placing his hand on Virgil's shoulder. "We are coming up to a door. Soon after we go through it we will be turning to your right so don't fall behind."

"Yes Mr. Geryon," Virgil replied. However, once the three of them had walked through the door and turned right, Virgil allowed himself to slip behind Mr. Geryon and Dr. Ness while their attention was directed toward an oncoming room.

"Dan-te, how are you?" Virgil whispered again, this time being more careful so that he would not be overheard.

"I am trying to control myself," Dan-te replied shakily. "I *Know* you remembered something in your past when you saw this 'muscle therapy room,' your white mental energy was sparking and becoming hazy as you remembered the past; especially after Dr. Ness mentioned they were all 'professional athletes,' whatever that means."

"It means they play sports for a living," Virgil clarified. "The wrestlers we passed back at the Hotel Avery would have been considered professional athletes."

"Well, that explains a lot," Dan-te whiffed, and Virgil could feel her hand tremble even more at the mention of the spectacle they witnessed back at the Hotel Avery. "These Hy-muns, each one of them is bursting with the same horrible red energy that Reye generated. They are here because of their own violent tendencies, violence against themselves and other people to be exact. Also, if, as you said, they are cut from the same stone as the Hy-muns I saw back in the Hotel Avery's arena, that would explain it even more. Yet, these Hy-muns still seem different from the arena's group."

"What's the difference?" Virgil whispered curiously.

"The Hy-muns back in the arena were filled with anger and wrath toward each other; but unlike the ones here, the Hy-muns in the arena had a 'limiter' on them."

"Limiter?" Virgil asked.

"They mentally limited themselves in the arena. It was the only place their wrath existed, the energy never went beyond the arena, and a spark of white mental energy caused them to check themselves before they went too far. The Hy-muns here, on the other hand, acted without that limiter; causing violence, mostly to themselves, through their own reckless actions which also resulted in the same actions being done to them in return."

Virgil thought about Dan-te's comparison for a second. He remembered his brother, Reye, and Raymond, all athletes in their own right, and the times he spotted each one of them in a facility like this. It was usually after they had pushed themselves so far during training or during an event that they ended up hurting themselves.

That would mean they acted without the limiter Dan-te is talking about, Virgil speculated, comparing the athletes, his friends, and brother with Dan-te's description of how she *Knew* the patients. *The 'limiter' must be our own natural mental safeguard to try to avoid pain or injury. To act without the limiter must be to Dan-te when someone pushes themselves beyond what they can physically or mentally do to the point where they injure themselves and possibly others along with them.*

"But all Hy-muns train themselves to improve and get better," Virgil replied, seeing one fault in Dan-te's *Knowing*. "Even I've pushed myself to become both a better scholar and fighter; I wouldn't be here otherwise, and I am guessing your people do, too. So how is that a bad thing?"

"It's the intention," Dan-te answered, taking Virgil's hand and placing it over his heart. "The place where that desire comes from and whom it is meant for. You're right, pushing oneself past the limiter is how we get better, and that's true for both of our peoples. But it's the intention that directs where that training will take them. The Members of the Remnant train so they can protect their families and the Remnant from Lord Tanas. I understand now that you trained not only to protect yourself from Hy-muns like the Hammers of the Orange Light but also to protect your family and Dominion to keep them safe and out of harm's way. But the Hy-muns here, they trained only for their own personal benefit, no more and no less. They're also angry with themselves, horribly angry, that they're stuck in here and couldn't hurt themselves more, and yet it's still just for their own glory and benefit. That's why they're radiating that horrible red energy, I'm just glad it seems contained to those boiling blood-like pools they were sitting in."

"Huh," blurted Virgil, a little surprised at Dan-te's comment and even more surprised at the level that he spoke. Thankfully, neither Mr. Geryon nor Dr. Ness—both engaged in their own conversation—seemed to notice. "What do you mean blood-like pools?"

"I mean those pools were boiling hotter than the Hy-muns sitting in them, and each one was glowing red from the horrible red energy being generated by its occupants, so red that the pools appeared to be boiling blood."

"Oh," Virgil replied, realizing now that Dan-te was just comparing the hot water baths to boiling pools of blood because of their appearance, not because of how she *Knew* them.

Of course, the pools would look like boiling blood if she's basing them just on appearance. Both blood and water boil hotter than a Hy-mun's natural body temperature, and with each of the occupants giving off a horrible red glow, it's going to make the water look red.

"Young Wood, keep up," Mr. Geryon called. Virgil, looking ahead of him now realizing that both Mr. Geryon and Dr. Ness had walked a little beyond him and were now waiting for him at the end of the hallway.

"I'm coming," Virgil answered, hurrying to catch up and deciding to accept Dan-te's assessment as just how she *Knew* this part of the Hy-mun world. He had long given up arguing with her ability to *Know* things. So, if she said that the patients in muscle therapy were generating the same horrible red energy that Reye was producing and that they were all violent people, to themselves especially, for no other reason than their own personal agendas, then he was willing to accept that.

"Now, gentleman," Dr. Ness began, opening a door after Virgil had rejoined them. "Right this way is our next room, the one we are most proud of, our life-support room. I believe this is the room where your friend Lawrence Mars is resting."

"It is," Mr. Geryon confirmed as Dr. Ness led the group into a room filled with people lying in beds, each connected to many machines.

Chapter 18

"This room wouldn't have been possible without contributions from the Platinum Throne and several Dominions, including your own Indigo Dominion." Dr. Ness said. "By working in conjunction with them and others, we have been able to recreate life-sustaining technology lost since the Great Rainbow War. These life-support machines are able to keep these patients alive almost indefinitely before illness or injury would have taken their lives. Now, let me take you to your friend, and also show you how our machines are functioning to keep him alive until he recovers."

Dr. Ness took them to a bed where a slightly disheveled looking Hy-mun slept while attached to several different machines. "Here is your friend, Lawrence Mars. Please excuse his bush-like appearance, his caregiver is arriving later to give him a haircut and clean him up a bit. But as you can see, despite being struck by an illness that ravaged his internal organs, he is still alive and perfectly comfortable. This machine stimulates his lungs, so he keeps breathing; this one is connected to the artificial heart we transplanted into him after the disease destroyed his original one. This one…"

Mr. Geryon continued to listen intensively as Dr. Ness described the machines preserving Lawrence Mars's life and his overall condition. Virgil, however, was tuning himself out of the discussion. He understood both the doctors' and the patients' desire to be put into such a state, but he harbored mixed feelings about the entire situation. On the one hand, Virgil knew and respected what doctors like Dr. Ness were trying to do, save the life of a dying patient, something that he would also want to do, and something the patient would also want. He also knew that for Mr. Geryon the situation was personal. Mr. Geryon had known Lawrence Mars his entire life and considered him the closest person he had to a brother. Virgil had met him once before he was struck with his illness, so he knew how inseparable the two of them were. But, seeing Lawrence Mars the way he was now, connected to machines, made him wonder if he could even be considered "him" anymore. Unfortunately, Virgil's own debate was the least of his worries.

Dan-te's grip has been tightening and her hands trembling from the moment we first walked into this room, Virgil thought to himself, worried as to how Dan-te could be *Knowing* a room filled with people on life-support equipment. *If her grip gets any tighter, I think my hand might start showing signs that it's being held. Not only that, I can tell she's scared to get near any of the patients. As we approached Lawrence Mars's bed, I could feel her dragging her feet. She wants to be away from him, and the rest of the Hy-muns in this room, as soon as possible.*

"Just hang on," Virgil whispered to her. "We'll be out of here soon enough."

Dan-te did not respond beyond squeezing Virgil's hand twice. She was thrilled he was by her side in that room.

"Are you alright, young man?" Dr. Ness asked, catching Virgil slightly off guard. "I just noticed you look a little tense. Is everything okay?"

"I just need to use the lavatory, Dr. Ness," Virgil answered, seeing a way he could get Dan-te out of the room. "If I may ask, can my master take me to the nearest one so I can relieve myself while the two of you continue your discussion."

"Not at all, Young Wood," Mr. Geryon replied. "Is there a lavatory nearby, Dr. Ness?"

"There's one just outside the life-support room Mr. Geryon. Feel free to take care of your ward, we can continue to discuss Lawrence Mars's treatment after you have seen to him."

"Thank you, Dr. Ness," Mr. Geryon said as he led Virgil and Dan-te out of the life-support room and into the bathroom which was thankfully empty. "As soon as I am finished checking up on Lawrence's progress with Dr. Ness I'll be back for you. Wait here until then."

"I understand, Mr. Geryon," Virgil answered, dropping his disguise persona as soon as they entered the bathroom. Once Mr. Geryon left, Virgil and the cloaked Dan-te entered a handicapped stall to wait for Mr. Geryon. Once inside, Dan-te ripped the Veil off her head revealing herself, ran to the toilet, and vomited in it.

"Dan-te, it's ok, we're out of there." Virgil rubbed Dan-te's back as she continued to vomit into the toilet. Her entire body trembled under his hand, and he could see beads of sweat running through her hair and down her face.

"Please, Dan-te," Virgil begged, trying to get her to talk. "Take a deep breath, tell me how you *Knew* the room."

It took Dan-te a minute, mostly because she was still throwing up almost every piece of food she had eaten since arriving in Virgil's room. But eventually, she took his advice and began to breathe deeply, her muscles relaxing with each breath until she slumped down in front of the toilet.

"It was completely unnatural, Virgil," Dan-te whimpered as Virgil reached over and flushed the toilet. "I *Know* a part of you felt it, too."

Virgil did feel uncomfortable being surrounded by patients hooked up to life-support machines. But Dan-te was not finished yet, as the words tumbled out of her with each breath.

"Those Hy-muns, they've been rooted to their beds and the very floor itself. The silver energy of life, normally flowing throughout their bodies, turned a dark charcoal color as it continued to be corrupted by the machines and forced to root the Hy-muns in place. They don't even smell alive, nor do they smell dead; they're giving off a metallic smell from the machines that is mixed with a rotting smell coming from their own flesh and perspiration. They're becoming trees, part metal, part flesh, with no real life flowing within them. All they do is just sit there doing nothing, serving no purpose, some of them—like Mr. Geryon's friend Lawrence Mars—even *want* to die, but they all know they can't *do* anything."

It did not take too much imagination for Virgil to understand how Dan-te could *Know* the patients as trees made of metal and flesh.

Dan-te's way of Knowing *them is actually an accurate description of how they looked, even by Hy-mun perspectives,* Virgil thought to himself. *Each one of those patients, including Lawrence Mars, is permanently confined to his or her own bed, and all of them have at least one machine that serves as a replacement for one of their organs or operates a body function. Like Dan-te put it, those patients "just sit there doing nothing, serving no purpose" while the machines keep them alive. Looking at Lawrence Mars, all tangled up in machine wires and life-support equipment, I could easily see him turning into some kind of half-Hy-mun half-mechanical bush or tree. I can also see how he would* want *to die, considering the state he is in now and comparing that to the person he once was—vibrant, active, and full of life—before the disease struck him.*

"But the worse part was their feelings," Dan-te continued, breaking Virgil out of his thoughts.

"Feelings?" Virgil asked.

"Yes, their feelings," Dan-te explained. "Those Hy-muns can't do anything, but they *can* think and feel, and every one of them is nursing feelings of pain, envy, and hopelessness. They have completely given up on the hope of returning to life. Each one of them remembers who they were before they were placed in those beds; the hazy spark of white mental energy in each of their heads helped me *Know* that. But now, they know that they will spend the rest of their lives—if it can even be called *living*—in the state that they're in now; feeling the pain from the loss of the life they once had and the life they could have had. What's worse, the more machines that get rooted and entangled to a Hy-mun, the more those feelings grow throughout them. Especially the feeling of envy."

"Envy," Vigil remarked.

"Yes, envy," Dan-te continued. "All around the dark charcoal energy that's flowing through them and the machines, there's a bright green energy of envy radiating and canopied over each of them. The Hy-muns planted in that room are growing envy like moss over a stone. It's directed to the doctors that see them every day, their family members when they visit, everyone. They envy their mobility, their freedom, their ability to *live*. They can't take that they are now planted like trees while everyone else is able to move around, going wherever they want. It leaves them with nothing to do but grow more envious of everyone around them."

"That doesn't surprise me," Virgil conceded. He often thought that each of those patients—if given a choice, might eventually decide for themselves that their situation is hopeless and would rather have died instead of being put into a life-support bed. "Have they really lost all hope?"

"You doubt my ability to *Know* now?" Dan-te asked, somewhat offended.

"I'm sorry," Virgil apologized. "I do know better than to doubt your ability to *Know*. Still, the idea that every one of them has completely given up on hope, especially since they chose to enter life-support because they hoped a cure could be found, it just sounds tragic."

"It *is* tragic, but it's true," Dan-te reaffirmed. "They've lost all hope that their lives are going to get better. What's worse, they've realized they can't do anything about it, and their hope for the future has become envy for those who want to help them. All they can do is remain planted where they are, static and unmoving, their silver life energy becoming more and more entwined and corrupted by the machines while they nurse and grow more envious of the healthy. It's just too tragic."

Dan-te's shaking subsided, but her voice still trembled. *Knowing* the patients on life-support had upset her more than even she thought possible. The encounter had also left Virgil with much to reflect upon. It was not that he doubted her, but her experience differed significantly from any argument he had heard before or come to believe.

Dan-te said the patients wanted *to die*, Virgil thought. *The patients kept on life-support chose that option, after being brought to the edge of death by disease, because they were afraid to die in the first place. Each one, including Lawrence Mars, hoped for an eventual recovery. The idea that they have given up on that hope, and now want to die, it's just...*

Virgil's own reflections were cut short as the door to the lavatory opened, and his head snapped toward the door of his stall. Dan-te, acting quicker, pulled the Veil of Shadows back over her head and disappeared back into Virgil's shadow. A few seconds later, someone knocked on their stall's door.

"Young Wood," Mr. Geryon called. "I'm finished with Dr. Ness in the life-support room. We are moving on."

"I am coming, Mr. Geryon," Virgil replied, squeezing Dan-te's hand to let her know he was still holding onto her.

"I realize I'm making you confused," Dan-te whispered as Virgil rejoined Mr. Geryon. "I know you told me back at Spectral Academy that hospitals were places of healing. I also *Know* that Dr. Ness believes he is doing the right thing. He's generating the same caring blue energy as you, and it's reaching out to all the patients here. But this just seems so different than what we do back home in Rem, and I don't know what to think. I'm sorry I just dumped all this on you."

Virgil replied by squeezing Dan-te's hand twice; he did not want to risk Mr. Geryon overhearing him. Walking out of the lavatory and readopting his blind persona, the group rejoined Dr. Ness.

"Well, we appreciate your time, Dr. Ness," Mr. Geryon said. "Now, if you could take us…"

"Dr. Ness!"

Mr. Geryon was interrupted by another doctor running up to them.

"Dr. Ness, could you please come with me to the Purification Chamber? We need you to administer a sedative to Mr. Lat."

The Purification Chamber, Virgil and Dan-te thought at the same time. They had heard that name before. It was where the Lead Fury sent the other Hy-mun after it was discovered he had a Tempter attached to him

"Very well," Dr. Ness huffed, annoyed with having to be called only to administer a sedative. "If you and your ward will excuse me for a few minutes, I'll be right back."

"Actually, Dr. Ness, if it's alright we would like to join you," Mr. Geryon requested, shocking everyone present. "I wouldn't mind seeing Tri-Dominion City's Purification Chamber, and I don't think anyone will notice if my ward comes along, just as long as he is *with me*."

Both Virgil and Dan-te realized the real meaning behind Mr. Geryon's request. It would be a perfect way for Virgil to be seen at the Purification Chamber and allay any suspicions that might be following them because of the Furies.

"Very well," Dr. Ness agreed. "But it's a dangerous room so you will have to stay in a designated safe zone. Afterward, I will take you to the airship port on the roof. An airship is going to meet you there to take you to your hotel, The Sand Spa Hotel."

"Thank you, Dr. Ness," Mr. Geryon replied.

"You're welcome, please follow me."

Chapter 19

Dr. Ness and the other doctor led Mr. Geryon, Virgil, and the veiled Dan-te up to the top floor of the hospital. All throughout the floor sunroofs let sunlight shine freely in from the outside, and airships passed overhead as they docked and left the hospital's airship port. At the end of a hall, they all entered a room with the word "Purification" written over the top. The room was lightly furnished except for a massive lamp-like device set near a sunroof and a sealed side room.

"This procedure only takes a few minutes," Dr. Ness explained. "And my part will take even less. Now if you will step this way, you can watch the procedure from in here."

Dr. Ness opened the door to the side room and ferried Mr. Geryon, Virgil, and Dan-te, inside before sealing it shut behind them. The side room contained a few chairs and a large window that allowed the three of them to observe what was happening in the Purification Chamber. Soon afterward, a team of doctors entered the room dragging an old, and very scared, Hy-mun with them. Dan-te and Virgil recognized him immediately.

The man the Furies sent here, Virgil and Dan-te thought at the same time.

"Who are those two and why are they in here for this procedure," another doctor asked, noticing Mr. Geryon and Virgil in the side room.

"This is Mr. Geryon," Dr. Ness defended, indicating Mr. Geryon. "He is a great contributor to this facility and a dignitary from the Indigo Dominion. He also has clearance to be *anywhere* in this hospital."

"I don't care who he is and what type of clearance he has," the doctor snapped back. "This procedure is top secret, it's implications affect the safety of all the Dominions. I can't just let anyone stand by and watch."

"With all due respect, sir," Mr. Geryon countered. "I am *not* just anyone. I work directly for Virt Prince Hesiod Virt Indigo-Castitas. I know better than anyone how to deal with *classified material.*"

I'll bet he's talking about me, Virgil mused, thinking that Mr. Geryon's last comment was directed toward him.

"Also, if your procedure *does* have anything to do with the safety of the Indigo Dominion, then that's all the more reason why I should be here to witness it. Unless of course, you would deny the Indigo Dominion information it needs to protect itself."

"Humph," the doctor scoffed. "What about the other one next to you?"

"That is my ward," Mr. Geryon explained. "And as you can see, he's blind. I can guarantee he won't repeat anything he hears during this procedure. Or are you telling me you're worried about what a blind man could see during it."

The doctor merely scowled at Mr. Geryon before turning back to Dr. Ness. It was clear who had won the argument.

"Dr. Ness, just get this one sedated and then let us do our jobs."

Dr. Ness scoffed back at the other doctor and proceeded to the older Hy-mun where an attendant was waiting for him. The older Hy-mun was still as frantic as when the Furies first took him away.

"Please, what are you going to do to me," the Hy-mun screamed. "What is *Purification*? I'm as healthy as they get. Why am I here?"

"Sir, what's your name," Dr. Ness asked.

"Bruno, Bruno Lat," the man answered. "I'm from the Koa Palace in the Green Dominion. Why is this being done to me? What have I got that needs to be *purified*?"

"Okay, Mr. Bruno Lat, my name is Dr. Ness. Nothing is going to happen to you. Now I am just going to give you a quick injection, just to calm you down."

At the mention of an injection Bruno Lat began struggling again. This time, however, Dr. Ness was ready for it. As soon as Mr. Lat started to fight back, Dr. Ness and the other doctors took hold of him while the attendant opened a case and presented Dr. Ness with a needle and serum. Picking up both, Dr. Ness filled the needle with the serum and injected it into Mr. Lat, who fell limp soon afterward.

"That's all we needed you for," the first doctor barked. "You can get into the waiting room with your *guests*. Once we're done, then you can all leave."

Dr. Ness did not acknowledge the first doctor with a verbal response. He only nodded to him, walked to the side room, opened it, and then sealed himself inside with the others and watched as the other doctors did their work.

"Now that Mr. Lat is sedated, let's get him into position," the doctor directed as two more attendants hoisted him and strapped him onto a table near the lamp-like device. Once on the table, the two doctors maneuvered the table underneath both the device and the sunroof.

"Prepare to administer Purification Therapy," the lead doctor instructed, taking a spot at the controls of the device. "Everyone, take your positions."

The other doctors and technicians moved gracefully around the unconscious form of Mr. Lat. Some went to his head and feet, others went to his side, but none of them blocked the device's path. Watching from the side room, Virgil's group quickly realized that they had done this procedure before, but as to its purpose, they had no idea.

"Is there any danger to us, Mr. Lat, the other doctors, or the technicians from that device?" Mr. Geryon asked.

"None at all," Dr. Ness assured them. "The Lightning Lamp's radiation, Lightning Lamp is what I have heard the other doctors call that device, is harmless to us. Its purpose is revelation and purification. Besides, radiation is *not* what we need to be protected from."

"What do you mean?" Mr. Geryon, Virgil, and Dan-te asked at once; except Dan-te's voice could only be heard by Virgil.

"You'll see soon enough, Mr. Geryon," Dr. Ness answered, his voice shaking with every word. "In truth, I have only seen this procedure a few times, and I still can't believe what I see when it's done; and for your own safety and others, *do not* tell your ward or Virt Prince Hesiod Virt Indigo-Castitas about anything you are going to see."

"Dr. Ness is bubbling with the pink energy of fear," Dan-te whispered. "Not only his energy but his words and smells are also tainted with fear. Whatever is about to happen has him scared for multiple reasons."

"Agreed," Virgil replied, also whispering so the others would not overhear him. Thankfully, they all seemed engrossed in the doctors' preparations. Virgil himself wondered what was about to happen but was just as curious about Dr. Ness's warning.

Something unbelievable, scary, or both, is about to happen, Virgil realized as the doctors seemed to finish getting themselves ready. *And whatever it is, it is a secret that people will do* anything *to guard. Otherwise, there wouldn't be a need for Dr. Ness to tell Mr. Geryon not to tell anyone about it,* including *my father. If this procedure could affect the security of the Indigo Dominion, and Dr. Ness* doesn't *want him to know about it, then it must be an extremely dangerous secret.*

Virgil was no stranger to dangerous secrets. Both he and Dan-te were two walking ones. Still, the apprehension in the air made both of them feel like this would top them both.

"I am activating the machine," the lead doctor announced. "Commence purification."

Pulling a lever, the Lightning Lamp came to life and projected a beam of orange-yellow light down onto Mr. Lat. The light's effect was instantaneous as both Virgil and Mr. Geryon gasped in surprise while Dan-te suddenly tightened her grip on Virgil's hand in fear. The Tempter that Dan-te first noticed attached to Mr. Lat had been revealed. Pulled from the Reversed State, his Veil of Shadows had turned blue-violet, and just as quickly he found himself standing among a team of attacking Hy-muns; each one able to hold him under the sunroof as they pulled the Veil off the Tempter's face.

"Argh!" the Tempter screamed as the sunlight's effect on him acted just as quickly as the Lightning Lamp. The Tempter's face turned from blue to black, stripped clean of features as it burned in the sunlight. Other parts of his body equally changed as the doctors continued to tear off the Veil, exposing more of the Tempter's body to the sunlight.

"What *is* that thing?!" Mr. Geryon gasped as the Tempter continued to burn. "Honestly, I don't know," Dr. Ness replied, his voice trembling with each word. "The doctors chosen for the Purification Procedure are handpicked, and information about the procedure is strictly on a need-to-know basis."

"And you're saying I don't need to know."

"I'm saying *I* don't need to know. The most I've been able to figure out is that the entity the doctors are able to expose with the Lightning Lamp can be separated from the Hy-mun once it's been bathed in the Lamp's radiation. Afterward, it is burned away in the sunlight. It is some kind of 'negative aspect' that was discovered in Hy-muns shortly after the Great Rainbow War. I don't know why the discovery was kept secret, but the 'powers that be' have spent a lot to figure out how to use the Sacred Nag-el Relics to separate that aspect from Hy-muns; and even more to *keep it secret.*"

Mr. Geryon simply nodded at Dr. Ness's remarks, the meaning behind them clear. Watching the doctors as they stripped the Tempter, causing him to burn to death, left him with a sickening feeling of what others might do if he spoke about this. Virgil, did not dare speak, twitch, or make any kind of reaction that could betray the fact he could actually see what was happening; but he *wanted* to.

Stop it, stop it, please stop it, you're killing *him!* Virgil's mind screamed as he watched the doctors strip the Veil off the revealed Tempter and expose him to the sunlight, burning him to death. Unlike Dr. Ness, Virgil knew who "the entity" was, and even if the Tribe of Shadows considered themselves enemies of the Hy-muns, no enemy deserved *this* kind of death. The very existence of the procedure created more questions than anything.

How does anybody else on the surface even know *about Tempters,* Virgil asked himself. *Dr. Ness said it was after the Great Rainbow War, but still, when and how did anyone else find out about them and get the idea to look for them? I should be the only one who knows about them because of Dan-te. My goodness...Dan-te!*

Virgil was so disturbed by the procedure he did not even think to check on Dan-te, cursing himself for both his own stupidity and insensitivity. Dan-te, however, had not reacted at all to the procedure. Her grip had not tightened, trembled, or made any indication that she was scared. The fact both puzzled and worried Virgil at the same time.

"Dan-te," Virgil whispered, slightly tugging on her arm and finding himself suddenly supporting her entire weight.

"Young Wood, are you alright?" Mr. Geryon asked, noticing Virgil slump suddenly for no apparent reason at all.

"I'm just weak and tired," Virgil answered.

"Don't worry," Dr. Ness assured him. "They are almost finished, the two of you will be able to leave once they are done cleaning up."

"Thank you," Virgil and Mr. Geryon replied, both wanting to get out of that room as soon as possible. Virgil especially, since he now understood why Dan-te didn't seem to react to the procedure.

She fainted from it, Virgil thought to himself, struggling to set Dan-te onto his back so he could carry her. *Seeing this must have been so terrifying that it shocked her senseless. Not that I blame her. When she first told me about "The Coming," how her ancestors burned to death in the light the Nag-el first brought into the world and how they also suffered from their weapons, I could hear the ancient fear in her voice. Seeing this "Purification," watching that Tempter be exposed by the Lightning Lamp and then burned in the sunlight must have made every one of those stories seem like they were happening right now in front of her.*

Virgil shivered at the idea that Dan-te might have been reliving what her ancestors suffered, not that the whole procedure was not terrifying in itself. Looking out the window, the doctors were cleaning and bagging both the charred remains of the Tempter and his Veil like they were pieces to study instead of a recently living being. Besides them, Mr. Lat still slept sedated, the entire operation going on without him being aware of it. As soon as the doctors completed the cleanup, the head doctor came and opened up the side room's door.

"Get Mr. Lat down to another room and wake him," the lead doctor instructed. "Tell him the procedure went fine and he can leave immediately. Now, as for the rest of you, that completes the procedure. It's time for you and your ward to leave, *now*."

"With pleasure," Mr. Geryon replied, leading Virgil—now staggering under Dan-te's weight—through the door.

"You do understand that everything you witnessed is classified."

"As I said before, I know all about classified material. Just get us to the airship port."

"Right this way," Dr. Ness instructed, leading Mr. Geryon and Virgil out of the Purification Chamber and up to the roof of the hospital.

The roof looked like a much smaller and simpler version of the airship port where Virgil and Dan-te first arrived in Wanton City. Several small balloons and airships were continually leaving and reaching the hospital, bringing both doctors and patients to the hospital from all levels of Tri-Dominion City. One small airship, with a checkered pattern over it, had the word "Taxi" written on its side. Dr. Ness led Mr. Geryon and Virgil to the airship, shook each of their hands, and helped them on board.

"Safe travels to The Sand Spa Hotel," Dr. Ness called in a final good-bye as the airship slowly rose from the hospital and began ascending through the levels of Tri-Dominion City.

Chapter 20

"We'll be at The Sand Spa Hotel in a few minutes," the airship pilot said. "We just need to clear the summit of the plateau."

Since Tri-Dominion City was built into the side of the plateau, the pilot needed to guide the airship through many warm air currents spiraling through the clef. At the same time, he steadily increased the amount of hot air in the gas bag, raising their airship to the top of the mountain where the city met the Violet Dominion's Border. However, as the airship crested the plateau, Virgil noticed a strange sight in the distance toward what should have been the Tri-Dominion Caverns.

"Hey, is that a tent?" Mr. Geryon asked, guessing Virgil's own question and stating it for him since Virgil was not supposed to be able to see.

"Honestly, I don't know," the pilot replied. "It started going up a little over a week ago. It was hauled in from the Violet Dominion and completely covered the chasm entrances to the Tri-Dominion Cavern system. Since it's gone up, the locals have noticed huge covered machines being brought in, strange orange-yellow lights shining under the tent, and noises that sound like blasting going on at weird hours; I don't think anyone around here really knows what is going on. Today they are actually quiet, eerily quiet."

Orange-yellow lights, Virgil thought, the memory of the Lightning Lamp still fresh in his mind and his interest over why the Tri-Dominion Caverns would be sealed off now reaching new heights. *First, a device that can expose Tempters, then one that can neutralize their Veils, now a whole cavern system is sealed off—possibly so both devices can be used inside them, and the public is being kept in the dark?*

Virgil's paranoia was running full blast. The fact that all of this was being done, and no one was asking any questions or trying to find out anything about it, meant that whoever was behind it needed support at the absolute *highest* level; a level Virgil was very familiar with.

Four of the Virt Princes are already here, Virgil surmised, putting pieces together in his head. *A couple of weeks ago, I would have thought that the sealed-off caverns had something to do with their retreat. It wouldn't have been the first time the other Virt Princes decided to keep my father in the dark about their plans—not that he minds one bit. But now, after everything that happened since meeting Dan-te…*

Virgil let his thoughts hang for a moment as he turned his gaze back toward Dan-te. She was still out from the shock of the Lightning Lamp and lying veiled over Virgil's back like an invisible load. The revelation provided by Dan-te, the existence of the Remnant, the Tribe of Shadows, Tanas, their activities before and throughout the life of the Hy-mun race, and now these devices that target Tempters in the wake of the Great Rainbow War, were leading Virgil to suspect one thing.

I'm not the first Hy-mun on the surface to learn about the races living underground and their activities up here. Someone else has done it. Another Hy-mun did it after the Great Rainbow War and convinced a number of the time's Virt Princes that Dan-te's people and the Tribe of Shadows lived underground, that the Tribe of Shadows influenced Hy-mun activity, and that he or she wasn't insane in the process.

As Virgil said the words to himself he realized what it could mean; not just for himself, but for everyone living beneath the surface.

When Dan-te first showed up in my room, I warned her that if she went public, the first thing people would ask for was proof beyond her testimony that her story was real. That the only thing Dan-te could prove from her being here is the existence of non-Hy-mum beings living beneath the surface of Prism that can't stand sunlight, and that a supporter of the Tome's story would easily claim she was a follower of Tanas trying to tempt Hy-mums with lies. Personally, after my own experiences with the Hammers of the Orange Light, I was also worried that if she went public, she would "disappear" almost immediately afterward and her warnings be dismissed and forgotten. But if a Hy-mun managed to reveal the Remnant of the Tribe and the Tribe of Shadows to the Virt Princes after the Great Rainbow War, labeling them as if they were all followers of Tanas, then there might be more going on here than any of us realize.

Virgil knew his father's neutrality stance against the other Dominions, a position started by his grandfather during the Great Rainbow War, was both a strength and a weakness; especially when dealing with the other Virt Princes. Since Virgil's father took a neutral stance in matters concerning the other Dominions, there was no reason why they would need to include him in any joint projects, and whatever was brewing in Tri-Dominion City *definitely* had the mark of a joint Dominion project. Whatever that project is, Virgil knew he would find out as soon as he and Dan-te reached the Tri-Dominion Caverns. But first, there were more immediate things to take care of as their airship descended and docked at The Sand Spa Hotel.

"Everybody off!" the pilot cried as Mr. Geryon walked off the airship. Virgil hobbled behind, Dan-te still unconscious and slung across his back. Once they left, the airship quickly departed, rising back in the sky before dropping down into the levels of Tri-Dominion City. Alone, Mr. Geryon led Virgil into the hotel. As they walked through the main entryway, they passed some of the hotel's famous sand baths. The whiffs of sulfur and alkaline in the air from the volcanic sand not only tickled Virgil's nose but caused Dan-te to stir on his back, the first sign of movement she made since passing out at the hospital.

Excellent, she's starting to wake up, Virgil thought to himself. *It's not that I don't mind carrying you Dan-te, but after a while, you begin to feel really heavy.*

Virgil knew Dan-te would probably punch him in the arm for *that* snide remark, but he decided to allow himself some mental levity as he continued to shuffle through the hotel and up to the main desk, a step behind Mr. Geryon. Mr. Geryon simply handed the manager behind the counter an envelope, which he opened, read, and then quickly handed a set of room keys to Mr. Geryon before sending them on their way without a word. Once at Virgil's room, set apart from Mr. Geryon's room, he turned and genuinely addressed Virgil for the first time since before they arrived at Tri-Dominion City Hospital.

"This is where I leave you, Young Wood," Mr. Geryon whispered. He still used Virgil's alias in case someone overheard them, but his tone was reverent. He knew he was not addressing a staggering boy but the son of a Virt Prince and was giving him all the grace and respect due to him. "The package you sent me from Spectral Academy is already in your room. Is there anything else you need?"

"Just a means to get to the Tri-Dominion Caverns," Virgil said.

"You do realize what you are asking for will be difficult, to say the least?" Mr. Geryon asked.

Virgil did. The moment the airship crested the Violet Plateau, and he saw the tent draped over the entrance to the Tri-Dominion Caverns for the first time and heard about the orange-yellow lights shining within them he knew that reaching them was going to be far more dangerous than he had thought.

Especially for Dan-te if those lights are more Lightning Lamps like the one in the hospital, Virgil thought to himself.

"Young Wood?" Mr. Geryon asked again.

"I do," Virgil replied. "And that's all the more reason why I *have* to get to the Tri-Dominion Caverns. I can't give you the details. You need to trust me. Just find some way to get me there without being discovered."

Mr. Geryon studied what little he could see of Virgil's face through his disguise, it was nothing but determination. In all the years he had known Virgil there were only a few times he had ever genuinely asked for something outside the realm of what the son of a Virt Prince would typically consider appropriate, and every time Virgil displayed the same rock hard determined look he had on his face right now.

He's dead set on going to the Tri-Dominion Caverns no matter what I do, Mr. Geryon realized, seeing the resolve in Virgil's face.

"There might be a way you can get to the caverns," Mr. Geryon replied. "I need to talk to some people. If I can arrange transport for you, then it will be waiting for you behind the Eastern Sand Bath in five hours."

"Thank you, Mr. Geryon," Vigil smiled, realizing Mr. Geryon had probably helped him more then he realized. "One more thing, though."

"What?"

"Once you have secured transportation for me, get back to the Indigo Dominion, immediately." Even disguised, Mr. Geryon could see Virgil's face turning deadly serious. "Also, if you can convince anyone else to leave the city, do it."

He's speaking to me like the son of a Virt Prince, Mr. Geryon quickly realized. *Lord Virgil never does that. Something must be coming. Otherwise, why risk traveling here in the first place. The mystery involving the Tri-Dominion Caverns, Lord Virgil's desire to go there, it must be part of something big if it's necessitating all of this, what he might still go through, and why he wants as many people away from this city as possible.*

"I'll do my best," Mr. Geryon assured him before leaving him to stumble into his room with Dan-te still unconscious across his back.

Once Virgil and Dan-te were alone in the room together, he immediately went to work turning off every light, closing and sealing every window, making the room as dark as possible. It was not an easy task with Dan-te still draped over his back. Fortunately, she finally woke up while Virgil was sealing up the room; unfortunately, she woke up thinking she was still in the hospital while the "Purification" was still going on.

"Let's get out of here!" Dan-te screamed, completely abandoning caution. Rolling off Virgil's back and onto the floor she jumped up, bolting for the door, dragging Virgil.

"Dan-te, stop!" Virgil pleaded, dropping into a sitting position to keep Dan-te from pulling him closer to the door. Virgil knew that Dan-te was afraid, for a good reason. She had just witnessed Hy-muns use a device to neutralize a Tempter's Veil of Shadows and then execute him by exposing him to sunlight. Every story she had heard about "The Coming" had just come to life right before her eyes, and she was terrified she would be next.

"We have to get out of here," Dan-te panicked, pulling even harder on Virgil's hand and starting to drag him toward the door. "We have to get back underground we have to…"

Dan-te's voice cut off as Virgil felt her hand slip from his grasp. Dan-te just as quickly found herself trapped within the small confines of Virgil's shadow the moment she broke their contact, a terrible feeling of dread overtaking her thinking that a Lightning Lamp would shine on her any second now.

"Listen to me, Dan-te," Virgil begged, trying to sound as comforting as possible, holding out his hand to where he thought she was, and hoping that she would listen to him. "Look around, we're NOT in Tri-Dominion City Hospital, we're NOT in the Purification Chamber, and you are DEFINITY NOT under a Lightning Lamp and about to be exposed to sunlight. Look around!"

Dan-te did listen. It was the only thing she could do besides curl up into a ball inside Virgil's shadow. But it took a few minutes before she started to peek out and really look at her new surroundings.

This isn't the 'Purification Chamber. Dan-te said to herself as she slowly looked around and took in every sight and smell, noticing how they were different from the hospital. *This room has a lot of furniture, the room in the hospital hardly had any. There's a large bed, chairs, lots of tables, and no Lightning Lamp. The room in the hospital didn't even have half of the stuff in here; then there's the smell. The Purification Chamber didn't even have a smell at first; but after that Tempter was killed, the room stank of blood, ash, and burning flesh. This room, on the other hand, smells of sand and the same slightly rotting odors I first encountered back when me, Ice, and our group first approached the city of Nis.* "Are we getting close to it?"

It took a few minutes, but Dan-te eventually crawled back over to Virgil and took his outstretched hand, reestablishing their connection.

"Virgil," Dan-te whimpered, "where are we?"

"Far away from that Lightning Lamp, 'Purification Chamber,' and Tri-Dominion City Hospital." Virgil could feel the muscles relax in Dan-te's hand as he answered her. He knew she wanted to get out of there soon after she witnessed Mr. Geryon's friend, Lawrence Mars, hooked up to life support; but after seeing the "Purification Procedure," and realizing that it was a way to execute Tempters, that was far more then she could handle.

"We're at The Sand Spa Hotel," Virgil continued. "After you passed out I carried you on my back out of the hospital and onto an airship which carried us to this hotel at the top of the plateau. We *would* have gone directly from here to the Tri-Dominion Caverns, but something has happened."

"What happened?"

"The passage leading down to the caverns has been sealed off inside a large tent," Virgil explained. "I don't know what's going on, but Mr. Geryon is working on getting us transportation to the caverns. He told me to look behind one of the sand baths in five hours, and after what you've just gone through I think you need the rest."

"Yeah, I do," Dan-te replied, still not over what she witnessed in the hospital.

"Then hide under the bed," Virgil advised, leading Dan-te to the side of the big bed in the room. "Let go of my hand once you're under the bed, I'll block off all the light around the sides once you've done that. When it's completely dark you can remove the Veil. I'll join you as soon as I finish sealing off the rest of the light in the room."

"Ok," Dan-te whispered, crawling under the bed and letting go of Virgil's hand. Virgil responding by ripping the sheets, pillows, and blankets off the bed and took more out of the closet and stuffed them along the edges of the bed. He also noticed the box that he sent to Mr. Geryon from Spectral Academy sitting on the desk and stuffed that under the bed, too. When the bed was sealed, Virgil turned his attention back to the room, sealing off any remaining sources of natural light before talking to Dan-te.

"Dan-te, have you taken off the Veil of Shadows?"

"I already did," Dan-te replied from beneath the bed. "You can join me."

"Okay, I'm going to move a few of the sheets on your opposite side so I can slide under the bed with you. Don't worry about sunlight, I've completely sealed up the room."

Moving the sheets carefully, Virgil slipped under the bed, pushing the package he had mailed so that nothing was between himself and Dan-te. She wasted no words. As soon as she could see him, she pulled him close to her with all her might.

"Dan-te," Virgil coughed, "I need those ribs."

Dan-te did not listen, she did not want to. From the moment she saw the Lightning Lamp expose that Tempter, followed by the Tempter's execution by sunlight at the hands of the Hy-muns in the room, all she wanted was to wrap herself in Virgil's protective violet energy, the same energy that flashed from him the moment that "Purification Procedure" revealed the Tempter, the energy that he was still generating now.

"Please, just let me stay like this," Dan-te begged.

"Take all the time you need," Virgil answered. "Just ease up on your grip before you break something."

Dan-te opened her eyes to look at Virgil and quickly *Knew* she was causing him pain. She relaxed her hold and felt embarrassed in the process.

"Sorry," Dan-te apologized. "I forgot how much stronger I am compared to you."

"It's okay," Virgil coughed again. "No harm was done. If you need to hold onto me, go right ahead. You look like you need it. Just don't crush me."

Now that Virgil could see Dan-te again, he could see how upset she really was. She buried her head in his shoulder, her horn rubbing against the side of his head. Virgil could feel her whole body trembling as he held her close to his own body.

"The surface can't be our home anymore," Dan-te mumbled from within Virgil's shoulder. "How could *any* member of the two Tribes even imagine living in a world where that kind of death is a constant threat. The Tribe of Shadows' Plan, generations spent trying to remove that threat so they could retake this place—especially when they have a city of their own, it's all madness."

Virgil wanted to say something, but could not. Instead he decided to hold Dan-te's trembling body closer to his own.

What do I say to her? Virgil asked himself, racking his mind, trying to find something to say. *What* can *I say to her? We might have both seen that Tempter die in the sunlight, but for Dan-te, that was how scores of her people died in "The Coming" ages ago, and it's also the death she's constantly dancing with every second she is on the surface and exposed to sunlight, a death that's only prevented by the Veil of Shadows. Now that protection can't even be trusted, especially if there are more of those Lightning Lamps where we are going. Worse, those lamps were created and used by Hy-mums like me. Dan-te just watched a Tempter die not only because of sunlight, but because of Hy-muns capturing, revealing, and tearing his Veil right off him to expose him to the sunlight. How can I possibly understand what she must be feeling right now?*

Virgil did not have an answer to his own questions, a feeling he was very uncomfortable with. He always strove to find the right words to tell someone when they came to talk to him. He did that with Reye whenever she came calling, and he had been trying to do that with Dan-te, but this situation was entirely beyond him.

Obscuris vera involvens, the truth being enveloped by obscure things, Virgil recalled, remembering his Platin saying lessons. *How do I understand what Dan-te feels when its surrounded by my own lack of understanding of what it must feel like to live in fear of sunlight?*

"You being here is enough," Dan-te whispered, snapping Virgil out of his thoughts. "Just being here, right now, holding your body and feeling its heartbeat. Letting your protective violet energy and caring blue energy wrap around me like a blanket, seeing your white mental energy buzz and pulse through your head as you struggle to think of something to say, *Knowing* how much you care and worry about me. It's enough."

"It doesn't feel like it's enough," Virgil countered, still wanting to do more for her.

"And that is why it's enough."

Dan-te pulled herself closer to Virgil. Having him with her did help, but she knew it was only a minor reprieve. Soon she would have to face more of the surface world before she could rejoin the Remnant; assuming there would even be a Remnant to return to.

"If we live through this, I'm going to have to talk to Ca-to," Dan-te mumbled.

"Who's Ca-to?" Virgil asked, catching Dan-te's remark.

"One of our best healers," Dan-te explained. "When my group went to Nis he came with us. Now that I remember him, I don't even know if he's still alive. The last time I saw him was when Ice and I volunteered to become gladiators. He came with us to Nis in case any of us were injured physically, mentally, or spiritually. Covering ourselves up like this is actually similar to one of the Remnant's best spiritual healing processes."

"Sealing yourselves under a bed is how you start a spiritual healing process among your people?" Virgil asked curiously.

"No," Dan-te replied with a chuckle. "What you do is lay in a small pit, then you are almost completely covered—sealed—in cold rock dust under the ground, and *that* is only the start of the process."

Part 5: Reflections from a Different Point of View

Chapter 21

"Please, lay down here, Reye," Ca-to instructed.

"All right," Reye replied, still skeptical about the whole idea, but willing to try it for the sake of her friend, Ann.

How many times have I recounted the story and all the different and wrong choices I made since I first escaped from the Grand Coliseum and started running wildly throughout the city of Nis? Reye asked herself. *The wrong choices began with my first decision to go further into Nis instead of heading toward Lust Atrophied to see if Stella had been taken there and ended with me arrogantly challenging Tanas. He was able to completely subdue me with hardly any effort at all.*

Reye shuddered at the memory of her encounter and the state it left her in. She was lost in her mind with the screaming faces of every warrior she killed throughout Nis until Ann pulled her back to reality. Since then, Reye had slowly been regaining her strength, but she was still constantly haunted by her past actions.

"You need *to come to terms with what you've done," Ann told me after the nightmares had woken me up again for the third time,* Reye remembered. *"I've*

gone through this Reconciliation Ritual myself and while it can be a little rough, it works. Let's talk to him and see if you can go through the ritual as well."

Before her imprisonment in Maestri, the only members of the Remnant Reye had ever met were Ice and his sister Dan-te; and they were the only ones she wanted to meet.

***

"I never tried to learn much about their people from either of them," Reye had told Ann, more nervous about asking the Remnant for help then the ritual itself. "All I cared about was that they could help me achieve my goal of vengeance against the Tribe of Shadows."

"Now you have a chance to make up for that," Ann encouraged her, leading her to the Seat of Kindness. "So, get moving and show me some of that enthusiasm we both know you are known for and let's talk to the Seat of Kindness. You *really* need to do this."

Reye turned notably depressed at the mention of her "enthusiasm." That aspect of her personality was part of the reason she was here in the first place.

"Humph, you've just proven my point," Ann pointed out, seeing Reye's depression. "You *need* to come to terms with what you've done. I've gone through this Reconciliation Ritual myself and while it can be a little rough, it works. Let's talk to him and see if you can go through the ritual as well."

***

Ann's insistence is what finally convinced me to talk to the Seat of Kindness who introduced me to Ca-to and attempt the ritual, Reye reflected. *Ca-to seemed to be ready for both of us the moment we came to talk to him. I wonder if it's another way that the members of the Remnant can Know things, or if I just looked so damaged to them that they have been waiting for me to ask about it from the moment I woke up. According to Ca-to, the first stage of the ritual involved both the healer and the one being healed to ritualistically rub themselves down with smooth stones. It's a good thing there are plenty of them scattered about this cell. I still don't know what this "ritual" actually entails. Neither Ca-to nor Ann would give me any details. But she still said that she had gone through with it and that I "need to come to terms with what I've done." That's one point I don't deny one bit. Still, why are some of the other members of the Remnant digging a small pit? Are they planning on healing me or burying me alive?*

"Please, lie down and relax," Ca-to instructed her, gesturing to the pit.

Burying me alive, Reye decided, about to turn around and forget Ann even suggested this ritual in the first place. Except before she could turn around she felt Ann's hand reach around her back and grasp her shoulder. Looking around, she found not only Ann, but also half a dozen members of the Remnant behind her, all with encouraging looks on their faces.

Or they Knew *I was going to back out at the last minute*, Reye mentally sighed to herself, climbing down into the hole now that she realized that she *couldn't* back out. Once she was in the hole, Ca-to handed her a small cup of liquid.

"Drink this. Then we will begin," he instructed.

Relaxing in the pit, and not seeing any other options, Reye drank the liquid. Her whole body suddenly stiffened up and then relaxed. Her eyes glazed over, removing her sight.

What was that stuff, Reye wondered, until she felt cold dust and dirt covering her body. *By the Great Lord Ash Addiel, they* are *burying me alive!*

Reye was panicking now, and the fact that she could not move made it worse as more of the cold dust began to cover her body. She could feel the cold dust slowly surround her, yet her body did not shiver or tighten, it just stayed the way that it was until she noticed something new.

What's that smell? Smoke? It can't be. Smoke isn't fragrant, but it still feels like smoke. And what's that noise?

Besides the weird smoke being fanned into the pit, Reye also heard something just out of her hearing range that could have been praying or chanting.

Healing, yeah right, this is a funeral! They're cooking me, Reye whiffed, feeling the dust almost up to her neck now. *It seems the members of the Remnant are planning to kill me all along. Not that I deserve any better. After all, I have already eaten flesh from Hy-muns like me, killed more members of the Tribe of Shadows then I can count—providing them with martyrs and food in the process. It's no surprise they would do the same to me.*

A new sound entered Reye's mind, the screams of all the members of the Tribe of Shadows that she killed in her mad rampage through Nis.

Humph, I'm not surprised they would come back, Reye figured, expecting their return. *After I killed so many of them just to reach Yam-Preen so I could try to kill Tanas, it is no surprise that they would come back now just as I'm about to be killed myself. Isn't this exactly where a horror like me belongs, eternally surrounded by the screams of the dead and terrified; each one a victim of my own hands. Why did Ann trick me like this? If they all wanted to execute me, then they didn't need to make a production out of it. Why go through all this?*

"Because you chose to do it," a familiar voice spoke out in the darkness.

Reye recognized the voice immediately. Coming to full wakefulness, she jumped up expecting to be out of the smoke and dust-filled pit in the cell in Maestri. Instead, she found herself in far more familiar surroundings.

"A forest," she gasped. "An Amber-leaf forest."

Amber-leaf trees got their name from the shade of orange that their leaves perpetually held. It was the same color of amber as the Amber Ziggurat of the Orange Dominion, Reye's home. A vast forest of Amber-leaf trees rested near Reye's farm and was where she and her brother Raymond created plenty of memories together.

"If I didn't know any better," Reye said, looking up and around at her surroundings, "I would think this forest is the same forest as the one near my home. The only difference is that its night and the sky is completely black without a single cloud or star in it."

"It is the same forest," the voice spoke again from behind her. "And you won't see any stars no matter how hard you look." The sound of the voice was so hauntingly familiar that Reye did not want to turn around and face its owner. Yet the voice continued prompting her.

"Well, aren't you going to turn around and look me in the face? Don't tell me you're that afraid of me."

I am, Reye thought to herself. She was afraid of the voice's owner, and even more afraid of confronting him. She knew that the voice's owner could not be behind her; she had seen its owner's death with her own eyes. So, the only way that the owner's voice could be behind her now would be if she were dead herself. She could not think of any other way he could be here.

"Just turn around, Reye," the voice shouted this time.

Reye turned around, slowly and trembling, and standing before her in the dark forest was her dead twin brother, Raymond.

"It can't be," Reye squeaked. She knew that her brother was dead. "The two of us were part of the Demp Cavern Mining Project. It was attacked by the Tribe of Shadows and almost completely wiped out. Just before the attack, the Tribe of Shadows' warriors extinguished all of the artificial light in the camp and turned the cavern pitch-black. I could only hear you in the darkness, you and the Tribe of Shadows' warriors as they walked into the camp and started slaughtering like animals the other project members. I still remember the fear, wondering when we were going to be killed, even more so when they finally reached us. I remember hearing you hit one, and I dodged and hit another, but I knew we would be killed, too. I prayed to Ash Addiel for a miracle, for light."

"And then there was light," Raymond continued. "Only it was no miracle, and it wasn't caused by Ash Addiel."

"No, it was Sol," Reye answered. "During the attack, he launched a flare from a device he had hidden in his backpack. It illuminated the cave, gave all of us our first real look at the Tribe of Shadows' warriors. It also caused them to burn in pain. Their skin turned from blue to black as it burned, cracked, blistered, and filled the air with a rotting smell. Afterward, Sol took the opportunity to use the emergency one-man rocket to return to the surface. I had asked myself, 'Is Sol getting help? Is he leaving us? Is he running away,' before I heard a loud crack and you scream. I turned around and saw you on the cavern floor, your leg broken, the warrior responsible raising his hammer directly over your head, preparing for a final strike. I remember you looking at me, all of your adventuring excitement erased from your eyes and replaced by fear, worry, an eerie sense of calm acceptance before you said two words to me before the warrior smashed your head open with the hammer, killing you. I still remember the words you told me, 'run, fight.'"

"I said *three* words," Raymond corrected. "Run, fight, *live*. During the fight, I ended up letting myself get distracted by Sol running away. You *know* the only way I would have let myself get into a position like that is if I was distracted."

Reye did know. She had taken enough martial arts classes with Raymond to understand that the only time he was ever knocked on his back—one of the worst places a fighter could be—was when he got distracted.

"I got distracted and got my leg broken and my head smashed open because of it," Raymond barked, talking like his death was his own fault and not because of the Tribe of Shadows. "Not that we had any chance of getting out of there to begin with. When that light paralyzed the Tribe of Shadows' warriors, I wanted you to take Stella, run, and try to fight your way out of that mess if it were even possible, and to *live* through it. But true to form, you only heard what you *wanted* to hear. Then you lost all control of yourself and acted totally crazy, slaughtering every warrior in your path as if you were a crusader on a divine mission instead of taking care of what was *really* important. I should have known better."

Reye had now officially overcome her fear of seeing Raymond again. Now, she was extremely mad at him.

"What do you mean I only listen to what I want to and then act crazy?" she challenged him. I just lost you and my best friend! Now you're telling me off, saying I only listened to what I wanted to and then acted crazy like it was a bad thing. You don't think I have the *right* to act crazy after that? The Tribe of Shadows took *everything* from me."

"Let's examine those points," Raymond interrupted. "First, you've always just listened to what you wanted to. The fact that you thought my last words were just 'run' and 'fight' should be proof enough. If not, what about our group dinner at AB's before we left. I told you then that you needed to pay more attention when people were talking to you because you were ignoring Ann. You just brushed it off politely, but even Ann remarked how you needed to pay better attention when people are talking to you. Otherwise you would miss something important someday. Well, the day I died *was* that day. I tried to tell you something important, and instead, you missed it entirely and only heard what you wanted to, and it's not the first time you've done it either. Tell me, how many times have you ignored what other people were telling you because it didn't interest or matter to you? Are you *honestly* telling me you seriously listen to everything being said to you? Or are you really just listening to what you want to?"

If there's one thing Raymond could always do, it was cut straight to the heart of the situation. Especially when he started to preach and criticize, Reye thought to herself, having been on the receiving end of Raymond's harsher evaluations; and always whenever she did something terrible beyond reasoning or excuse.

Raymond's death certainly hadn't decreased his energy, his passion for talking, or his sharp tongue, Reye mused, trying to divert herself from coming up with an answer to his criticism. *What should I even say to him? I could never lie to him, and even if I tried, he's always been able to tell.*

"But I never act *too* crazy," Reye finally said, trying to downplay her actions.

"What do you mean you 'never act *too* crazy?'"

Raymond looked like he could not believe the words Reye had uttered.

"You've been going crazy from the moment I died, and every decision you've made before coming here has been one crazy decision after another."

"So, are you saying it would have been a sane idea to give up and die?" Reye asked.

"There you go doing it again," Raymond said exasperatedly. "Listening only to what you want to. It *was* a good idea to fight for your life. But holding an entire civilization responsible for the actions of one warrior—a warrior you killed long ago. Ripping through an entire city like you were a crusader on a divine mission—killing everyone in your path, and completely ignoring everything else because it either wasn't related to your goal or just didn't seem important, that *is* crazy. Sadly, that is also you, a wild Hy-mun who runs around crazy with joy. You did it when you learned we were accepted into Spectral Academy and you did it again throughout Nis. Only here there was no one to check you."

"You are *not* comparing the way I acted when I was accepted into Spectral Academy with my action in Nis, are you?" Reye viciously challenged him.

"Yes, I am," Raymond answered. "Are you telling me you didn't enjoy it, killing all those warriors, blowing up buildings, staircases, and homes while you ran through Nis? Joy is joy; it doesn't matter if your actions are good or evil, *you* are the one who decides what you're doing, and *you* are the one who finds the joy in it. Think about that."

Reye tried to think about it, but her mind came up blank as she stared at Raymond, trying to process what was going on. Elsewhere, while Reye confronted her brother in a dark Amber-leaf forest, her body rested in the pit the members of the Remnant excavated for her, the cold dust now up to her neck.

The liquid that she drank earlier putting her body into a semi-comatose state while the other members of the Remnant chanted and blew a strange smoke into the pit. Silently, Reye's friend, Ann, watched and waited.

This is going to be far tougher on you than it was on me, Reye, Ann thought to herself, remembering her own experiences with this ritual. *The attack on the project caused you to suffer a severe mental shock and collapse. Then you went crazy throughout Nis, making a lot of terrible decisions, leaving you broken internally and in a lot of pain. But if you come back from this, you will finally be able to dig yourself out of this pit and make your way back to us.*

Meanwhile, Reye was not the only one reflecting on a large number of bad past decisions.

Chapter 22

If it weren't for this suit, I wouldn't be able to keep my eyes open, the Tribesman mused. Making his way through the smoke-filled section of the Great Tunnel, the Tribesman struggled on toward the Keyblast Point where he hoped he might be able to stop the Third Great Attempt before it was initiated. But the suit's protection from the smoke could not silence his mind.

Each person working in the Tunnel is here on "volunteer service," "good leadership is key." Fragments from Lom-ardo, the crew chief the Tribesman encountered, still rang through his mind as he made his way down the Great Tunnel. His mind not only flashing back to his home, the city of Rem, and how its leadership ensured their survival; but also, how poor leadership—that his old self performed voluntarily, had destroyed his old self, an uncountable number of lives in Nis, and also almost destroyed Reye.

I still remembered how Ice felt when he first met Reye and decided to tell her nothing except what she already knew, the Tribesman thought to himself. Feeling the stone in the smoke and watching for the jam-tinted glow of other diggers from the Tribe of Shadows, the smoke almost swirled into the familiar images of Reye as Ice first *Knew* her.

Reunions, Reflections, and Reconciliations

She was hurt: physically, emotionally, and spiritually, and Ice made the dumb choice to tell her she was letting her injuries change her "for the worse," the Tribesman remembered, his memory from when he was Ice still in his head. Reye, who had never met a member of the Remnant, or the Tribe of Shadows before her encounter, was being introduced to our ability to Know *other beings and things immediately after suffering a traumatic loss and her abduction. A skill she couldn't understand and would repeatedly encounter in that short time she was in that cell. He also made the mistake of being too honest with Reye. Ice was always taught that it was a good thing to be honest. But he already* Knew *that when he, his sister, and Reye where locked in that cell and decided to tell Reye the fate of the other Hy-mun captives that he was destroying hope instead of cultivating it, as he had wanted to. He* Knew *the turmoil in Reye's mind and guessed that once she knew the truth, that she ate food made from Hy-mun flesh, and that any other survivors would be used for breeding, it would turn her into a wrath-filled fighting machine he could aim at Lord Tanas. In the end, when it really counted, all those lessons in Rem Ice was supposedly good at, the values of being both hopeful and a peacemaker, he ignored them all. Ice* Knew *what Reye really needed but instead chose, through his own free will, was to cultivate her wrath and get her to do his dirty work for him.*

"Come on you people, move it!"

The Tribesman's thoughts were interrupted by a shout echoing through the smoke. Taking cover behind a few rocks, the Tribesman soon spotted the jam and grey-colored radiance from five large lines of diggers returning to Nis. Each line was bound together in chains, pulling another one behind it, and joyfully glad to be going back to Nis. The Tribesman watched as the lines moved slowly but steadily. He Knew that whatever they were pulling must have been extremely big and extremely heavy; the grey stressful energy combined with the growing stink of sweat made that extremely clear.

"Come on, pull," the line leader shouted. "We got to get this machine back to Nis before we can start the Third Great Attempt."

The Tribesman looked silently on from his hiding place as the diggers dragged a large machine through the smoke and into view.

A Hy-mun digging machine, the Tribesman thought as the diggers slowly pulled a giant machine through the tunnel. The device took up almost the entire tunnel, leaving only a little room for diggers to move around it. It sat on two large treads that slowly moved as the diggers pulled at it, and it had a platform near the points where the chains were attached. On the platform, the Tribesman could see more diggers and the artificial glow created by the Hy-mun devices.

That digging machine must have broken down, the Tribesman guessed. *That must be why all those diggers are pulling it out instead of riding it out. I'll bet I'm looking at the back of it, that the actual "digging" part of it is on the other side.*

Oh, if only Reye were here, she would be able to, the Tribesman stopped himself mid-thought, chastising himself for even still having thoughts like that. *Using Reye for that kind of work is precisely what got Ice killed in the first place and left a mountain of dead bodies behind him.*

I still remember Ice's actions clearly, the Tribesman mourned. *Once Reye and Ice escaped the Grand Coliseum, Ice directed her straight down the path that led toward Yam-Preen. Even though he had the chance to put Reye on a course that could have led her to possibly other Hy-mun survivors, maybe even freedom from Nis, instead he sent her straight toward Lord Tanas, gambling she could kill it. Ice willingly chose to use Reye, increasing her wrath so she would do the work he knew he couldn't do himself—work he was afraid to do himself. He decided words would be wasted on her, standing by while he did nothing but guide her through Nis, hacking scores of warriors as they went. He was gambling on the hope she would be able to destroy Lord Tanas and turned a blind eye to the number of members from the Tribe of Shadows, members who were still blood kin to him, who died in the process.*

Watching the lines of diggers from the Tribe of Shadows moving down the tunnel, the Tribesman was ashamed of himself to find he fell back into the mode of thinking for a moment that killed Ice. He knew that if he continued the thought, he would be thinking that if Reye were here, she would be able to take out all of the diggers that were pulling the machine and leave it stranded in the tunnel. One of the diggers did say he needed to get the machine back before the Third Great Attempt could begin; so, any delay would put off the start of the Third Great Attempt.

"Have I really become so slothful I need Reye with me every time I need to do any kind of work?" the Tribesman muttered to himself under the noise of the dragging machine. "Am I really so lazy now I just don't want to face this one task on my own, or even try to face it?"

"Hey, who are you over there!"

The shout broke the Tribesman out of his contemplations. He suddenly realized he had been spotted while he was lost in thought. Cursing himself silently and moving quickly through the smoke, he hoped to lose the diggers that were now pursuing him and to put as much distance between them as he could. Unfortunately, the diggers *Knew* the Great Tunnel far better than the Tribesman, and it was not long before he was caught by them.

"Well, look what we found," one of the diggers puffed, looking into the Tribesman's helmet. "A Rodent managed to scurry its way into the Great Tunnel. How do you think it managed to get in here?"

"Ask Lord Tanas," another digger yawned.

"You wish," a third digger replied. "We haven't heard anything from Nis since the Hy-mun raid over a week ago."

And I am grateful for that, the Tribesman silently added. Contact between the diggers in the Great Tunnel and Nis took a long time under the best conditions, so it only happened rarely. Considering that they were just calling the Tribesman a "Rodent," the usual derogatory curse for members of the Remnant, instead of an associate of the "Hy-mun Horror" meant they did not know who he was.

In fact, considering all of the destruction Reye caused, and that there is only minimal contact between Nis and the diggers, I'll bet they haven't even heard the news about what has happened to Nis or about us yet, the Tribesman guessed.

"So, what do you think we should do with this Rodent?" one of the diggers asked.

"Let's just kill him and toss the body," a digger replied.

"No," another digger objected. "If we're going to kill him, why not have some fun with him. Let's leave him here and let the drilling machine be dragged over him."

"Whatever we do, we're going to have to do it now. The taskmaster is going to need us back on the chains pulling the drilling machine soon," the first one said. "Personally, I like Benu-Re's idea. Let's just leave him here, and whether he's crushed by the drilling machine or dies slowly, he'll be gone, and we can have the satisfaction of knowing we exterminated one more Rodent."

"Excellent idea," the digger identified as Benu-Re exclaimed. "Let's do it!"

The other diggers were just as eager to leave the Tribesman to die in the Grand Tunnel as the Tribesman was to be rid of them. The Tribesman also liked Benu-Re's idea, but for an entirely different reason.

If the diggers leave me behind, then I will only have to deal with three of them, the Tribesman considered, weighing his options. *The three of them versus me, especially if they plan to leave me here to die, is a lot better than my chances against all of the diggers—especially if they want blood. The other diggers might also ignore me if they think I'm being executed, whereas if I fight or run they won't* ignore me. *Of course, there is a risk with this plan. There's no guarantee the other diggers might not decide to kill me where I am. Plus, I have to worry about the digging machine itself. I need to find a way to dodge it quickly.*

The Tribesman knew it was a dangerous risk, but also an acceptable one, and one he needed to take if he planned to continue down the Great Tunnel.

Reye and Dan-te took all of the risks before, the Tribesman thought to himself, remembering all of the dangers Reye and his former sister Dan-te took when he was still Ice and stayed in a relatively safe location. *Now it's my turn to take a risk instead of just relying on someone else.*

With that thought, the Tribesman let himself be bound and left face down in a ditch in the center of the Great Tunnel. The digger named Benu-Re kicked him a few times for joy and good measure.

"Well, that will be one less Rodent to deal with," Benu-Re laughed as they walked back toward the machine that they were pulling. The Tribesman was laughing, too, in his mind, because he managed to escape them with his life—for now—without having to rely on someone else. Unfortunately, as the noise from the other diggers and the machine came closer, the Tribesman realized this was where the real challenge began.

I can't let myself feel anything, the Tribesman thought to himself, trying to silence his own mind in the process. *No fear, shame, regrets, joy, determination, expectations, nothing that would let my energy bubble up any more than it is. Don't even think!*

The Tribesman silenced himself with that thought and was soon as still as the stones around him. He already knew that the most dangerous part of this risk would be when the other diggers passed him. They were the ones who needed to ignore him. If they passed by him, he would have a short time before the machine rolled over him to move away. It was not long before he heard the first diggers and their taskmaster passing by.

"Hey, what's this thing doing here," the taskmaster bellowed, stomping the Tribesman with his foot. The Tribesman, however, did not twitch at all to the prodding.

"Just us having some fun with a Rodent," Benu-Re answered from down the line. "Just leave it to be crushed. You said it yourself that we have to get this machine back to Nis so let's pull, and pull it right over that thing while we're at it."

The other diggers and the taskmaster all laughed and cheered at Benu-Re's remark and were soon pulling the machine again. Meanwhile, the Tribesman ignored them, keeping as still as possible, and listened until they all slowly passed by, while the machine rumbled closer; the stone beneath it cracked and dipped slightly under the increasing weight.

It won't be much longer now, the Tribesman mused, his first thought since the taskmaster approached him. *They should be far enough away now, now all I have to do is...*

The Tribesman's thoughts and blood froze as he tried to twist himself face up, only to bump up against metal. *By the Ancient Tribe, I'm already under the digging machine!*

The Tribesman did not know if he should feel terrified or elated. In truth, he felt both. Turning his head slightly, he managed to see the digging machine's threads not far from him and at the same time discovered why he was not crushed when it was pulled over him.

"I sank into a ditch," the Tribesman blurted out, unable to believe his luck. "The ground cracked around me from the machine's weight, I sank slightly, and the diggers pulled the machine right over me thinking they had crushed me with it. All I need to do is wait."

The Tribesman also knew he needed to keep quiet, silencing himself again until the machine had been pulled entirely over him. He did not want the diggers to realize he was still alive. Watching from the ditch, he soon saw the front of the machine and its piercing drill staring him in the face. Unfortunately, propping himself up to shave off his bindings on the drill proved next to impossible, especially considering the machine was moving.

Fine, the Tribesman fumed, tired of trying to cut the binding on a drill that was continually moving away from him. But now, encouraged by his recent brush with death, he moved with fresh determination. *If I have to crawl on my belly for now, so be it. I'll find another way get these ropes off, and then I'll reach the end of this tunnel and get to the Keyblast Point. I will get to it, and I will stop the detonation.*

Meanwhile, back in Nis, several others were facing their own reflections.

Chapter 23

"Enough! You don't want to kill the pathetic thing, do you?"

The warrior looked at his training partner and spit on him. His master was right, he did not want to give the thing the privilege of becoming a martyr. That was an honor reserved for the pure-blooded members of the Tribe of Shadows.

"Get out of here and back to your duties," the warrior hissed. "If we need you to be our practice dummy again, we'll find you."

"Thank you for the training session," Met-on squeaked, receiving another kick to his rear as he staggered out of the training arena in the Fourth Circle of Nis, Envy Opal-Lo.

Met-on, the child of a member of the Tribe of Shadows and the Remnant of the Tribe, scurried away from the completed combat session. Even though he had been beaten bloody, he knew no pure-blooded member of the Tribe of Shadows would ever give him the honor of turning him into a martyr.

"Becoming a martyr for the Plan is an honor reserved only for pure-blooded members of the Tribe of Shadows and those who have earned their brandings," Met-on muttered to himself. The same words had been repeated to him more times than he could count. "Be thankful for the duties you are given, leave the rest to the real warriors of Nis."

During the Hy-mun Horror's rampage, he had been denied the chance to join in the chase for the Horror. He was not permitted to see it when it made its grand debut in the Grand Coliseum. At the time, it would have made him feel even more like the garbage the pure-blooded members of the Tribe of Shadows believed him to be. But as he found himself walking toward the Third Circle of Nis, Lust Atrophied, he realized he was thankful for the Horror. She gave him the opportunity to not only fulfill his own duty, one that could earn him a branding, but she also let him really get to know Stella.

Stella, Met-on mused, as he remembered the Hy-mun girl in Lust Atrophied. Stella recently picked up a new glow about her, a secondary level of silver life energy radiating from her that he had not noticed before. Met-on did not know what it meant, nor asked anyone to explain it yet; he did not want to. He knew their relationship had been anything but routine, and considering his "routine," he wanted it to go on as long as possible.

I still remember the first time I met Stella, Met-on recalled. *I was part of a class in Lust Atrophied. Our teacher had brought one of the females out of her room so he could show us what a female body looked like and demonstrate Joining procedures so that when we Joined with one for the first time, we would know what to do. It was also a vital part of the Tempter Training since tempting Hy-mun to Join with each other, the same way we Joined with each other in Lust Atrophied, resulted in more destruction among the Hy-muns than anything else the Tempters did. In fact, it's often joked that if there's a Fourth Great Attempt, it would be based on making the Hy-mun Join with each other even more until it destroys them.*

After class, we were guided by the Warden of Lust Atrophied, Cha-Les, to the females that were expecting us. Since I was the only member of the class with Rodent-blood, I had to pick last. The Warden also told us that besides the waiting females, there was also a Hy-mun girl who was captured in the raid that brought Nis the Hy-mun Horror that we could use. However, none of the other members of my class wanted to Join with a Hy-mun girl, they wanted pure-blooded females from the Tribe of Shadows. I wanted one like that, too, but eventually decided I would take Stella. Otherwise, I wouldn't be allowed to Join with anyone. When I reached the door that led to her room, I activated the relaxing gas, just like I was supposed to, removed my clothes, and walked in.

So, this is what a Hy-mun looks like, Met-on remembered thinking to himself the first time he saw Stella. He had never seen a Hy-mun before. Every time he tried to get into a class that would let him use a Veil of Shadows he was denied. So, unlike Tempters or trainee Tempters who first see Hy-muns on the surface, he was seeing one here in Lust Atrophied for the first time; and she was all his. Admittedly, he felt a tickle of joy.

She's taller than I am, older too, she has different colored skin than mine, shorter ears, and no horn—lucky. Met-on's black horn, one of the marks of the Rodent-blood within him, was often ridiculed by pure-blooded members of the Tribe of Shadows who had no horn at all.

Well, let's get started, Met-on eagerly thought to himself, walking through the gas and climbing up to the Hy-mun girl. *She's face down. The instructors said I should begin the Joining Procedure by examining her. I guess I should start with her legs, they're the closest thing to me. Remember, be extremely careful, Hy-muns are physically weaker than we are. If I go too roughly, I could kill her by Joining with her. That's how I've heard other Hy-muns have died here.*

Met-on began feeling Stella's legs. Stella did not twitch as Met-on checked and caressed each of them.

I hope I am doing this right, Met-on worried. *This is supposed to comfort, stimulate, and make the other know I mean no harm. I can tell that her legs are strong and sturdy. Whatever she did on the surface must have worked them thoroughly. She's also afraid, the pink energy of fear and its acrid stench is starting to rise off her. But the instructors said that would be normal, "if the female isn't afraid—and she has a lot more to be scared about then you do—then you are not performing correctly." Just keep examining her, Met-on.*

Met-on did, finding the rest of her body was just as developed as her legs were.

Her body feels tight but firm, Met-on thought to himself, holding Stella's naked body up against his own. *I can feel her lungs and heart through her chest. They feel excited. I wonder how much more excited they would be without the gas relaxing her. Her arms are also strong. She's used to lifting heavy loads. I wonder if she would be able to pick me up?*

Met-on's examination was leaving him with more questions than answers. It did not make him any less confused about the Joining Procedure. The only thing it did do was make his manner stiffen.

I'll bet the other members of my class are getting more vivid and better instructions from the pure-blooded female members of the Tribe of Shadows, Met-on lamented, cursing his own inexperience. *Meanwhile, I'm here fumbling around and trying to figure the whole thing out on my own. Still, I will admit that makes it a little more interesting. It's a good thing, though, that Hy-muns are almost physically identical to us except for their size, ear shape, and skin tone. I guess it time to complete the Joining Procedure.*

Met-on placed Stella face down again the way he had found her. The instructors had demonstrated several Joining Methods he knew he could use, and this was the one Met-on had taken a particular interest in, positioning himself in the proper place above and behind her.

Now, I take my manner, I press it forward into here and…wow!

Met-on's mind went blank from the sensory overload. He had overheard stories from other members of the Tribe of Shadows about their first Joining, the feelings that raced through their head and body the moment they became one with a female. But at that moment, he *Knew* none of those stories did the actual experience any credit.

This is incredible, Met-on whiffed. *It's so soft, slimy, and slippery; but it feels like we are becoming one ecstatic being. I can* Know *the Hy-mun girl's feelings. Her pain, fear, confusion—that* must *mean I'm doing this right. I can also feel her ecstasy, desire, and pleasure. Despite her mixed emotions, she's enjoying it as much as I am.*

Met-on continued to Join with her, moving steadily and in pace with her body right up to the final moments of the experience when he felt them both release what was inside of their bodies. Afterwards, he separated himself from her to catch his breath. It was then that he noticed the Hy-mun girl looking right at him, her face a mixture of fear, shock, and wonder. Best of all, she was still alive; he had succeeded in Joining with her without killing her.

I Know *she enjoyed the experience*, Met-on surmised. *She's afraid, the pink fear energy and its acrid scents are pulsing off her now, and the instructors told me that if she's not scared, then she's not enjoying it; so, she must have* really *enjoyed it. This must also have been her first time Joining with another person, just like me, I guess we're both a little shocked by the experience.*

Met-on sat there, looking at the Hy-mun girl, the room, everything. He took in everything he could from both the experience and the circle in which he found himself.

This *is Lust Atrophied,* Met-on thought proudly. *This is where the Tribe of Shadows Joins with its women. It was established by Lord Tanas and the Seven Vices of the time when the current city of Nis was built to produce children. I was born here. It is all for the Plan so that we could one day return to the surface. Still, I wonder why this Hy-mun would be sad? The Hy-muns are the successors to the Beings of Light who stole the surface world from our ancestors and made it impossible for us to return. I would think she would be a little happy about trying to give back what was ours originally. The Hy-mun* must *know about us and what both they and the Beings of Light have put us through.*

Met-on could still hear the booming lectures about Hy-muns that echoed through Envy Opal-Lo. They would be screaming, "The Hy-muns are evil! Created by the Beings of Light to guard a world they conquered. A world they slaughtered our ancestors to take from us. Do not trust them."

The Hy-muns must know their own history, Met-on figured. T*hey must know how the Light Bringer and the Beings of Light conquered the surface from the Ancient Tribe, although, I guess she would be a little surprised to see a descendant of those survivors up close. If it wasn't for Lord Tanas, all of the steps and measures he taught us and instituted, the Tribe of Shadows wouldn't have grown and survived until now. Still, this Hy-mun girl's shock, it seems like she's confused. I guess I should let her know how extraordinary that felt and how good she was.*

"T…That…" Met-on panted, struggling to find the right words to say. "That…was *INCREDIBLE!* I had no idea it would feel this good. You were great, sis."

The Hy-mun girl stared blankly in reply.

I wonder if I didn't compliment her right, Met-on worried, his mind racing faster than it ever had before. *I told her she was great, called her "sis" per our tradition. Is something still wrong?*

Met-on's "tradition" of calling someone in the Hy-mun girl's position "sis" stretched back to just after "The Coming," but before the arrival of Lord Tanas. The story went if you think every woman you are with is part of your family, you never have to worry about discreetness.

Maybe I should explain myself more, that should help her to understand what's happening better, Met-on reasoned. The feeling grew stronger after the Hy-mun girl gasped a single, "What," in response to his first sentence.

"Yeah, they gave me you for my first time since I'm half-Rodent and you're a Hy-mun," Met-on explained, "but I'm glad they did, it was incredible! I'm going to ask if they'll reserve you for me. I doubt it will be a problem since no one is probably going to want a Hy-mun, especially now. I got to go, I'll see you again soon; the name is Met-on."

"Met-on," the Hy-mun girl called back.

"That's right! You can say my name! I'm so glad you are my sis," Met-on chirped before leaving her in the room and walking back out into Lust Atrophied proper.

I know it's unlikely, highly unlikely, that the Warden of Lust Atrophied would ever let me reserve any woman, even a Hy-mun woman, Met-on sighed. *After all, I'm still just a Rodent-blood child with no brandings to my name. But that doesn't mean I can't ask. I know some women, from time to time, are reserved by warriors for particular purposes. I also know that none of the other members of my class wanted anything to do with her. I might have a shot.*

Met-on would not admit it, but the simple reason why he wanted to reserve her was that he merely wanted to see her again. He did not understand why Joining with her was the most exciting experience of his life, but he wanted the chance to find out, and he wanted to Join with her more.

I already know all the women in Lust Atrophied are supposed to be available for every man in Nis so they can increase the population, Met-on considered. *But now, since I've Joined with her, the odds should be low that anyone else would even want to Join her; unless it was to kill her. A warrior would probably just Join her to death to reduce the number of Hy-muns out there. Yeah, I think I have a chance. I got to talk to the Warden.*

Finding Warden Cha-Les was easy. He waited for everyone to return from their first Joining, so Met-on decided to ask right away.

"Great Warden Cha-Les," Met-on begged him, prostrating himself before him. "I, Met-on, know I am a pitiful member of the Tribe of Shadows cursed with the blood of the Rodents, but I beg you to listen to my request."

Warden Cha-Les completely ignored Met-on's opening statement, as would anybody if the speaker was a member of the Tribe of Shadows possessing Rodent-blood.

"I beg of you," Met-on continued. "Please grant me an exclusive reservation to the Hy-mun girl. I realize I am only a pathetic Rodent-blooded child, worth less than nothing to the Plan, but even I realize no one might even want to touch her after I have Joined with her. She can teach me much about how I can tempt others from how I tempt her. It has to be some aid for the Tribe of Shadows, the Plan, and Nis."

Met-on knew better than to hope for anything. He had Rodent-blood running through his veins, no branding, and had only started with his studies. The possibility that Warden Cha-Les would *ever* consent to letting him reserve a woman was almost nonexistent.

I wonder if Warden Cha-Les, will *answer me,* Met-on wondered in his deep prostration. *But just because he doesn't right away, that doesn't mean an automatic "no." I just need to be patient. But if he does refuse, then I will have to wait until she is available again. No, I'll have to wait until I am allowed to* see *her again.*

"Met-on…"

Immediately Met-on forced himself into an even deeper position.

Warden Cha-Les spoke to me, Met-on whiffed, his mind racing. *He's not only paying attention to me, but he's also planning to answer me.*

Met-on did not hold out hope that the Warden decided to grant his request. He realized it would be far more likely for him to be sent to clean out the Great Tunnel for merely suggesting that *anyone* in Lust Atrophied be reserved for him, especially with his Rodent-blood.

"I'm going to give you the opportunity to earn a branding."

"A branding," Met-on exclaimed, immediately checking himself for letting his joy and excitement get the better of him.

"I will let you have the Hy-mun girl you Joined with remain reserved for you, and I want you to make that Hy-mun girl fall in love with you. That and provide the city of Nis with a child born of our two races. If you can do that, or even just make her say that she loves you, then you will earn your first branding."

Met-on's eyes would have popped out of his head in surprise and joy if he was not keeping his eyes closed and his body to the ground in prostration.

The Warden of Lust Atrophied has just given me a mission to earn my first branding. The thoughts swirled in Met-on's head. He realized that a rare and valuable opportunity had been given to him. *Most members of the Tribe of Shadows with Rodent-blood like me usually earned only one branding, at best, throughout their entire lives; and I've never heard of anyone receiving all four brandings. This is my chance to earn my first branding.*

"Yes sir," Met-on replied cheerfully and obediently. "I will make the Hy-mun girl that I have Joined with fall in love with me, confess her love for me, and make sure she provides a child for Nis. That will be my mission to earn my first branding."

Met-on never asked how he was to accomplish that mission; he knew doing so would be insulting to Warden Cha-Les. Any task for a branding needed to be completed by himself. That was a rule for all the citizens of Nis. Still, he was overjoyed, for multiple reasons.

I have a mission to earn my first branding, Met-on sang to himself as he backed away from Warden Cha-Les. *Now I can also see that Hy-mun girl again anytime I want to without having to compete with anyone else in Nis. She's all mine.*

Warden Cha-Les, however, was as unreadable as the walls of the Great Tunnel, but inwardly he was amused.

This will be an intriguing way to pass the time, the Warden thought to himself. *That old experiment about making Hy-mun women fall in love with the ones they have Joined with is a perfect way to get a simple Rodent-blood out of the way until the Third Great Attempt starts. If the Hy-mun dies in the process, one less Hy-mun to worry about and I can have him punished for failing a mission. And if he somehow does succeed in the task I just gave him, I can have them both killed—a win-win situation.*

Chapter 24

That was the reasons why I started continually visiting Stella, and why she's never Joined with any other member of the Tribe of Shadows besides me, Met-on thought to himself. *When we started, I really didn't know what I could do to make her "fall in love" with me like Warden Cha-Les ordered. All I did know was that I wanted to see her again, learn more about her, and definitely Join with her again. And Joining with others is exactly what was done in Lust Atrophied. So, Joining with her was what I did, every time I got the chance. Thankfully, that turned out to be a lot easier than I had thought since the other members of the Tribe of Shadows seldom paid me any attention except for menial tasks or to use me as a sparring partner; and then there was the "Hy-mun Horror's" rampage.*

Met-on remembered the special Hy-mun who earned the nickname the "Hy-mun Horror" and how she originally was going to fight in the Grand Coliseum. He had tried to get into the Grand Coliseum to see the "Horror," but a Rodent-blood was not allowed to see her fight.

Not seeing her turned out to be a blessing, Met-on remembered, thinking about the flash of Light that burned the Coliseum's attendees after the First Envy's Veil of Shadows was destroyed and the destruction that followed it. *After the "Hy-mun Horror" escaped, she began rampaging throughout all the Circles of Nis from Wrath Eras all the way to Yam-Preen. When she was in Greed U-Sez, she managed to destroy an E-gle Building, cutting off a third of the Nis's communications. After that, the other two E-gle Buildings and a good number of the warriors of Nis became so tied up compensating for it that someone like me was able to slip away and become completely unnoticeable. I still remember sharing those opinions with Stella not long after it happened.*

***

"I really have to thank whoever destroyed the E-gle Building if I ever meet them, Big Sis," Met-on remembered saying between panting breaths. "Practically no one paid any attention to someone like me before because of my Rodent-blood. Now they don't notice me at all, and I can see you as often as I can."

Met-on did not know if Joining with her as much as he wanted was going to make her fall in love with him any faster, but it was the only thing that he could think of doing.

She's not showing the same response as she used to, Met-on realized. *Her energy isn't pulsing like it did the first time I Joined with her. It's dimming instead. Am I doing something wrong? Do Hy-mun women like something else?*

Unfortunately, Met-on did not know anything else he could try. All he was ever taught in Lust Atrophied was how to Join with a woman, and while he admittedly only Joined with her, he *Knew* it wasn't enough.

"Well, I got to go, Big Sis," Met-on sighed. As much as he did not want to go, he knew he was not making any progress with her now and thought some time away would give him new ideas. But this time, he heard a voice behind him and a hand grasp him.

"Please…stay…talk to me."

Met-on's eyes bulged. It was the first time that the Hy-mun girl had ever really spoken to him, and she asked to talk to him. Usually, no one ever talked to him because of his Rodent-blood; but Met-on knew she was serious, because she pulsed white mental energy from her head. She genuinely wanted him to talk to him.

"Want to…learn…about you…your people."

Met-on could not have been more delighted if he had been honored by Lord Tanas himself. He went to the door, opened a panel above it, pulled a rope inside that slowed the flow of the gas, and began to clear the room. He then lay down next to the Hy-mun girl and started talking.

"Well, Big Sis, as you already know, my name is Met-on of the Tribe of Shadows. I was born here, in the Third Circle of the city of Nis—Lust Atrophied."

"I am…Stella." the Hy-mun mumbled.

***

That was the first time I heard Stella say her name, and it wouldn't be the last, Met-on remembered, thinking back to that first real conversation between the two of them. *It was during that first conversation I told Stella about where the tradition of calling women in Lust Atrophied Big Sis came from. I also told her our history and how my people used to live on the surface until "The Coming" when they were forced underground by the Beings of Light and then split into the Greater Tribe and the Remnant of the Tribe. This was followed by the coming of Lord Tanas and his Legion of Shadow, which was when the Tribe of Shadows first took the name the "Tribe of Shadows." Considering the golden energy of shock and awe that burst from her when I told her our history, I wonder what they must teach Hy-muns on the surface. Maybe Hy-muns just don't have a sense of history. I think I've told Stella more about myself than anyone; in fact, I don't think I've ever spoken before to anyone for as long as I have with her.*

After the capture of the "Hy-mun Horror" by Lord Tanas, life in Nis returned to normal as preparations for the Third Great Attempt's commencement continued. Chief among those meant more sparring sessions with warriors in training. Yet despite the constant pain and torment he received from both sparring and carrying Rodent-blood, Met-on found that every time he approached Lust Atrophied his cares for his mission weakened and his thoughts for Stella only increased.

Why am I thinking this way? Met-on asked himself. *I know that getting Stella to admit she loves me is the minimal I have to do for me to earn my branding. So, why am I thinking more about her then the branding?*

Could that secondary level of silver life energy radiating from Stella be a sign of love? Met-on wondered, suspecting that perhaps she might have fallen in love with him. *Even if it is, I can't just tell Warden Cha-Les or the guards I've*

171

witnessed a strange glow around her. I need her to confess her feelings at the least or show evidence that she is carrying a child at the most. Otherwise, they'll never believe me.

Met-on did not get much more time to think about Stella and her new glow as he entered Lust Atrophied and found Warden Cha-Les walking toward him. Met-on immediately fell to the ground in prostration away from his path to let him pass by. Instead, the Warden stopped in front of him and began to speak.

"Met-on, has the Hy-mun girl confessed to having fallen in love with you yet?"

"No," Met-on replied honestly and obediently.

"There will be a gathering of all those like yourself soon in the Grand Coliseum to signal the start of the Third Great Attempt. Be sure to listen for the announcement. Be there when you are summoned." The Warden walked off after that leaving Met-on stunned where he was.

The Grand Coliseum, Met-on whiffed. *I've never been allowed to sit there, and I'm going to be standing* in *it!*

Met-on knew that when Warden Cha-Les said "those like yourself" he was referring to members of the Tribe of Shadows with Rodent-blood like him. He had only encountered a few of them over his life. They were all purposely kept apart.

If they gather all of the members of the Tribe of Shadows with Rodent-blood in their veins together in one place, I wonder how many of us there might actually be, Met-on wondered, his excitement building. *More importantly, we will all be standing in the Grand Coliseum, and we'll be signaling the start of the Third Great Attempt. I can't wait to tell Stella.*

If he did not need to keep himself composed and submissive, Met-on would have jumped for joy, shouting loud enough so everyone from Lust Atrophied to Yam-Preen could hear him. Met-on knew he could not do those things while he was still in public, but once he was alone with Stella, he knew he could be as happy as he wanted to be.

Chapter 25

Met-on waited until he heard Warden Cha-Les walk away from his prostrated position before he arose from the ground again. He hurried to Stella's room, the news from the encounter still racing in his mind.

I'm going to be in the Grand Coliseum, in Wrath Eras!

He found Stella still had that new silver glow about her. It was also becoming stronger. Stella's primary glow, mostly fearful pink and mixed with several other colors, was now being encompassed by the new silver glow emanating from her midsection. But right now, Met-on had other concerns than the new glow around her. Closing the door, grinning from ear to ear, he wrapped her up in an embrace that completely surprised her.

Met-on's much stronger than I imagined, Stella realized, surprised by his sudden display of excitement and shear strength. *If it comes to it, he might be harder to subdue than I thought. Also, if this is the strength a teenager is capable of, then how strong are the* adult *members of the Tribe of Shadows?*

Stella knew that despite everything Met-on had done, her own survival in Lust Atrophied was partially due to Met-on's fancies. She also knew that he was both her and her child's only hope of successfully escaping the city. But those plans also hinged not only on how quickly she could convince him to take her to the edge of Nis but also how quickly she could get away from him.

Once I make it out of the city, I'll have to knock Met-on unconscious or...

The thought hung in Stella's head. She knew that the only way to make sure he did not report her or try to chase her was to kill him once they were out of the city. Yet despite everything that he had done to her, all of the pain and disgust she now felt toward herself because of him, and all the fury she harbored toward him, a part of her still did not want to kill him.

Despite all of the times he's been here—Joining with me, Stella recalled, *Met-on's never done anything beyond just that. Just Joining and talking. Even without Met-on being present, I still would have ended up in Nis, and if he's* really this *strong, then he must have been treating me with extreme care and tenderness. If he didn't, or if he didn't reserve me and someone else came in here and did what they liked with me...*

Stella would have shuddered at the revelation if she was not being swung in the air by Met-on. His strength made her realize how much her own survival actually did depend on Met-on's behavior.

"So, why all of the excitement?" Stella gasped, feeling a little out of breath, and definitely curious about what had brought on Met-on's sudden outburst of joy and strength. "The last time you were here you ran out again after a quick Joining, so why all the celebration? Are you getting a branding?"

"No brandings, I'm afraid," Met-on replied as he calmed himself and put Stella back on the floor. "But something else almost as good just happened. I ran into Warden Cha-Les as I was entering Lust Atrophied. You'll never believe what he told me."

"Something that made you excited," Stella said. Stella had heard about the Warden in charge of Lust Atrophied from the guards outside her room, but this was the first time she had heard his name.

"Extremely excited," Met-on chirped. "The Warden told me I'm going to be appearing in the Grand Coliseum! There's going to be a gathering, all the members of the Tribe of Shadows like me with Rodent-blood are going to be welcomed into the Grand Coliseum to start the Third Great Attempt. I've never even been *inside* the Grand Coliseum. Now I finally have the chance. As well as the chance to meet other members of the Tribe of Shadows that are like me. I hardly get the chance to see any of them around the city. This is going to be fantastic!"

Stella, however, was not as excited as Met-on was, and he quickly *Knew* it. From the moment Met-on said, "There's going to be a gathering, all the members of the Tribe of Shadows like me with Rodent-blood are going to be welcomed into the Grand Coliseum to start the Third Great Attempt," her fearful pink energy flared, along with white mental energy. The guard's words echoed in her head.

"The rumor is that all half-Rodents are going to be wiped out before the Third Great Attempt starts," Stella remembered, the guard's words now sounding like ice in her mind. *That's what the guard said. Tanas is planning to gather all of the members of the Tribe of Shadows with mixed parentage like Met-on into the Grand Coliseum to wipe them all out.*

"What's wrong, Stella?" Met-on asked, a mixture of both confusion and curiosity crossing his face. He *Knew* the news was upsetting her, but he could not understand why. "I've told you before how much every member of the Tribe of Shadows wants to be in the Grand Coliseum, and how few members of the Tribe of Shadows I see throughout Nis who are also like me. I thought you would be happier for me. I'm going to be standing on the greatest stage in Nis alongside every other member of the Tribe of Shadows with Rodent-blood while we start the Third Great Attempt. We could hardly ask for anything better."

I know you could hardly ask for anything better, Stella thought to herself, trying to force the words from her mouth. *I know both of those facts very well. You've told me, many times, that one of the dreams that all the members of the Tribe of Shadows have, whether they be warriors or not, is to stand and fight in the Grand Coliseum. Just standing there would be a thrill in itself for any member of the Tribe of Shadows. It's where the finest warriors are forged and where you can earn one of your brandings. Dying there also meant the extreme honor of being declared a martyr. Then there's the fact you'll be surrounded by other members of the Tribe of Shadows with Rodent-blood, I know how much that means to you.*

While mining Met-on for information about Nis, Stella once asked him how many other members of the Tribe of Shadows he had met in his life that also possessed Rodent-blood like him.

"I have only met one other like me in my entire life," Met-on had answered, surprising Stella at first who imagined that there must be more in the city. "But I do know there are more. I hear about them from other members of the Tribe of Shadows. The one I met was my first teacher in Envy Opal-Lo, probably the oldest member of the Tribe of Shadows you will ever see. He was so old he couldn't even remember his own name. He actually managed to earn two brandings and taught me the way to behave around pure-blooded members of the Tribe of Shadows. He was also the first one to tell me that there were a lot more members of the Tribe of Shadows like me than I thought, even if I didn't see them. They were kept purposely scattered and placed into the most out-of-sight jobs so that they could, 'Use the skills they inherited with their Rodent Blood.'"

Met-on recited those words so perfectly he must have had them drilled into his head, word for word, from an early age, Stella thought, thinking back to when Met-on told her that. *Met-on's teacher is probably right about there being more members of the Tribe of Shadows that were like him scattered around Nis. But I highly doubt it's so they can "use the skills they inherited with their Rodent-blood." I'll bet it's so they can't organize and support each other.*

Stella had seen it plenty of times at Spectral Academy when bullies would target Sol and other students from the Yellow Dominion. The bullies always bothered them when they were alone. But when they were together, they did not dare approach them.

I can't even imagine what it must mean for Met-on just to see *more members of the Tribe of Shadows like him, and to see them in the Grand Coliseum, no less. But if they go to that gathering, if Met-on goes...*

"What is it Stella?" Met-on asked more worriedly now, breaking her out of her thoughts. "Something is really bothering you. Your white mental energy is frazzling. What is going on?"

I have to say something to him, Stella realized. *But what? I can't lie to him, because he'll be able to tell by his ability to* Know. *Nor can I tell him what I overheard from the guards, he'll never believe me. So, what do I say?*

"Well," Met-on pressed.

"I don't want you to go to the Grand Coliseum," Stella blurted out.

"What?" Met-on gasped.

"I don't want you to go to the Grand Coliseum," Stella repeated. "Instead, I want you to take me outside the city."

"Stella, I can't just take you out of Nis. Women never leave Lust Atrophied, they are too valuable to the Plan and the future of the Tribe of Shadows. And I am *not* turning down an invitation to the Grand Coliseum. Think about it, it's the *Grand Coliseum*, the dream battleground for every member of the Tribe of Shadows. Not only that, but I'll be surrounded by other members of the Tribe of Shadows who have Rodent-blood like me."

"If you go to the Grand Coliseum, you'll die," Stella screamed, not caring now if the guards heard her outside.

"Of course, I could die. Thousands upon thousands have died there, and if I die, I will be recorded as a martyr and be remembered forever on the walls of Nis, just like those before me. But I doubt there will be a coliseum battle. We are going to start the Third Great Attempt."

"No, you *will* die. Please, you need to trust me. Don't go. Instead, take me outside the city. I'll do anything for you if you can do that, I'll even tell you that I'm in love with you."

Met-on was struck speechless by Stella's declaration. His mind raced as the implications settled in.

Stella will tell me she loves me. The thought echoed in Met-on's mind, along with what that declaration would mean for him, the risks it would entail, and what it would cost him. *She'll tell me she loves me, and she's* not *lying. I can hear the honesty ringing in her voice. All I needed to get from her was a declaration of love, and I will have successfully completed my mission. I will have earned my first branding. But to do that, I'll need to take her outside the city. Will the guards outside even let me take her outside this room, let alone Lust Atrophied or Nis itself? The guards are there to make sure she remains reserved for me; would they have to follow us? Then there's the Grand Coliseum. If I want Stella's declaration then I'll never be able to go into the Grand Coliseum, I might never meet another member of the Tribe of Shadows like me if I do that, but I could still get a branding. Yet…*

Met-on's mind burned with indecision. He wanted both the branding and to go to the Grand Coliseum. But Stella had locked him into a position where he could only have one or the other.

If the gathering at the Grand Coliseum weren't going to happen, this choice would be so much easier, Met-on fretted. *If there were no gathering, then I would try to get Stella out of the city so I can get her confession.*

Similarly, Stella's mind also burned with worry. *This gathering couldn't have come at a worse time*, she feared. *My escape plan depended on Met-on doing anything if it meant getting a confession of love out of me so that he would earn his first branding. But this gathering in the Grand Coliseum could be one of the few things that would make him do otherwise, and it's also where the Tribe of Shadows plans to exterminate its members that are like Met-on. Meaning if I don't get Met-on to help me now, we're* all *dead.*

Stella remembered the rest of the guards' conversation.

"After the purge, kill the Hy-mun," that's what the guard said. The memory made Stella shiver, not just for herself, but for the child she carried. She knew she was just about out of time.

Met-on, however, could not get past his indecision or his confusion. Stella pulsed and fizzled with fearful pink energy and white mental energy while being wrapped in the new layer of silver life energy. He *Knew* she was scared and worried, but also that she was counting on him, for what he could not understand.

Wait, could she be testing me, Met-on concluded, remembering Tempter classes he managed to listen in on. *Hy-mun women, even without a Tempter's whispers, are prone to tempting and testing men, especially if they harbor feelings for them. At least, that's what the teachers are always saying. If Stella is in love with me that would explain why she's doing this, it's a test. She's trying to make me chose either her or Grand Coliseum because she's scared of losing me to my own ambitions. The teachers here in Lust Atrophied were right—this is an essential part of Tempter Training.*

A happy smile crept upon Met-on face over the prospect that Stella was testing him because she secretly loved him. He could feel that he was just one step away from reporting to Warden Cha-Les that his mission was a success. Then he would be able to go to the Grand Coliseum *with* a branding. All he needed was to hear the admission from Stella's mouth.

"Stella, do you love me? Is that why you are afraid to see me go? Is that why you're testing me this way?"

Stella's eyes popped as a golden flash of shock pierced the other energies surrounding her. He *Knew* he had surprised her with his question.

"You think I'm testing you?" Stella asked.

"Aren't you?"

I am, Stella realized. *But it's not what you think, but that doesn't mean it could* be.

"More than a test, this a challenge from me to you," Stella declared.

"Ha! I thought so," Met-on laughed. "Well, I definitely love you, Stella. Tell me you love me, too, and I promise I will always be here and *will* take you outside the city."

Of course, you will, Stella thought sarcastically. She did not doubt that Met-on would just tell her "I love you" and then promise to take her out of the city if she replied in kind. *You need me to tell you "I love you" to complete your mission, and if I do that we're both dead here and now.*

"No Met-on, you will not get to hear those words that easily. The purpose of a challenge is that it has to be passed for you to claim the reward. Instead of going to the Grand Coliseum, come here instead and take me outside the city. Do *that*, and I'll tell you exactly what you want to hear."

Now it was Met-on's turn to be shocked. He thought Stella would admit to being in love with him if he revealed he knew she was testing him. Instead, she's was pushing the test forward.

"Why?" Met-on squeaked, feeling torn from Stella's challenge.

"Like I said, it's a challenge, I am challenging *you*," Stella restated. "If you can't give up going to the Grand Coliseum, give up being able to stand there with the other members of the Tribe of Shadows like yourself, and instead come to me and take me where I want to go. Then you do not deserve to hear me say that I am in love with you."

Now Met-on looked crushed, and Stella could see it.

I just forced him not only to choose between his people or me but between two different kinds of honor: branding or standing in the Grand Coliseum, Stella mused, weighing the two options. *If he helps me, it's because he's trying to get me to say I love him, completing his mission to receive his first branding. But then Met-on will lose the chance to be in the Grand Coliseum and meet other members of the Tribe of Shadows like himself. On the other hand, if he goes to the Grand Coliseum, he meets other members of the Tribe of Shadows like himself but he fails in his mission to receive a branding. And if he goes to the Grand Coliseum, we're both dead. And if I just come out and tell him what I overheard he would never believe me. He's too loyal to Tanas, the Tribe of Shadows, and the city of Nis to think they are going to butcher him. All that would do is prove I'm just trying to escape, which would still get us all killed. Live or die, whether my "challenge" is going to work depends on Met-on now.*

Whether or not it would work, Stella did not know. As for Met-on, Stella's challenge left him confused and divided over the choice she presented him with. Without further acknowledgment, Met-on turned around, opened the door, and left Stella's room. He had a lot to think about.

Meanwhile, back in Maestri—the First Circle of the city of Nis, Ann waited patiently for her friend, Reye, to complete the Reconciliation Ritual. She was remembering her own experience with the ritual and wondering what Reye must be witnessing.

Chapter 26

When I went through this ritual I was confronted by a copy of myself from before the mining project, Ann remembered, thinking back to her own experience with it. *She forced me to face the reason* why *I was so pessimistic. It was because I was too scared to hope and believe in something better. Reye, however, is confronting much more than my pessimistic past. The death of her brother, her rampage as the Hy-mun Horror, as well as anything else that might be hiding in her conscience, it is all going to be pulled up by this ritual. I only hope she comes out of it okay.*

Ann did not mention it, she was not allowed to, but there was a risk involved in the ritual. Depending on how Reye faced that risk would determine whether or not she would awaken as the same person, or a better one.

"She'll make it, I know she well," Ann whispered, more optimistically than anyone had ever heard her speak before as she stared down at Reye's still form. Her mind, however, was anything but still.

In her mind, Reye was standing in the Amber-leaf forest near her home in the Orange Dominion unbelievably facing her dead twin brother, Raymond. The reunion, however, was anything but happy. Raymond had been harshly chastising her about not paying attention and listening to him when he told her to run, fight, and live, choosing instead to only hear what she wanted to. He went so far as to say she not only acted crazy as the Hy-mun Horror, slaughtering almost everything in sight but that she also actually enjoyed being a murderer.

"You haven't answered me, that's unusual for you," Raymond remarked, waiting for Reye's reply. "So, have you thought about what I just said, or are you not listening again."

Reye was thinking about what he had said, how could she not? Her dead brother had just chastised her about how she had a tendency to go crazy and enjoy it.

Joy is joy, it doesn't matter if your actions are good or evil, you are the one who decides what you're doing, and you are the one who finds the joy in it, Reye repeated in her head, the words sounding almost like an accusation than a statement.

"Did I enjoy it, yes, Raymond, I enjoyed it! Are you happy now?" Reye angrily asked. "Tell me, how could I *not* enjoy it. You were gone, Stella was gone, everyone on the project was gone. I even *ate* the processed flesh of one of our teammates from the project. And it's all the fault of these creatures.

"From the moment I was given the signal to fight in the Grand Coliseum until I faced Lord Tanas in Yam-Preen, I've been swinging that ax through every creature the Tribe of Shadows produced, and yes I was enjoying every minute of it. I was taking revenge for you, for Stella, for everyone who had ever been victimized by them and ensuring they couldn't do it again. Are you telling me that I was wrong? Do you think I would have still done it if I didn't lose any of you? Do you think I just don't know myself?"

"That's right, you don't," Raymond replied. "And you don't know others as well as you think you do either. That is why you ended up a crying and broken wreck after you faced Tanas and every person you killed became a martyr for the Tribe of Shadows. Not only that, every single body you left behind was processed into more food for the Tribe of Shadows. You weren't weakening them, you were making them stronger. Also, what makes you think they killed your best friend?"

"Stella is alive?" Reye asked startled.

"You tell me. Do you think Stella is alive because I say she is still alive, because you think that since I'm dead I would know for certain? Did you ever believe she was still alive in the first place?"

Reye did not answer.

"You had the chance to go and find her in one of the outer circles like Maestri or Lust Atrophied after you broke out of the Grand Coliseum; instead, you decided to go deeper into Nis instead of trying to escape it, find Stella, and take her with you. Tell me why?"

Reye did not respond. She opened her mouth like she wanted to say something but nothing came out of it. Shame and guilt robbed her of her voice.

"Ice and Dan-te told you that if any Hy-muns were still alive, they would either be gladiators or sent to the Third Circle of Nis, Lust Atrophied, where they could be used for breeding. So, why did you write your *best friend* off as dead? Why didn't you think Stella could be alive either in Lust Atrophied as a breeder or in Maestri as a gladiator? Ann even *confirmed* that there is a Hy-mun girl in Lust Atrophied. Why can't that be Stella? And why didn't you try looking for her yourself when you had the chance?"

"But why would Stella even be in a breeding farm," Reye finally burst out. "Why would any creature reproduce their children like livestock. I just can't…"

"You can't believe it," Raymond said, completing Reye's sentence. "So, you couldn't believe that the Tribe of Shadows would set up in a system, similar to how we breed livestock back home, and since you couldn't believe it, you decided it didn't exist, and that meant that Stella was dead."

"No! That's not true," Reye frantically denied. "I do admit that when Dan-te and Ice first told me that there was a section of Nis that was used for breeding, I couldn't believe it, but that is not why I didn't see if I could rescue her."

"Then why didn't you?" Raymond asked again.

Reye knew from Raymond's stare and repeating questions that he already knew exactly why she did not go looking for Stella. Whenever he chastised her like this, he always asked her questions that she already knew the answers to. He only wanted to hear the words come out of her own mouth.

"It was because I *wanted* to kill Lord Tanas," Reye admitted.

Despite how many times Reye told herself she could have gone and saved Stella in her rambles about what she had done in Nis; in truth, she knew in her heart she just wanted to kill Lord Tanas.

"I didn't care if Stella was alive or dead," Reye continued. "Nor did I care about what might be happening to her, or what any of our families on the surface must be going through. All I wanted was to kill Lord Tanas, and I wasn't going to let anyone or anything get in my way."

"So, you abandoned any hope that your *best friend* could have been alive all because you wanted to kill someone. Is that how you value friendship?" Raymond accused. "Or was the Tribe of Shadows right to call you the 'Hy-mun Horror?' Maybe you should just paint yourself blue and join up with them full-time. I think you'll fit in with them perfectly."

"Hey!"

That was it. Reye had heard Raymond's lectures before, granted this one was the strangest, but she knew even he had limits to how far he would reprimand her.

"I have thought about everything you've just said and taken everything with all of the humility I can muster; which isn't easy, considering how much you're shaming me. But for you to even consider that I really am a 'Hy-mun Horror,' or that I should join the Tribe of Shadows, especially after what I've had been through, is beyond even the worst lecturing that even you have ever given me. Who do you think you are telling me I would be better off joining the Tribe of Shadows? I am not one of these creatures. I am a Hy-mun!"

Reye's last words were followed by a punch, hitting only air the second it would have connected with Raymond's face.

"I said, 'Maybe you should just paint yourself blue and join up with them full-time,'" Raymond repeated, now standing behind Reye. "'*Maybe*,' not '*Why don't you*,' and that just further proves my point. You still only want to listen to what you want to listen to, knowing and understanding only what you want to instead of what is actually true. You just said a little while ago, and I quote, 'You don't think I have the *right* to act crazy after that? The Tribe of Shadows took *everything* from me.' If that is how you truly know and understand your situation, then you really are no better than the warriors from the Tribe of Shadows that killed me."

"I am not the same," Reye denied. "There is no way you can relate what happened to me, losing you and Stella, to them."

"Oh, really," Raymond said, his tone telling Reye she should have already realized the point that he was about to make. "Again, you weren't listening to Dan-te and Ice when they told you about the Tribe of Shadows' history, were you?"

Reye did not answer. She had forgotten the history lesson Ice and Dan-te had tried to give her about their world before the battle in the Grand Coliseum. At the time, she was not paying attention to it. All she wanted to do was kill as many members of the Tribe of Shadows as she could because of what they did to her.

"Before the fight in the Grand Coliseum, they told you about 'The Coming' and how the Ancient Tribe was almost destroyed by the 'Beings of Light,' the ones we call the Nag-el. The members of the Ancient Tribe all lost friends, family, *and more* in that one genocidal attack. They lost their whole world and had to bear the knowledge that their destroyers were building a new world all for themselves, and later for us, on their ashes. How do you think that would make anyone feel?"

"But that was different, that was ages ago," Reye whispered until Raymond cut her off.

"How is it different?" Raymond snapped. "Why would the amount of time make a difference? All the members of the Ancient Tribe lost someone; brothers, sisters, if not entire families to the Nag-el's devastation. More than that, they lost their entire world to invaders that regarded them as little more than monsters while they, believing themselves to be the superior beings, acted the most monstrous of all. Worst of all, the Ancient Tribe's world was left in a state where they couldn't return to it even if they wanted to. You don't think they felt hurt, angry, or thought that they were also due vengeance. Before you encountered Lord Tanas, have you ever once thought that either the Tribe of Shadows or the Remnant of the Tribe feel the same emotions we do?"

Again, Reye did not answer. She tried, but the words choked in her mouth. Raymond's question had caught her, and she could feel it vibrating in her head as his words echoed there, forcing her to think.

All that time I spent charging through Nis, killing every member of the Tribe of Shadows I came across, have I ever thought if they, or Ice or Dan-te for that matter, were capable of the same emotions as me? Reye asked herself. *Ice and Dan-te seemed all about their ability to* Know *and how it was different from the way I perceived things. As for the Tribe of Shadows, they were nothing more than killers and kidnappers; the Cave Snatchers of myth, demons and monsters. That was what I remember from Worm's books. I know they don't feel guilty about killing and eating one of their own, and I've never felt guilty about killing them. At least, until I encountered Lord Tanas.*

The memory of her encounter with Lord Tanas still sent a shiver down her spine. It was not just because of the absolute submissive feeling he evoked in her, but because he forced her to see every warrior she killed anew without her own crusader's zeal. It was the first time she identified the warriors of the Tribe of Shadows as beings like herself dying at the hands of a monster, and if not for Ann, it might have destroyed her.

"Well, have you?" Raymond pressed.

"No, until I faced Lord Tanas I didn't think of the Tribe of Shadows in the same way as I thought of Hy-muns," Reye admitted. "And why would I? The Tribe of Shadows are a cannibalistic society, they live only to breed, kill, and eat themselves, claiming to be making some kind of attempted attack on the surface. An attack I still don't believe they can pull off. They die when exposed to sunlight. How could anyone from here even survive on the surface, let alone attack it? As for the Remnant of the Tribe, if Ice and Dan-te are any indication, they're just a pack of dying scavengers, thin, weak, and living off the scraps of the Tribe of Shadows. How could I possibly think them capable of feeling in the same way as we do?"

"Because they feel pain, joy, fear, determination, and reverence, just like us," Raymond answered, looking disappointed at his sister. "I guess I should have known better. You would judge whether or not they have any emotions simply by their society's appearance."

"You *cannot* compare Hy-mun emotions and society with the Tribe of Shadows," Reye challenged. "Before the Great Rainbow War, our civilization was great. We were able to build great cities across the Cherubi Continent; ships that could sail the sands of the Yellow Dominion, the waters of the Great Lagoon of the Blue Dominion, the Seraph Sea, and even the skies. Explore channels of magma with ease and save lives that were on the brink of death. And while the war might have all but destroyed that technology, Hy-muns are still picking themselves back up and trying to rebuild what they once had."

"And you are *still* judging whether or not we can feel by what our society looks like, not by what *we* look like," Raymond replied. "And isn't what we're doing right now the exact same thing that both the Tribe of Shadows and the Remnant of the Tribe are doing? The Tribe of Shadows and the Remnant were once one people, the Ancient Tribe. They also built for themselves a great civilization until the Nag-el came and reduced their civilization to almost nothing. Just like the Great Rainbow War reduced our own civilization to almost a preindustrial state. Afterward, the Ancient Tribe split into the Remnant of the Tribe and the Greater Tribe and like us have also been trying to rebuild their civilization using whatever they had at their disposal."

"So, what are you trying to tell me?" Reye challenged. She was getting tired of both this lecture on her behavior against the Tribe of Shadows following his death and hearing him compare both her and Hy-mun society to the very same Tribe of Shadows that killed him.

"What I'm saying to you is the Tribe of Shadows, the Remnant of the Tribe, and the Hy-mun people are a lot more alike in ways you've never even bothered to try and understand. You had no problem butchering them and destroying their city when you considered them 'creatures' different from yourself, but once you started thinking of them in the same way as you would other Hy-muns, you cracked. What's worse, you know it, and a part of you is still refusing to believe it. At this point, maybe you should think I was merely killed by another Hy-mun."

Now Reye retreated from her brother; he had said something she couldn't accept, something she couldn't believe her brother would say.

"No, you're lying! You're not Raymond, whoever you are, whatever you are, you're lying!"

"The only person you are lying to is yourself," Raymond countered, inching toward Reye as she crept away from him. "Trying to create a difference between yourself and what you've done, to what Hy-muns constantly do, to what the Tribe of Shadows has been doing for generations. What you need to do is accept what you have done, accept the fact that you are no different than the Tribe of Shadows that killed me, and that the Tribe of Shadows is no different than we are."

"No," Reye shouted, turning away from her brother and running as fast as she could. "I refuse to accept that I am the same as those creatures. I am not like them. I come from a world of light, not this dark city. I don't have 'other blood' running through me like they do. I am a pure-blood Hy-mun woman."

Reye did not look back as she dove into the Amber-leaf trees to get away from Raymond. He did not run after her but said one sentence in response to Reye's last statement.

"But you are wrong," Raymond said, his voice echoing behind her. "About the Tribe of Shadows, even about the 'other blood,' and you know it. Otherwise, why are you running?"

Reye heard Raymond's last words as clearly as if he were still standing right next to her, which made her run faster. All she wanted to do now was run away and find a way out from the Amber-leaf forest that she now felt trapped in.

Elsewhere, while Reye believed she was still running through the Amber-left forest, her body was actually still in the cell with Ann and the other members of the Remnant in Maestri. Ca-to and the other members of the Remnant were physically performing the Reconciliation Ritual through a mixture of chants, smoke, and cold dust that all but buried Reye in the pit. As the ritual entered its final phase, Reye's entire body was now being completely submerged in the cold dust. Silently, at a small distance away, Reye's friend, Ann, watched the ritual with nervous anticipation.

I was the one who had convinced Reye to go through with this ritual, Ann worried. She already did it herself, but that did not mean she was not scared about how it would go for her. She never told Reye what to actually expect in the ritual itself. *I didn't tell you anything to be mean, Reye, it's because the crucial parts of the ritual involve not knowing how it works. You need to experience it yourself firsthand. When I decided to take part in the ritual, Ca-to didn't tell me about any of the things I would experience, just that it was a way for me to "put the past to rest" and that it couldn't be told, only be Known. At the time, I knew that it was a cryptic answer and I was as skeptical and pessimistic about the whole idea as I could be. But after coming to Nis, fighting in a Maestri coliseum, watching the other project survivors get killed one by one, while I was protected by the Remnant of the Tribe and spent my free time talking and learning from them, I figured I had nothing left to lose so why not trust them and go through with the ritual?*

After experiencing the Reconciliation Ritual herself, Ann knew that there were two main parts to the experience. The first involved coming face-to-face with her conscience, which would confront her with all that she had done wrong and the reasons why she should have known better.

When I did it, my conscience appeared as myself, Ann remembered, trembling from the confrontation. *I wonder who Reye might be seeing.*

The second part, which Ann knew Reye would be entering now, involved the confrontation with one's own inner demons; the part of oneself that would drive a person to evil ways.

After I completed the ritual, I was told why its details were never explained to me. For the ritual to work, I had to experience it as if it was real. Looking back on it now, if I had known from the start what was going to happen to me, I wouldn't have reacted the way I did. I can only guess who Reye might be seeing.

Chapter 27

"I have to get away," Reye panted, running through the Amber-leaf forest. "Away from him, from Nis, the Tribe of Shadows, this Reconciliation Ritual, all of it. I have to get home!"

Reye did not know how long she had been running, but that she had to keep running. The more she ran, the further away she was from Raymond.

"I just have to keep going, soon I'll be out of the forest, back in the light, back home."

Reye knew the Amber-leaf forest, which had grown darker since she ran away from her brother. It was going to break soon. She had already run through it enough times that she knew where she was and how long it would be until she was out of it. After confronting Raymond, she had completely forgotten about the Remnant's Reconciliation Ritual. All she wanted was to go home, back to her family's farm in the Orange Dominion, the world she knew. One without any blue creatures living underground who ate their dead, who held gladiatorial matches, and used women for breeding. When she did make it out of the forest, Reye felt like she had been running for a lifetime, but she immediately recognized the landscape.

"The hill," Reye exclaimed, catching her breath, and feeling a renewed sense of hope over the familiar landmark. "A single, solitary, hill that rose up and separated the Amber-leaf forest from my family's farm. I can even see the daylight shining on the hilltop just like it does at dawn and dusk. All I have to do is climb the hill, and on the other side home will be waiting for me."

"Home," Reye repeated, psyching herself up as she made her way toward the hill. "No more Raymond lookalikes, no more creatures living under the ground, no more madness, just the home I've always known." However, as Reye made her way further and further up the hill, she soon realized that the light was not coming from the sun shining on the hilltop like she thought, but instead from a person.

The person generating the light was the most beautiful person that Reye had ever seen. At first glance, the figure appeared to be a man, but Reye had never seen a man like this before. He sat on the grass dressed in some kind of armor while writing notes in a book. Every part of him radiated the most beautiful light that Reye had ever seen.

"Who are you?" Reye barely whispered, her voice almost taken by the sight of the man before her.

Instantly, Reye felt a pull toward the man.

What is this feeling, she asked herself. *I want to be with this man, sit with him, live with him. Why does this sensation feel familiar? Why does* he *feel familiar?*

For a second, Reye was tempted to look away from the man, but he was just too dazzling and too beautiful not to look at. As Reye continued to look at him, she started to notice other things about and around him.

If he stands up, I'm guessing he's a little bit taller than me, Reye estimated. *He also has pointed ears. Not as pointed and long as the Tribe of Shadows' ears. His are only slightly pointed, they don't stand out as much. Wait, are those* animals *by his feet?*

Looking closer and through the light, Reye could now see that there were three baby animals at the man's feet, a leopard, lion, and wolf. Reye immediately dropped to her knees and placed her head on the ground. She finally realized why this man seemed so familiar to her, he was a Nag-el.

I've seen pictures of the Nag-el writing in books and welcoming souls into the stars from high places for as long as I can remember, Reye thought to herself, the incredibility of the situation astounding her. *Does this mean I died? Did the members of the Remnant kill me and this Nag-el is here to take me to the stars? I mean, he looks exactly like every picture I've seen in my life. He's writing in what some believe to be the Tome of the Ouroboros, others the record of our lives, and sitting before him at his feet are the Three Loyal Creatures who are favored by and protect the Nag-el. I wish Worm were here. He's the real expert on the Nag-els and what they did. But now that he's here what do I do now?*

"Hello, Reye," the Nag-el said. His voice was so beautiful and mesmerizing that it took Reye a minute to realize that the Nag-el had spoken to her and said her name before she was able to mutter a reply.

"You know my name," Reye muttered, regaining her composure somewhat, but still in awe of the Nag-el before her.

"Of course, I know your name," the Nag-el continued, pausing from his writing to look at her. Reye, at a speed that could only be called instinctive, placed her head deeper into the ground in supplication. "I have been writing your deeds down in my book for a while now. I must say that I am quite impressed."

Impressed, Reye thought, confused at the Nag-el's words. *I considered my recent actions to be many things, but I would never have thought they would have "impressed" anyone.*

"Yes," the Nag-el said. "I have been very impressed by you, from the moment when you began your journey and you willingly left the world of light to enter the world of darkness. Once you were trapped in that world, surrounded by the darkness, you didn't succumb to it. Instead, you picked yourself up, grabbed an ax, and began cutting your way through the darkness toward your goal of returning to the light. I find that very impressive indeed. I even have your ax right here." The Nag-el reached behind him and produced a twin-bladed ax, Reye instantly recognized it as the same one she used during her rampage throughout Nis.

"I can't believe what I'm hearing," Reye stuttered. "You, a Nag-el, are praising me for everything I have done. All I've ever felt is regret over what I've done, and even more for what I didn't do, and the chewing out I just received from Raymond's ghost hasn't helped me make any of those feelings go away. If anything, Raymond just dragged them up and threw them in my face. Yet here you are telling me I did a good job, that I didn't succumb to darkness but cut my way through it toward my goal, even though I never reached it."

"Now that is where you are wrong, Reye. It's not that you never reached your goal. It's just that you haven't reached it *yet*, but you are close. One last difficult trial remains before you. If you can complete it, then you will finally be able to return to where you have always belonged. I will personally ensure that you get there."

"What do I have to do?" Reye asked. She could feel her excitement growing. "If all I have to do for you is complete one trial and then I can return home, the place where I belong, then I'm willing to do just about anything. Please Nag-el, tell me what I have to do."

The Nag-el turned his head down toward the opposite side of the hill, beckoned to Reye, and pointed downward.

"Look down the hill," he instructed. "Tell me what you see."

Reye looked down the hill, seeing what she had been longing for since she first woke up in the city of Nis. Sheltered on the side of the hill, so that sun set behind it early in the afternoon, was her family's farm, where Reye grew up and left from when she first went to Spectral Academy.

"It's just how I left it," Reye cried in joy over the familiar landscape. "I can see the animal pens, the three silos where food is stored, the large tables that everyone uses to eat together outdoors. The fondest memories of my life were made right here on this farm." It was then Reye noticed something else on her farm, creatures like the ones from Nis moving throughout it.

"What's going on?" Reye panicked, frantically turning to the Nag-el for answers. "Those things shouldn't be here, they can't be here." Reye was disturbed over what she was witnessing. "Why are they here? What are they doing on my family's farm? Where is my family?" Instead of answering the Nag-el presented her with her ax.

"This is your trial, take up your ax one more time and destroy the invaders to your family's farm that are now before you." Reye quickly took her ax from the Nag-el, fear that her family would meet the same fate as both Raymond and the mining project students fueling her actions. Yet she quickly realized something was different, something that forced her to wait.

The ax, it feels heavier than it did before, Reye noticed, struggling now to lift the weapon that once felt weightless in her hands. *It also stinks of blood, the blood of all the warriors and citizens of the Tribe of Shadows that I cut to pieces.*

Reye turned and again looked down the hill toward her farm. She knew that if it were only a few days ago, she would have charged down the hill and into the creatures before her, killing them without mercy. This time, however, something inside her forced her to stay still. Smelling the blood on her ax, Reye vividly remembered the faces of every warrior that she had cut down during her mad dash through Nis, all the ones she cut in half, their blood and organs staining both herself and the ax replaying itself quickly and gruesomely throughout her head.

"Why do you hesitate?" the Nag-el asked. "Your enemy is before you attacking your home, you must go down and attack."

Reye took a step down the hill when Raymond's words came back to her. "You really are no better than the warriors from the Tribe of Shadows that killed me."

"You must strike now," the Nag-el pressed. "If you don't your home will be destroyed and lost to you forever. Don't you understand me, your *home*, you must strike!"

Reye still hesitated, she wanted to attack, to do what the Nag-el asked of her but could not. Inside her head, she could hear Raymond's voice telling her, "All the members of the Ancient Tribe lost someone; brothers, sisters, if not entire families to the Nag-el's devastation. More than that, they lost their entire world to invaders that regarded them as little more than monsters while they, believing themselves to be the superior beings, acted the most monstrous of all."

"Fine then," the Nag-el said, clearly frustrated at Reye indecision. Rising from his position he walked over to Reye and extended his hand to her. It was the first time that she had ever seen the Nag-el's face that close up. It was the most beautiful face she had ever seen, and it also seemed eerily familiar.

"If you need my help to make up your mind, then take my hand and let me help you," the Nag-el stretched out his hand, and in that hand, Reye began to believe that no matter what she could trust him. "Let me take you back to where you belong, and together we will bring upon these creatures a curse of destruction a thousand times over!"

Instantly, something clicked in Reye's mind. Without hesitation, she used her ax.

Chapter 28

The light from the Nag-el was fading quickly. The Three Loyal Creatures scattered the moment he hit the ground; Reye's ax sticking out of his chest. Reye could barely keep herself on her own feet and could not stop shaking. She felt afraid, confused, and shocked. The more she looked at the Nag-el's face, which was becoming more visible in the dimming light, the more familiar he became to her. The Nag-el himself was still alive. Reye, however, knew he would not be for much longer. But looking at him, all she could do after mortally wounding him was repeat the last words he said to her.

"If you need my help to make up your mind then take my hand and let me help you," Reye repeated. "Let me take you back to where you belong and together we will bring upon these creatures a curse of destruction a thousand times over!"

Reye had heard those final words before, almost those exact words, spoken the same way not too long ago. They were preached by Lord Tanas to the Tribe of Shadows after he had beaten her. He told the Tribe of Shadows' warriors, "What has happened to this Hy-mun will be visited upon all Hy-muns, like a curse of destruction a thousand times over."

Seeing the face of the Nag-el, a passage Reye read from the Tome of the Ouroboros in Worm's room, which now seemed like a lifetime ago, appeared in Reye's mind. It was a passage that she had forgotten about soon after she had read it but now found that she was able to remember it entirely. Looking at the Nag-el dying in front of her, she had to repeat it.

"So, Light Bringer gathered a sum of the Nag-el, forces he himself had led to the new world, and began a vicious war against Ash Addiel and the Nag-el loyal to the Great Master, a war lasting seven years, each battle more vicious than the last," Reye repeated, now realizing who was lying before her. "When the war finally ended, the Great Master stood victorious. For his treason, Light Bringer's 'light,' the very soul of a Nag-el, was stripped from him, leaving him neither living nor dead. Light Bringer, along with his followers, was then banished to a dark prison, to watch as his followers slowly died around him, eventually leaving him alone in the dark for all time.

"You're Light Bringer, you're Lord Tanas," Reye concluded, more for herself than anyone. In the Nag-el's dimming light she could clearly see his face now, and despite its beauty, it was unmistakably the face of Lord Tanas. His face still had the same features he had at Decca-Ju Tower. She also recognized that instinctual feeling she felt when she first saw him as the same submissive impulse she encountered when she challenged him. But it was his words that really identified him. He spoke not only the same words, but he spoke them with the same emotions behind them as when he preached to the Tribe of Shadows. It was those words that made Reye realize that the Nag-el before her, and the ruler of both the Tribe of Shadows and the city of Nis, were the same person.

"What have you done," Lord Tanas gasped from where he lay on the ground. "I was going to take you back to the light. Didn't you want to go back? You've been looking for the light, chasing after it, ever since you found yourself in Nis. Why would you kill it?"

Reye did not answer. She could not; maybe it was because he was dying, but she did not feel like submitting to him now. All she wanted to do was back away from him while her mind processed what was going through it.

First was Raymond's ghost chewing me out over what I did, what I didn't do, or even what I tried to do, and how I might be more like the Tribe of Shadows then I wanted to admit, Reye wondered, piecing together her thoughts. *Now this*

Nag-el version of Lord Tanas comes along, praising my actions, promising to take me back home again. All I needed to do was charge into a massacre or take his hand and let him pull me into one. Is it true, am I really that blind, have I always been that blind?

Everything was spinning inside her head. When Reye did speak again, she did not know if she actually thought about the words or not; she just let them come out of her.

"You're right," Reye said. "I want to go back to the light. I still want to go back, and I have been a blind fool searching for it. I spent so long looking at the light, making it my goal, for so long it left me blind. Blind to what I was doing to myself, to those around me, and to what I was not doing. I might as well have still been on the surface looking directly at the sun until I was blind. Raymond was right, maybe I should have joined the Tribe of Shadows. All of us are single-minded blind fools. All we seem to do is follow you without thinking."

Despite having an ax in his chest, Lord Tanas actually began to laugh at Reye's words. The laughter left Reye feeling confused.

"What's so amusing?" Reye asked. "Did I say something funny?"

"You did," Lord Tanas answered gleefully. His reply made Reye back away from him slightly. "You actually think that you and the Tribe of Shadows have just been following me blindly without thinking. You couldn't be more wrong."

Lord Tanas began laughing again. In his laughter Reye could hear a prideful taunt, almost like someone had played a joke on her and everyone caught it, except for her, and she still did not get it.

"The Tribe of Shadows haven't been following me blindly without thinking," Lord Tanas explained, now sounding exactly the same as when she heard him at Decca-Ju Tower. "Didn't that Rodent tell you anything?"

Reye did not answer. She knew well that she had ignored and had forgotten everything Ice had told her about the Tribe of Shadows' civilization. All that had mattered to her was reaching Lord Tanas so she could kill him, creating as much devastation as she could along the way.

"Yes," Lord Tanas continued. "You did ignore that Rodent a lot. Well, pay attention now. The Tribe of Shadows worship me, I am practically their god, in the same way that Ash Addiel is god for you Hy-muns. I gave them what they wanted, a way to fight the invaders."

"But *you* were that invader," Reye countered, remembering another passage from the Tome of the Ouroboros.

"Light Bringer searched and found a world shrouded in darkness and chaos, a world in need of the glory of the light," Reye recited. "Light Bringer *brought* his people *to* that world, making it ready for the coming of the Great Master, bringing light to the darkness and shaping order from the chaos he found."

"Do you think they knew that back then?" Lord Tanas asked smugly. "Do you think these savages recognized me when I found them in the caverns? Did *you* recognize the me before you and the me I later became after I was banished?"

Again, Reye did not answer because she knew he was right. If not for those few words, Reye would have continued to think of Lord Tanas and the Nag-el she first encountered as two separate beings. Realizing that whatever "light" was stripped from him, "leaving him neither living or dead," also left him unrecognizable to anyone he encountered.

"I gave those savages a way to fight the Nag-el and later the Hy-muns. I gave them a civilization! Honestly, they had no idea what one was. In return, they gave me a place for me and my Legions to live. Do you honestly think you are the first Hy-mun to encounter me and my forces since I came here? The first one to realize I am 'Light Bringer?'"

"Yes." Reye did think she was the first one to have made that connection. "Considering how much the Tribe of Shadows hates the 'Beings of Light,' I thought if they knew you were the leader of the ones that attacked them in the first place then they would have killed you. Instead, you've been the unopposed head of the Tribe of Shadows. If the Tribe of Shadows thinks for itself, then someone must have connected you to the story of Light Bringer recorded in the Tome. The Tribe of Shadows must have heard it."

"Oh, they've heard of it," Tanas replied with a gasp. "But as far as the story in the Tome of the Ouroboros goes, it's just an instruction book made for Hy-muns to follow after we forced the Nag-el back into space. As for the members of the Tribe of Shadows who *have* made that connection, they are no longer with us. I doubt those Rodents from the Remnant even know of its existence. Even if they did, what could they do? After all, *I* am with the Tribe of Shadows constantly while the Nag-el, the 'Beings of Light,' have long since left this world, and the

Hy-muns and are in no position to argue. Who do you think the Tribe of Shadows will believe?"

Reye did not admit it, but Lord Tanas had a point.

It would be easy for him to deny what had happened, Reye thought to herself. *Especially if he called himself "Light Bringer" during "The Coming" instead of "Lord Tanas." The first Tome of the Ouroboros was said to have been written by the last Nag-el to leave Prism, and we can't question that Nag-el about its contents. The Tribe of Shadows, on the other hand, has Lord Tanas, in their presence all the time; even if he keeps himself secluded from them. He can speak about the past, lie all he wants, and no one is going to contradict him.*

"The Tribe of Shadows worship me as a deity, seeking me out for specialized decisions, which is a bother, but the actual governing of it is done through the bureaucracy in the Circles you ripped your way through to reach me. I set the Tribe of Shadows up that way so I could be left alone to my own devices and not have to deal with them. So yes, they don't 'follow me,' they think for themselves, and they follow their Plan to retake the surface, no matter the cost. All I ever did was give that Plan proper direction, one that will grant both the Tribe of Shadows and me precisely what we want; just like I was trying to give you what you wanted."

Despite having the ax still embedded in him, Lord Tanas stood up; the light draining from him faster than his blood. Despite his injury, he looked like he could take on an army and win. In fear, Reye backed away as he suddenly seemed to loom over the hilltop. Yet Reye did not miss his last comment about how he was trying to give her what she wanted. Despite her fear, she was going to argue that.

"You're wrong." Reye said. "You weren't trying to give me what I wanted."

Lord Tanas broke out laughing that made Reye back away even more.

"Not give you what you wanted," Lord Tanas said. "I have always given you what you wanted. You wanted revenge, I gave you revenge. You wanted a world of light, and I was giving you a way to reach that world. All you had to do was finish off those pathetic creatures down there, and you would have been able to return home to your world of light. But now you are going to have to stay here in a world of darkness."

Before Reye could reply, Lord Tanas quickly grabbed her by her throat, just like he did in front of Decca-Ju Tower. This time, however, Reye did not feel the penetrating cold that she encountered the first time or the flood of negative memories emerging into her head. She felt only a tight grip around her throat as he lifted her up off of the ground. The light was leaving him faster now as he held her up next to the ax impaled in his chest

"You've made your choice," Lord Tanas coughed. "Now live with it."

Lord Tanas tossed Reye down the hill as effortlessly as he had from Decca-Ju Tower; the last visages of light fading from him as Reye tumbled down the hill toward her family's farm and stopped in total darkness. Lying on her back, Reye struggled to see anything, but the darkness was complete.

I guess this is it for me, Reye thought to herself. *The Tome said that only the good become stars,* remembering the other passages she read in Worm's books. *I once asked Worm what happens to evil people after they died and he told me that they are imprisoned in eternal darkness. I definitely qualify. I'll never go home again.*

Reye felt a tear roll down her cheek. She knew she was crying not only for what she had done throughout Nis but for what she had failed to do.

I could have escaped, possibly found Stella, rescued Ann sooner, but instead I just cast them aside to pursue vengeance, Reye lamented. *An act of vengeance that I should have known better to peruse if only I paid more attention to the world around me, but I didn't. My own aloofness and hardheadedness lead me here. The worst part is that I was told beforehand, but I just didn't want to listen. Instead, I just denied that anything could go wrong and kept acting like normal.*

Closing her eyes, which made no difference in the darkness, Reye curled up on her side and continued to cry. It was then that she heard them.

Footsteps, Reye thought to herself.

Reye opened her eyes and tried to look around but saw and heard nothing. Closing her eyes again she could hear the footsteps again, a sudden memory flashing back into her head.

The attack on the project, Reye thought, remembering how the attack started that cost Raymond his life and left her in Nis in the first place. *They are coming back for me. Well, this time they can have me, I won't fight them.*

Reye waited as the footsteps came closer and the tears rolled down her face; there was no challenge or defiance in her. Whatever purpose these footsteps heralded, Reye decided she would accept and submit to them, keeping her eyes shut as the footsteps came closer and closer until they were almost right on top of her. Reye waited for a sword, a hammer, something to come down onto her and finish her off, but instead, she felt was a warm hand on her head.

"Open your eyes," a familiar voice said to Reye.

Scared, Reye opened her eyes to the most wondrous sight she had ever seen.

Chapter 29

The land was glowing. Reye was lying face down, but she could see that the land had begun to glow. No longer blind, Reye looked up and saw her brother's face staring back at her. Only this time, her brother was not "exactly" a Hy-mun but a member of the Remnant. He had all of the characteristics of someone from the Remnant; the gold and silver horns that created a coronet and joined into one horn on his forehead, the white skin that had never seen sunlight, the pointed ears, the increased size, and silver eyes, but the face was "definitely" Raymond. Almost like Raymond dressed himself up with makeup and props to look exactly like a member of the Remnant.

"Don't get up," the Remnant Raymond instructed. "Look around, tell me what you see."

Reye did, immediately noticing that it was not only the ground beneath her, but also everything was glowing. The land, plants, animals, even the buildings making up Reye's home, which she could see clearly now, had all taken on the same glow.

"Everything is glowing," Reye whispered. "Blues, yellows, greens, violets, and colors I can't even begin to describe."

"What else can you see?" Remnant Raymond asked, smiling.

"I can see other members of the Remnant," Reye answered, looking around her home. "They're working alongside my parents and the other Hy-muns who work here. In the light provided by the glowing land, they look more alike now than I initially thought they could be. They're all sitting down together at the long outdoor table—which is also glowing—and starting the Evening Supper. The big meal we all eat together outside when it's warm at the end of the day. I can see members of the Remnant eating, laughing, having fun with my family and the people I grew up with, and enjoying each other's company."

"And what does all this tell you?" the Remnant Raymond asked.

Reye looked at the Remnant Raymond, he wanted an answer from her, and he was not going to stop questioning her until he received one. Watching the members of the Remnant and her family eating together in peace she realized she did have one.

"It tells me that my family can eat and live in peace with members of the Remnant," Reye answered, hoping it would satisfy the Remnant Raymond.

"Very good," the Remnant Raymond replied, but not satisfied. "What else does this tell you?"

"It tells me that they can work well together," Reye hesitantly continued. "The Evening Supper is a big deal, it takes a long time to set up. The Remnant members and my family need to work well and quickly together. Otherwise they would never get it ready."

"And you didn't think they weren't working together to set this up?" Remnant Raymond asked.

"No, I didn't," Reye answered. "It doesn't look like it took them the time it usually does. Normally everyone back home would have started making the supper preparations over an hour in advance. I remember we used to help everyone make those preparations; and when we weren't helping, we would watch them from the hilltop and…"

Reye's voice instantly silenced itself the second the words passed her lips, the realization hitting her. A smile also appeared on the Remnant Raymond's face. He had been waiting for her to reach this moment.

"I was watching the members of the Remnant move through the farm on the hilltop with Lord Tanas," Reye muttered. "I thought they were warriors from Nis invading the farm and putting my family in danger. Lord Tanas also wanted me to think my family was in danger, to run down and kill everyone. But my family was never in any danger at all; they were just preparing for Evening Supper. If I did what Lord Tanas wanted, I would have killed everyone, members of the Remnant who have no connection with Nis or Lord Tanas, maybe even my family too if I didn't realize Lord Tanas was who he was.

"I really have been a blind fool." Reye was crying now, tears rolling from her eyes as she sobbed and continued to lament how close she came to destroying her home. "I lived here my whole life, and all it took was a few slight changes, different people joining a common practice, a different perspective, and not only was I not able to recognize what was going on but I also almost destroyed it; just because of those changes. Just like you said, I really am no better than the members of the Tribe of Shadows."

"True," the Remnant Raymond agreed. "You have been blinded by too much 'light' in your eyes."

Reye did not even try to argue with the Remnant Raymond anymore. She knew he was right, about everything that he had said about her actions in Nis, and before that when she was still on the surface. However, while Reye did not want to argue, she still had some questions that she needed to ask, regardless if she liked the answer or not.

"Tell me, where are we really?" Reye begged. "I'm not really back home at the Evening Supper, am I? You're not really my brother, and that Nag-el wasn't really Lord Tanas. So please, what is all this?"

"What do you think it is?" the Remnant Raymond asked.

"I don't know," Reye said. "I thought I was dying, that the members of the Remnant were cooking me and going to eat me like the Tribe of Shadows do in Nis with their dead. I thought everything I saw so far was whatever you were supposed to see before or after you die."

"Then why did you get into the pit in the first place?"

"It was Ann's recommendation," Reye replied. "She told me she took part in this 'Reconciliation Ritual' before and that it would be the best way for me to reconcile with my past."

"So, despite Ann's recommendation, and her claim to have done it before, you quickly thought that the people from the Remnant were going to kill you the moment they started doing something you didn't understand. Is that how much you trust Ann?"

Reye realized the same thing. *Ann convinced me to take part in this ritual,* Reye thought to herself. *And I've known her for almost as long as I've known Stella. Ann was the one I cried out my story to once I started coming back to my senses in Maestri and had been there through every bloody retelling up to the end where I faced Lord Tanas. Yet all it took was one shred of doubt to make me think that she had betrayed me and was turning me into food for all of them. I really didn't trust her at all.*

"Do you know what the word 'reconciliation' means?" the Remnant Raymond asked.

Reye wanted to say "forgiveness" but quickly decided not to. If she had learned anything from this encounter, it was that she had often twisted things in her head to suit whatever situation she desired. Instead, she just hung her head low and shook it from side to side.

"Reconciliation means resolution," the Remnant Raymond said. "It also means reunion, understanding, and settlement. Ann told you that this was the best way to reconcile yourself with your past, and that is *exactly* what's been going on. Whether we are talking about the Hy-mun or Remnant's culture, you first have to know and understand your injury before you can heal it. That is why this ritual is so good for healing, it serves as a means of resolution. It also lets you reunite with who you were before an injury, understand what is injuring you, and settle your feelings with it."

"Are you saying that you're me," Reye asked confused, trying to understand what the Remnant Raymond had just said.

"I am your twin," the Remnant Raymond answered, "I have always been your twin; equal and opposite to you. I know everything about you. I know everything you know and everything that you don't want to know or have forgotten. Also, like any good twin, I only want to protect you and see that you are all right. But when you do something wrong, it is my job to make sure you understand and realize what it was that you have done wrong. Do you understand?"

Reye let the Remnant Raymond's words sink into her, and she found that she was starting to understand. *The being before me that's taken the form of my brother, continually chastising me about my actions just like Raymond would, is my conscious*, Reye concluded. *The Remnant Raymond is right, he is my "twin." Before, Raymond always acted as my conscious's voice whenever I did something wrong. So, why shouldn't I be surprised to find my real conscious looks just like him? No wonder he is so mad at me.*

Reye realized now that all of the chastising "Raymond" had given her was really her own conscious, her own self, disciplining her.

"But what about the Nag-el that I thought was Tanas?" Reye asked. "Who, or what, was he?"

"He is someone who is inside every Hy-mun," the Remnant Raymond explained. "An inner demon that is a part of you that can be traced all the way back to the Nag-el and is also part of both the best and the worst that the Nag-el can be; a paradox of a deceiver who tells no lies."

"A deceiver who tells no lies, what do you mean by that?" Reye asked, confused by the Remnant Raymond's words.

"What I mean is that he tells you only the truth, and that is how he deceives you. Do you remember what he told you?"

Reye thought for a minute, thinking back to her encounter with Lord Tanas in his form as a Nag-el and tried to remember his exact words. "He said that he was 'quite impressed.' That once I was 'surrounded by darkness' but 'didn't succumb to it. Instead, you picked yourself up, grabbed an ax, and began cutting your way through the darkness toward your goal of returning to the light.' He seemed very impressed about that."

"Correct," the Remnant Raymond said. "And he wasn't lying. He said you didn't 'succumb' to it, you didn't succumb to your surrounding but instead cut through them, literally, toward a goal of returning home. According to the Remnant, the Nag-el did no less when they first arrived. They refused to submit to the local environment and cut it down to create a new one with the goal of recreating their home. Of course, the Nag-el would be impressed by something similar. What else did he say?"

"That I had 'one last difficult trial' remaining," Reye repeated. "That if I completed it then I 'will finally be able to return to where you have always belonged.' He told me to look down the hill, and I saw, what I thought at the time, were warriors from Nis raiding the family farm. Lord Tanas, who I thought was a Nag-el at the time, told me that 'This is your trial, take up you ax one more time and destroy the invaders to your family's farm that are now before you.'

"I admit that not too long ago I would have charged down and attacked without a second thought. But this time, I hesitated, the memories of my rampage through Nis kept me from moving. Lord Tanas then asked me, 'Why do you hesitate, your enemy is before you attacking your home, you must go down and attack.' I actually took a step down the hill that time, but then I remembered your words about how I was no different than the Tribe of Shadows. Yet Lord Tanas kept persisting saying that I 'must strike now. If you don't your home will be destroyed and lost to you forever. Don't you understand me, your home, you must go now.'

"Still, I was hesitant to go. Lord Tanas finally said, 'if you need my help to make up your mind take my hand and let me help you, let me take you back to where you belong, and together we will bring upon these creatures a curse of destruction a thousand times over!' That was when I recognized him as Lord Tanas since I heard him say almost the exact same thing to the Tribe of Shadows, and I used my ax on him instead."

"I'm glad you remembered it this time," the Remnant Raymond said smiling. "Nothing that the Nag-el Lord Tanas told you was a lie. The deception was in how you perceived it. The Nag-el told you that you had one last trial before you could 'return to where you have always belonged.' He also constantly said that 'your enemy is before you attacking your home' and that 'you must strike now. If you don't your home will be destroyed and lost to you forever.' However, he was really referring to *himself* as the enemy you had to attack. The trick was in the perception, making it look like the people here on the farm were the ones you had to attack instead of him. The challenge was not to be blinded by him, and I mean that both figuratively and literally, and to know what you really had to do."

"So, what happens now?" Reye asked. "Do I just get up and enjoy the Evening Supper with everyone else now? Why is the land glowing? What is this?"

"This is the Glow the members of the Remnant speak of; and the dream of the world," the Remnant Raymond said.

"What?" Reye asked, still confused.

"The world has never forgotten what it was like before the Nag-el first came to it, and the world dreams of returning to what it was once was. This is the world's dream, one where it can shine with the Glow again and live in harmony with *all* its people."

Reye sat up and began to really look around her family's farm, now lit by the Glow she had heard Ice talk about before in the cells. Seeing both the beauty of it and the peace her family and the Remnant members were sharing together, she finally understood how losing such a world would be devastating to the Ancient Tribe. Reye did not notice the tears running down her face anymore. She only wanted to gaze at the beauty of the landscape until smoke began gathering around and obscuring her vision of her home, the Glow, and her brother.

"Raymond," she called.

"The Nag-el Lord Tanas wasn't lying to you, remember?" the Remnant Raymond's voice echoed from the smoke as a hand reached out above her. "It is time for you to 'return to the world where you have always belonged.'"

"Raymond," Reye cried as she grasped a hand above her as it pulled her up.

Reye sat up to find herself in a pit covered in dust that she cleaned off herself. Still feeling a hand holding hers, she looked up to see Ann's smiling face. Standing around Ann were the other members of the Remnant, including the Seat of Kindness, now feeling far more like family and friends to Reye then they did when she was first thrown into the cell in Maestri.

Chapter 30

"Welcome back, Reye," Ann whispered to Reye as she sat next to her in their cell in Maestri.

"Ann," Reye coughed, dust coming out of her mouth. "Just now, I saw…"

"Whatever you witnessed during the Reconciliation Ritual was meant for you and you alone," Ca-to hushed, placing his hand over Reye's mouth. "It is not meant to be discussed with anyone else."

"Still, I wish you could have told me more about what I was going to see," Reye muttered from beneath Ca-to's hand.

"You weren't told anything about what the ritual entailed because you needed to believe that the visions you were experiencing were real for them to be effective," Ca-to explained, taking his hand off Reye's mouth. "Do you truly think you would have listened to anything the visions said to you if you knew what they were from the start?"

"No, I wouldn't have," Reye replied.

"Well, looking at you now, I *Know* you are far better now than when you were first brought here. Maybe now you and Ann can really catch up."

"And we need to catch up," Ann added, taking Reye's hand and drawing her attention while Ca-to walked away.

"So, what happened to you after the attack?" Reye asked. She knew she had talked enough, and now it was Ann's turn.

"Well I never went rampaging through Nis," Ann began. "Not that I didn't want to at first. The other few survivors and I were forced into the gladiatorial arenas here at Maestri to train the prison guards. The first survivor was killed the day after the attack. The remaining four went one a day until I was the last one left. By that time, I thought to myself, 'This is it, just like I thought, they were going to save me for last,' but they decided to hold off fighting me until some 'big event' in the Grand Coliseum was over."

Ann tossed a mischievous look to Reye who turned away shyly. They both knew the "big event" was the fight that started Reye's Hy-mun Horror rampage through Nis.

"Thankfully, until the event was over the guards decided to toss me in here with the other members of the Remnant," Ann continued, sounding extremely grateful. "And after you started going crazy through Nis they completely forgot about me. Once I met the members of the Remnant, got over the culture shock, and also experienced their Reconciliation Ritual myself, we began to share information about our cultures. I was able to identify Lord Tanas, the Light Bringer from their stories of 'The Coming,' and the Light Bringer in our own 'Tome of the Ouroboros' as the same person. It turns out the Seat of Kindness, the other members of the Council, and other highly placed members of the Remnant's society like Ca-to already knew about it. They discovered the truth from a defector from Nis at the end of the Second Great Attempt; but when members of the Remnant attempted to tell the Tribe of Shadows, they laughed it off as 'Hy-mun propaganda' and killed them. That's why the information is kept only to a select few. The most frightening thing to learn about was the Third Great Attempt.

"From the few details I've been given, I've figured out Tanas's plan. He's going to set off a super volcano here in Nis. The Tribe of Shadows thinks it's going to happen in the Red Dominion. They've spent generations digging to a magma vein where they believe they can set off a charge that will cause the volcanoes to erupt and blacken the sky so they can attack the surface. But it's a lie. The blast is meant to send magma here, filling this entire cavern—already stockpiled with explosives—up with magma. Artificially creating a super volcano that will erupt right here. I just don't know when it's going to happen."

When Reye heard Ann's description, she mentally kicked herself for not paying more attention to what Ice was trying to tell her about the Third Great Attempt.

I thought that the Tribe of Shadows wasn't capable of being able to do something that could actually harm the surface world, Reye cursed herself. *But hearing Ann describe how the Third Great Attempt is going to be executed, and she's the best when it comes to volcanoes, it does make sense. Heck, I'm trying to become a terranaut, I should have known this, too. Yet I wasted all my time going after Lord Tanas when I should have been trying to stop the Third Great Attempt. Am I only just listening to her because she's a Hy-mun like me?*

"So, we're all dead." Reye mourned, realizing both her own mistakes and scale of what was about to happen. "All that time I was charging through the city as the Hy-mun Horror, I could have been fighting my way out of it to stop whoever was working on the Third Great Attempt."

"We're not dead yet, Reye," Ann said, her eyes glowing with determination and optimism. "I haven't just been fighting for my life, learning about, and talking with the people from the Remnant. I've been listening for any information the guards might leak about the Third Great Attempt and making my own plans to escape and stop it."

Ann knelt down and began drawing in the dirt with her fingers. Soon, she had sketched a rough map of the entire continent of Cherubi, complete with the Dominions' borders and other noteworthy sites.

"Unlike you, I wasn't unconscious after the attack on the camp. After the attack, the warriors from the Tribe of Shadows loaded us onto a transport vehicle and brought us here through the Great Tunnel. Now I've been riding transport vehicles all my life with my father, so I have a pretty good idea of where we are now. The transport left the Demp Caverns by the Great Tunnel, going under the Orange Domination, Yellow Dominion, traveling underneath Sand Break Border—the border between the Yellow and Green Dominions—until we were almost under the Violet Plateau. That should put the city of Nis right here." Ann tapped a spot on the center of the map with her finger.

"We should be somewhere underneath both Tri-Dominion City and the Tri-Dominion Caverns where the Yellow, Green, and Violet Dominions intersect. That also means we should be near the Prison Caverns." Ann touched another part of the map where the desert of the Yellow Dominion met the Violet Plateau. "If I'm right, and I'll bet I am, we are near this point. If this is also where Lord Tanas was banished to when he was still Light Bringer, and where the Ancient Tribe fled during 'The Coming,' it makes sense that Nis will be here and that we'll be able to find multiple ways back to the surface."

"Okay, so now we know where Nis is and have two possible ways to get back to the surface," Reye observed, carefully following Ann's explanation this time. "But what is your plan for stopping the Third Great Attempt?"

"Like I said, I've been listening to the guards and gathering information, as have the other members of the Remnant, and you'd be surprised what a guard will let slip when they think you're no danger to them. The Third Great Attempt is going to be triggered soon, but not until all of the mining machinery, and workers are pulled out of the Great Tunnel. *That* is when we put our own plan into action."

Ann reached into her clothing and pulled out a rusted key. Reye's eyes widened as she quickly realized it was the key to the cells. But before she could say anything, Ann placed her hand over Reye's mouth and shook her head, silently telling her to be quiet, before quickly slipping the key back into her clothing.

"I actually have you to thank for allowing me to get my hands on that," Ann chuckled. "The rampage you caused throughout the city drew so many guards and attention to the city's interior that the remaining guards became so lax we were literally able to take it from under their noses. Now, let me explain our plan."

Ann pointed to the circle she drew on her map to show the location of Nis. Next, she made several smaller circles across Sand Break Border along with a series of lines running through the Yellow Dominion to the Seraph Sea. "Once the magma starts flowing through the Great Tunnel we won't be able to stop it. But we can divert it and force it to go elsewhere."

"Your land-based volcano theories," Reye mumbled, remembering the dinner they all had together at AB's before all this happened.

"That's right. The plan is to use one of the digging machines the Tribe of Shadows is using to alter the Great Tunnel. We want to create miniature volcanoes across Sand Break Border on the side of the Yellow Dominion, so the lava flows across the Yellow Dominion instead of the Green Dominion. I have been teaching the Remnant members everything I know about drilling machine operation, and I am certain we can do it."

"What about damage to the surface?" Reye asked, realizing that what Ann was suggesting was to create volcanoes across it. "Weren't you the one who was preaching about damage to the surface. Like how 'if a volcano popped up in the Yellow Dominion and cut the Great Line River in half the Dominion's chief water transportation route and habitable zone would be destroyed.'"

"I'm glad you actually remember," Ann grumbled, her mood quickly turning sour. "Please *do not* think I don't remember and realize that. Sand Break Border and the area around it has thankfully been mostly deserted since the Great Rainbow War, so there shouldn't be much collateral damage to it. The border is also a good distance away from the Great Line River so the lava *should* stop before it reaches it. But if it flows into the Green Dominion, then it *will* ignite the agricultural planes. Besides, no matter how destructive the volcanoes might be to the Yellow Dominion and the surface, it's still far better than what will happen to both the surface and the underworld if the Third Great Attempt is successful."

Reye noticed Ann's face now carried the familiar look she had whenever she started doom talking. She had not seen it since she found Ann in Nis. Only this time, whether because of everything that had happened to her or if she just wasn't dismissing it, the look felt more real now and far more frightening.

"Is a super volcano *really* that destructive?" Reye asked, hoping that Ann's theory might have been exaggerated.

"Reye, I personally think my theory doesn't even begin to accurately describe what will happen if this super volcano erupts," Ann replied, fear tainting her voice. "We've both seen videos of volcanoes erupting in the sea, as well as the minor eruptions that happen in the Red Dominion, but I don't think they could even compare to this. Think about how some of the volcanoes in the sea create small islands around themselves, only to be destroyed as the volcano further explodes and collapses in upon itself. Now, imagine that the whole Cherubi Continent *is* one of those islands. Once the eruption starts, magma and volcanic hail will rain down on all except the most remote and isolated parts of the Red, Blue, and Indigo dominions that are furthest away from the eruption. Then there is the ash cloud. It will cover and darken the entire planet. Temperatures will drop, and the ash will make seeing, breathing, and living almost impossible."

"But why is Lord Tanas and the Tribe of Shadows doing all of this if it's going to destroy them?" Reye asked. "The Tribe of Shadows wants to return to the surface. They don't want to destroy it."

"The Tribe of Shadows *do* want to return to the surface," the Seat of Kindness said, joining Ann and Reye's conversation. "They believe without a doubt that the Third Great Attempt will give them the freedom to return to the surface. However, we have long suspected that Lord Tanas couldn't go to the surface for one reason or another and has been using the Tribe of Shadows to perform its dirty work. After speaking with Ann, we've not only been able to confirm that, but we're also certain that what Lord Tanas is trying to do with the Third Great Attempt is free itself."

"Free himself from what?" Reye asked confused.

"Well, first we need to assume that the passages in the Tome of the Ouroboros are based on some truth," Ann explained. "Worm and I were talking once, and he read me a passage telling how after 'Light Bringer' was banished, *'Eight sentinels took watch across the land to make sure that Light Bringer would never return. Should he try, the sentinels would ensure that he suffer an even worse fate than what he had already been condemned to.'* One of Worm's top guesses about who the *'Eight sentinels'* were is the Platinum Throne and the Seven Ziggurats because of how they reacted on the Day of the Rainbow Light. If those are the sentinels, and Tanas can get past them, maybe he will be free to leave Prism and do whatever he wants."

"And he's sacrificing everything else," Reye whiffed. "The Tribe of Shadows who worship him, the Remnant, the Hy-muns, all the life that lives on and below the surface, the entire planet, just for his own personal freedom. Is he really that selfish? Does he really think nothing at all about any other life but his own?"

"Yes, to both questions," Ann and the Seat of Kindness answered in unison.

Reye was beside herself. She was more than familiar with being selfish. Thanks to the ritual, she realized she had spent a good portion of her time in Nis selfishly pursuing a foolish vengeance instead of actively trying to save anyone. Ann's description of the super volcano's eruption only further made her realize how selfish she had been—thinking about her agenda instead of seeing what was really at stake. However, Lord Tanas's plan had now put him *beyond* selfish.

No matter how bad I acted as the Hy-mun Horror, Reye fretted. *How many warriors from the Tribe of Shadows I killed, how often I ignored Ice when he was continually trying to tell me about the Third Great Attempt and the dangers we faced from it; casting it off as being unimportant. I still cared about the Hy-muns on the surface and didn't want what happened to Raymond to happen to any more of them. But Lord Tanas, he doesn't care about anyone. Once the magma starts flowing through the Great Tunnel, it will fill this cavern and quickly destroy Nis and everyone in it, flowing through the rest of the tunnels to the Remnant's home, obliterating it and the Remnant too before anyone can do anything about it. Afterward, it will erupt on the surface just like Ann said, wiping out all the Hy-muns. All that death and destruction, not just now but throughout our history, just for one person to free himself.*

Reye only shuddered. The idea of all that devastation across the generations being partially orchestrated by one person trying to free himself was both mind-boggling and frightening.

"Even if you do manage to get the drilling machines and create land-based volcanoes, can that still stop the super volcano?" Reye asked. "There's no guarantee that the magma won't still find its way to Nis and from here to the Remnant's home."

"We don't know," Ann admitted. "But it's the best we can do, the only thing we can do, and it's better to do something than nothing."

"But then shouldn't we get going now?" Reye pleaded. "If we have a key and the means we can…"

"Have patience, child," the Seat of Kindness interrupted. "I know you want to act. And there will be a time for action, but this is not it. The best thing for you, for any of us to do, is to conserve our strength: physical, mental, and spiritual, for when we know the time is right."

"Our friend is right, Reye," Ann said, not wanting to speak the Seat of Kindness's title aloud. "I know it's hard, believe me, I want to get going too, but we have to wait. If there is one thing we all agree on is that Lord Tanas likes to put on a grand production. He won't start the Third Great Attempt without making a spectacle of it first; his ego won't allow him to do otherwise. When all of the mining equipment gets back, and he gets his spectacle started, that is when we make our move, when the entire city has its eyes on Lord Tanas."

Reye knew they were both right, but it was still hard to wait. Waiting meant remembering all that she had seen in the ritual and all that she had done during her rampage throughout the city of Nis.

If by some miracle I live through this I'm going to remember it for the rest of my life, Reye thought to herself, sitting down next to Ann. *But when the time does come, what am I going to do, and also what happened to Ice?*

Chapter 31

How much longer will this take? The Tribesman was growing restless. When he fell into the ditch that protected him from being crushed by the drilling machine, he thought it was a stroke of luck. Until he realized he couldn't free himself or climb out of the ditch.

"Come on," he moaned beneath the third drilling machine as it passed overhead.

The Tribesman had been rubbing his wrists and legs against some rougher rocks, hoping to saw through the ropes binding his arms and legs, until he could feel blood running down his limbs.

"Snap stupid ropes, just break already."

A sudden loud crack in the ground followed by the digging machine inching closer to the Tribesman silenced all his complainants. Fear that his sanctuary would soon be crushed, him along with it, gripped him like the Tribe of Shadows' warriors that first bound him outside of Nis when he was still Ice. Thankfully, the ditch held, and even better the ropes finally broke.

Now I can get moving again, the Tribesman mused, crawling out of his ditch and underneath the drilling machine's massive drill that rested overhead until he was face down in the dirt and smoke, tucked into the side of the Great Tunnel.

Now that he was moving again, he could see that more mining equipment was being driven through the Great Tunnel then he initially thought. The taskmasters' shouts now echoed just under the screeching noise of the machines as they were driven through the tunnel.

"Come on diggers, move it!"

Wow, the Tribesman realized. *The Great Tunnel is being filled with Hy-mun digging machines. The first one was merely the start of the procession. If they're moving this much equipment, then that means they must be starting the Third Great Attempt soon. On the other hand, there's no way I can keep myself hidden and get past all of those workers. What am I going to do?*

The Tribesman was still watching the oncoming diggers when his hand found something abandoned on the ground. Picking it up, the Tribesman saw a strange package, the first of many leading down a side tunnel, with a bizarre label on it.

"Peaches provided by the Deep Earth Mining Corporation," the Tribesman whispered, reading the label out loud. He did not know what "Peaches" or the "Deep Earth Mining Corporation" were but opening up the packet he could soon tell what it contained, real food.

The Tribesman hurriedly ducked down the side tunnel picking up the packets as he went. Ripping off his helmet, he began eating the contents faster than he ever thought possible. In his helmet, he managed to see his reflection.

"I'm changing," the Tribesman whispered hopefully. "The umber colored contentment and dark green gluttonous energies are fading, and blue energy of resolve is growing in their place. I'm also physically changing, but perhaps not for the better."

The Tribesman laughed at his own joke, tearing open another packet and eating the food inside. The food was stone-like and tasted like it was drained of all water, but it was beyond doubt the best food he ever ate in his life, and he needed it. Looking at himself in the helmet, the Tribesman also noticed that his body had wasted away to almost skin and bones.

After refusing to eat the flesh of dead Remnant members in Nis for over a week when I was still Ice, the Tribesman reflected. *Followed by the mad rampage through the city which 'killed' him, working the quarry at the mouth of the Great Tunnel, and now the walk down it which has taken me who knows how far from*

Nis, it's no wonder I'm skin and bones. It's actually a small miracle I just haven't dropped dead from malnutrition or exhaustion. But if there's one thing I've learned from Reye, it's that a person can do just about anything once they've committed themselves to it completely. I wonder if there's more food like this lying around?

The Tribesman continued down the tunnel, finding more packets filled with food which he gratefully devoured, finally relieving himself of the hunger that had constantly gripped him since he and Dan-te first entered Nis. However, it was not long until the Tribesman encountered another smell, one he knew too well, the scent of death and decay.

Should I turn around and head back to the Great Tunnel? the Tribesman asked himself, realizing quickly that would be a fatal mistake. *I can hear the echo from the machines, and that means they're still being moved past the tunnel entrance. If I go back now, it will be a suicidal walk right into the Tribe of Shadows' diggers. Not only that, I Know that if I walk away from the scent of death, it's because I'm afraid of it. I need to find its source, for myself if for no one else.*

The Tribesman continued down the tunnel toward the smell of death. He soon found himself in a large cavern facing a grisly sight.

"What happened here?" the Tribesman gasped at the sight before him. In the cavern was the remains of a Hy-mun camp, a big camp, and throughout it, Hy-mun bodies were left to rot.

By the amount of mossy green, decaying brown, and sickly yellow rotting energies emanating from their bodies, the Tribesman figured, *none of these bodies couldn't have been dead for more than a little over a week.* The Tribesman soon realized precisely where he was.

This is where it happened, the Tribesman thought to himself as he walked through the remains of the camp. *This was where Reye first came down from the surface, where she and the other Hy-muns were attacked by the Tribe of Shadows, where her brother was killed.*

The Tribesman's eyes soon became fixed on one point throughout all the rot. A single headless Hy-mun corpse with pieces of, what must have been, his head decaying just above the neck. Around the corpse, the entire area was devoid of any sign of the massacre. It was almost as if someone had cleaned the area around that corpse of any other bodies and just decided to leave that one alone where it was; which he realized is *precisely* what happened.

"Before Reye woke up, I heard bits and pieces of her exploits that earned her the nickname, the Hy-mun Horror," the Tribesman muttered, dragging his feet toward the headless corpse. "The say she created a mountain of martyrs, that she danced from opponent to opponent creating a ring of bodies around her that just kept piling up. When she was finally captured and taken from this place, the Tribe of Shadows would have carried their own dead back to Nis with them to prepare them as food for the other warriors and gladiators. But you, the Tribe of Shadows couldn't give a care about you. But as far as Reye was concerned, you meant far more to her than anyone else on or beneath the surface world, and I failed her."

The Tribesman finally broke down, dropping to his knees, crying. "I'm sorry," the Tribesman wailed. "When your sister was first thrown into the cell across from the person I once was, I knew she was hurt and needed help. But I also knew she could be used in a desperate plan to stop the Third Great Attempt. So, instead of trying to help her, that person led her down a bloody path of vengeance that only hurt her more and, in the end, broke her spirit and her mind. I'm sorry for what he did to her, what I did to her, and for what I didn't do. Please forgive me, Raymond!"

The Tribesman knew the corpse was not going to answer him, but he still felt the need to apologize to it. He remembered Reye describing her brother Raymond's death while she was unconscious during that first week she was in the cells of Wrath Eras and again during their mad dash through Nis. He knew that Raymond had died when a warrior from the Tribe of Shadows smashed his head open, and from the guards' stories that one death was the trigger that turned Reye into the Hy-mun Horror. It was no surprise that his corpse would be the only one isolated from the other Hy-mun bodies once the Tribe of Shadows carried away their own. After crying out all of his tears, the Tribesman picked himself back up.

No amount of tears is going to make Raymond's corpse, or any of these corpses rise up and offer me comfort or forgiveness, the Tribesman thought, gazing out over the ruins of the camp. *Judging from the commotion coming from the Great Tunnel, I'm going to have to wait until all of the drilling machines have passed before I can continue down toward the Keyblast Point. But I must be close to it now. From what I heard back in Nis, Reye's camp was attacked because it was near the Keyblast point in the first place. So, while I'm waiting, there is something I can do, something I have to do.*

The Tribesman started searching the camp. He knew most of it was pillaged by the Tribe of Shadows, but thankfully he soon found what he needed; a shovel. Returning to Raymond's body, he knelt down again and put his hand on the rotting shoulder.

"This is all I can do for you, for any of you," the Tribesman whispered, looking around Raymond's remains, and those of the other Hy-muns scattered around. "I am sorry if this isn't your custom, it's a custom of my people when dealing with the dead, so I ask that you, please take no offense." The Tribesman took the shovel and began to dig a grave. He would not let the bodies of these Hy-muns just sit and rot; especially Reye's brother. When the Tribesman considered everything Ice did to Reye, using her, refusing to help her, leading her on a bloody vengeance-filled rampage through Nis while he, as Ice, stood relativity safe behind her like one of Nis's Tempters, he knew he had to give Raymond a proper burial.

They all deserved to be buried so their bodies can become part of the land and their spirits journey to the Glowing Land of their forbearers, the Tribesman prayed. *Or whatever "Glowing Land" the Hy-muns believe in. No matter what we believe, we all die eventually, and when we do, we will all go to where our forbearers are waiting for us. Besides, I've let others do the "dirty work" for me while I was a passive participant long enough. I can do this at least. And if I have to wait for the Great Tunnel to clear, I'm going to bury every corpse in this camp if it's the last good thing I do.*

Part 6: Reunion with the Ghosts of the Past

Chapter 32

"So, let me see if I understand how this works," Virgil asked from under the bed. "After placing yourself in the pit, you drink an elixir which puts you into what you call 'a penitent state.' Afterward, the person undergoing the ritual is slowly buried in the dust while smoke is blown over them while prayers are chanted above them."

"Unfortunately, that is all I know," Dan-te admitted. "I've never taken part in the Reconciliation Ritual myself, and even if I did, I couldn't tell you what happens to 'me' once the ritual starts. Anyone who undergoes the ritual can't tell anyone else what they experience. That's part of the reason why it works so well. Since no one talks about what they see it remains an extremely personal experience. I can only tell you about what I have witnessed looking at it from the outside. But I can say that after watching people take part in the ritual, *Knowing* the changes in their energies and smells as they are resting in the pit, I can guess the experience must be unlike anything you or I would imagine or expect it to be."

"I don't doubt that," Virgil admitted.

Virgil and Dan-te had been hiding under a bed since they arrived in their room at The Sand Spa Hotel. Virgil had sealed the room from natural light, and he and Dan-te were now waiting for the transportation to the Tri-Dominion Caverns that Mr. Geryon said would arrive, if available, in five hours. In the meantime, the two of them were talking about the Reconciliation Ritual the Remnant performs. It was a distraction Dan-te desperately needed.

"From what you're describing," Virgil guessed, "the beginning of this rituals sounds like a process where the participant is put into a deep hypnotic trance or a state of near death. But what they might see in that state: ghosts, their conscious, best and worst of themselves, anything to put whatever issues they have to rest is beyond me."

"Beyond anyone, Virgil," Dan-te giggled, amused at his confusion. "I know you are trying to understand the Reconciliation Ritual, but it's not something you can understand by listening to me tell you about it. You have to do it and experience it for yourself."

"Well, if or when I meet this Ca-to, I'll be sure to ask him about it."

"You don't need it," Dan-te replied confidently. She had learned a lot about Hy-muns in general while she had been traveling on the surface; none of it had been good. But regardless of what she learned, Virgil still stood out as the one exception that continued to give her hope for the rest of the species.

"Now, why don't you tell me about that package," Dan-te finally asked. "I've been wondering what's inside it since I first saw it back at Spectral Academy and even more so after I saw it again here. It looks like a tube and is a little bit longer than your arm. I also *Know* that you regard it with mixed feelings of dread, fear, pain, thankfulness, and trust. Every time you touch it a bolt of those energies swirl around where you make contact with it. I *Know* whatever is in it stirs up painful feelings and memories, makes you worry about the future, but at the same time offers you comfort and reliance. Your white mental energy is telling me that much. I can also tell that whatever is in that package is something you can trust with your life, has saved your life, and has never let you down before. You're counting on it for help right now."

"Then, I'll show you what it is," Virgil replied, somewhat reluctantly. "I had planned on showing you this before we arrived at the Tri-Dominion Caverns, but this is just as good a time now. Especially if you're that curious."

Virgil opened the case. Inside was a single-edged sword with a blade made of a slightly transparent material and a strange animal with a horn similar to hers on its pommel. It was held in a scabbard that looked far too big for it. As Virgil picked up the hilt, Dan-te started to realize why Virgil had mixed feeling about it.

"You've used that sword before," Dan-te mumbled, watching how Virgil handled the sword between them, seeing his energy running up and down it like it was a part of his body. "I *Knew* you were a skilled fighter from the moment I first saw you in your room. You've trained with that particular sword for years and *Know* exactly how to use it. I'll bet this sword also saved your life when you escaped the slaughter of the Alien Astronaut Movement."

"Right on all counts," Virgil confirmed. "This sword and I were together during the attack on the AAM. Back when I fought against the Hammers and out of the AAM's camp and started the long journey home. It saved me from both Hammers and robbers, taking many lives in the process."

Maybe he does need the Reconciliation Ritual, Dan-te reconsidered, hearing the pain in Virgil's voice. She *Knew* he never wanted to be responsible for anyone's death, and the pain of taking those lives still haunts him. But when he was forced to make a tough decision, in his mind, he chose to live instead of dying.

"When we left Spectral Academy, I sent the sword ahead of me to Mr. Geryon from the post office at Minos Airship Port with instructions concerning what to do with it. The sword's design is one-of-a-kind. If there are Hammers around who were a part of the AAM raid, there's a good chance they would recognize it."

"I knew there was a reason you left it at that office at the port," Dan-te interrupted. "But I'm still curious. I can see why you would be comfortable, nervous, and pained about holding it, but you seem a little bit too conflicted about a sword."

"It's not *just* the sword," Virgil chuckled, squeezing the scabbard and causing a piece of it to open up. Dan-te instantly noticed Virgil's energies becoming conflicted and erratic as he removed a series of papers from inside the scabbard.

"The scabbard is also a photo album," Virgil explained. "It contains all my family pictures. Now, I believe you once asked me about why I felt so confident about not being recognized as Homer's twin brother."

Dan-te took the picture from Virgil and felt her eyes about to burst in shock.

"This…is your *brother*?" Dan-te asked completely dumbfounded. The person standing next to Virgil could not have looked less like Virgil if he had tried. Where Virgil was small, thin, lean, and almost stick-like, Homer was a solid mass of muscle, over a head taller than him, and almost looked like he would have been found in a Hy-mun arena.

"I did say we were fraternal twins," Virgil explained. "But even as fraternal twins go, we're a mismatched set, and you're not the first one to ask about it. Homer, despite his intimidating size and appearance, is as friendly and social as they get. Best of all, he's *always* posing for pictures, so if anyone sees this picture I can honestly say I was getting my picture with him and no one would doubt it."

Dan-te only snickered in reply, realizing Virgil was right. He had nothing to fear in regards to being recognized as a member of the Indigo Dominion's Virt Indigo-Castitas family.

But that also explains why Virgil would have mixed feeling about carrying it around, Dan-te realized, watching the way Virgil reacted to the other photos. *The sword might be able to link him to the attack on the AAM camp, but the pictures inside of it identify him as a member of the Indigo Dominion's royal house, a fact which Virgil had already explained had been both a blessing and a curse.*

"Say, Virgil, if those pictures prove that you're Hesiod Virt Indigo-Castitas's son, why do you carry them with you in the first place?" Dan-te asked. "Why do you even carry that sword in the first place if it's really one-of-a-kind? Wouldn't it have been smarter to get rid of them?"

"It would have," Virgil agreed. "And I admit I've thought about doing just that many times. Still, call me a loyal and sentimental fool, but a part of me can't let them go completely. I'm alive because of this sword, and yes, I realize it's just a sword, but it still feels like a betrayal to just throw it away. The same with my family pictures. I'm alive because of my family, and despite the pressure that comes from being part of the Virt Indigo-Castitas family, it's still the reason why I've been able to do everything I've wanted to do, including this."

Dan-te could hear both the loyalty and the pain echoing in his voice as his energy became erratic as he talked. She *Knew* now he was not going to completely sever himself from his past. Unfortunately, that started to raise doubts about him.

"Say, how much of *this* does your family know about?" Dan-te asked.

"For the time being, nothing at all," Virgil answered honestly. "When I was making the preparations at Spectral Academy the only people I contacted were close friends. Each one helped me get home after the AAM camp was attacked and knew my real identity. I only told them I needed transport to get to the Tri-Dominion Caverns, I would be traveling in disguise, and I might need help with security. I also sent a letter to the Head of Spectral Academy announcing my withdrawal from school along with instructions on when my belongings are to be sent back to the Indigo Dominion. It's in my belongings where I've included a sealed letter to my family explaining you, the Third Great Attempt, everything else that's happening, and to pronounce me dead should the need arise."

"And when will your family *get* that letter?" Dan-te worried.

"Not until next week," Virgil assured her, placing his hand on Dan-te's shoulder. "By then, regardless of what happens, I doubt any of us are going to have to worry about Tanas, the Tribe of Shadows, or the Third Great Attempt ever again. Besides, you should *Know* I plan on seeing this journey straight through to the end, whatever that might be."

"I do," Dan-te replied, watching as the blue energy of resolve rose up and enveloped him.

I've Known *from the beginning,* Dan-te reminded herself, feeling foolish for thinking otherwise. *From the moment we left Spectral Academy, you were determined to take me back to Nis. After that, you've already decided that you can only do one of three things, die trying to stop the Third Great Attempt, succeed and then stay underground, or return to the Indigo Dominion and never leave it again.*

"Anyway," Virgil said, breaking Dan-te out of her thoughts. "We had better get going, Mr. Geryon said, if possible, he would have transportation waiting for us. We need to get to the Tri-Dominion Caverns."

"Exactly," said Dan-te, realizing that Virgil was right. They needed to move. Putting the Veil of Shadows back on, she noticed Virgil abandoning the cane he used to alert others that he was blind; also he exchanged his hat and glasses with ones that were in a closet and adopted a long coat in which he concealed his sword.

"You are not going to act like you're blind anymore?" Dan-te asked soon after she reformed her connection with Virgil.

"Not this time," Virgil explained. "The staff and guests saw a blind person walk in, they'll be watching for one to leave. Besides, now is not the time to act blind."

"Good point," Dan-te replied. "We need to move as quickly as we can now to make up for any lost time and get to the Tri-Dominion Caverns as quickly as we can. Personally, I'm ready to get back underground again."

Dan-te was more than ready. Her journey across the surface had taught her several uncomfortable things. She learned the Tribe of Shadows and the Hy-mun race were far more alike than either one would admit. She learned that more Hy-muns on the surface knew about the Tribe of Shadows then either she or Virgil ever suspected—Hy-muns who were extremely hostile to the Tribe of Shadows and developing ways to fight them. Finally, she learned the absolute folly of the Tribe of Shadows' "Plan." There was no way for either the Tribe of Shadows or the Remnant to live on the surface again. The surface world was irreversibly lost to everyone residing beneath the surface. Now they needed to try and stop the Third Great Attempt before both the surface world and the underworld beneath it were completely destroyed.

Chapter 33

Leaving the central hotel, Virgil and Dan-te quickly made their way to the Eastern Sand Bath, his sword invisible in the folds of his coat.

Virgil's coat was made for carrying the sword inside it, Dan-te observed, as the two of them quickly moved through guests and staff to where Mr. Geryon promised transportation would be waiting for them.

"Accord to Mr. Geryon, the transportation we'll use to get to the Tri-Dominion Caverns should be waiting for us just behind that bath," Virgil whispered through the rush of guests and staff. Even though the sun was going down, the sand baths were still extremely active. Large numbers of guests were all buried up to their necks in the hot sand while staff saw to their needs.

"What's the purposes of these sand baths?" Dan-te whispered to Virgil, her veiled grip tightening slightly as she asked.

"Hy-muns use them for skin treatments and body relaxation," Virgil replied, but he could feel the tension in Dan-te's grip rise from passing the sand baths. Virgil remembered Dan-te's stories about "The Coming" and how some members of the Ancient Tribe attempted burying themselves in sand to escape the effects of Light, only to be literally cooked where they were buried.

Dan-te's seen enough shocking sights up here, Virgil thought to himself. *She doesn't need anymore, especially ones that might look like they came right out of a retelling of "The Coming."* Picking up his pace slightly, he decided to get out of the sand bath area as soon as possible to where, he hoped, Mr. Geryon had arranged their transportation, a fact Dan-te was incredibly grateful for as she observed the Hy-muns in the baths with interest.

Why do these Hy-muns purposely hurt themselves, Dan-te wondered as she and Virgil crept around the edge of the Eastern Sand Bath. *Virgil said the reasons for taking these sand baths were "skin treatments and body relaxation," but what's going on is something entirely different. The heated sand that's wrapped around the Hy-muns where they lay is only opening up their skin to more injury. The more it is heated, the more it opens up, and the more sand and heat are able to crawl into their skin like bugs into a wound; festering and hurting their skin even after the Hy-muns get out of it.* Dan-te thought of sharing her opinions with Virgil, but she *Knew* that right now he was focused on getting them out of the baths and finding the transportation that Mr. Geryon promised so they could start making their way to the Tri-Dominion Caverns. The two of them were almost to the back of the Eastern Sand Bath, going through some trees and bushes that lined its back wall when voices from the sand bath suddenly made Virgil freeze and drop to the ground.

"Virgil, what's wrong," Dan-te whispered, crouching down next to Virgil. Dan-te *Knew* from the moment he froze that something was wrong. He was exploding with fearful pink energy. Virgil was scared, afraid, nervous, and now more cautious then she had ever seen him. She also *Knew* that unlike what had happened at the Stone Gate with the Medusa Machine, the fear Virgil was feeling was familiar. His white mental energy was bursting just as much as his fearful pink energy. The fear he was feeling was a familiar danger.

"Virgil, talk to me, tell me what's wrong," Dan-te asked again, crawling next to him and whispering into his ear. Virgil only looked and listened intensively to a small group of people that was sitting alone in the sand bath.

"Just a moment, Dan-te," Virgil answered, his face pale as he turned his focus back to the people in the sand bath. Dan-te, *Knowing* how much Virgil was disturbed by them, also listened to their conversation.

"Our hammers will soon be striking the Lord and Master's Divine Light through Tanas's darkness," one member of the group boasted to his companions.

"Have all of the roads to the Tri-Dominion Caverns been closed off?" another asked.

"All of them," a third answered. "Only our brother and sister Hammers of the Orange Light have access to the roads. If anyone else wants to get even remotely near the caverns, it will be on foot."

"Assuming they can walk that far," the first one joked, bringing the group into a round of laughter. But from behind them in the bushes, Dan-te quickly understood the reason behind Virgil's fear.

The Hammers of the Orange Light, Dan-te thought with a shock. *Those Hy-muns are members of the same extremist group that wiped out Virgil's friends in the Alien Astronaut Movement. No wonder Vigil is suddenly on edge.*

Dan-te remembered Virgil telling her about the Hammers of the Orange Light.

Publicly, they were wiped out at the end of the Great Rainbow War, the Second Great Attempt, but secretly they continued their founding purpose to destroy anything, no matter who or what it was, that they considered an obstacle to Ash Addiel. Dan-te was lost in her memory for only a second until she recalled something else that they had said. They were blocking all the roads to the Tri-Dominion Caverns, the caverns that they needed to get to.

"I can't wait to get underground and shine the light of our hammers into the face of Tanas and his monsters." another one cheered.

"Keep your voice down," the first said in quick response. "Considering how much backing we've been given, the last thing we want is to tip our hand, especially if Tanas's veiled spies are around."

"Okay, now I'm *really* interested," Dan-te whispered. "Those Hammers just said that they can't 'wait to get underground and shine the light of our hammers into the face of Tanas and his monsters.' I already learned the hard way that Hy-muns know about Tempters, that they can expose them, and make their Veils of Shadows useless."

Dan-te shivered at both memories: first the Medusa Machine at the entrance of Tri-Dominion City that exposed and captured a Tempter in the shadow of the Hy-mun he was tempting. Then the Lightning Lamp at the hospital that neutralized the Veil of Shadows, leaving the Tempter to be captured and have his Veil stripped off him and burned to death in the light.

"The Hammers of the Orange Light must be connected to both of those devices," Dan-te surmised. "That first one said they needed to keep their voices down, 'especially if Tanas's veiled spies are around.' He used the word 'veiled,' the Hammers have to know about Tanas's Tempters veiled in the Veils of Shadows. Just like the Furies with the Medusa Machine and the doctors with the Lightning Lamp. The Hammers must also know about Nis's very existence and are trying to get there themselves; and have lots of backing, meaning they're prepared for whatever they're going to come across." Dan-te and Virgil slowly inched away until they were quickly heading back in the direction toward where their transportation would hopefully be waiting.

"Now what do we do?" Dan-te whispered as they made their way through the bushes. "If the Hammers somehow manage to invade Nis, it will be the biggest disaster *ever*. One of the few things that the Remnant of the Tribe and the Tribe of Shadows ever agreed upon was the common fear of a 'Second Coming.' We've both been afraid that either the Beings of Light or later the Hy-muns, would invade the new home we created and finish the slaughter the Beings of Light begun generations ago. The Hammers of the Orange Light sound like they are positioning themselves to do just that."

"I know," Virgil replied, sounding as worried as Dan-te. "And I agree with you. But all we can do is keep making our way to the Tri-Dominion Caverns and hope we can make it to Nis before the Hammers, and that just got harder."

"What do you mean?"

"You heard what that Hammer said, they have all the roads blocked off so they can plan their assault privately. That means to get to the caverns we'll need to travel off-road, and that is *not* an easy trek."

Virgil was worried, and Dan-te knew it. She knew that what they were attempting to accomplish was already hard enough. Now there was the added problem of the Hammers of the Orange Light.

"Right now, what we need to do is find Mr. Geryon's transportation, assuming he was able to get it and figure out how we can use it to get us to the Tri-Dominion..." Virgil paused suddenly as great white muzzle suddenly shoved itself into his face.

Dan-te had not seen many of the other creatures besides Hy-muns that had inhabited the surface since she first arrived in Virgil's room. But this creature was easily the strangest thing she had ever seen. It was tied to a tree and emitted a cloud of powder calm energy. It was white like her, had four legs, and a big head with an elongated face. It wore something that looked like a seat with a folded piece of paper on it. Dan-te *Knew* despite its calmness that it was a muscular creature, far stronger then it seemed. It was used to transporting heavy loads and could easily carry both of them if it had to. Dan-te also realized that Virgil knew what this creature was; his white mental energy flashed the moment he saw it.

"A Waa Pony," Virgil said, naming the creature before them.

"Is this our transportation?" Dan-te asked.

"Yes, it is, look at this," Virgil picked up the small piece of folded paper on the seat. Inside, there were only two words and a signature: "Good Luck, Mr. G."

"Mr. G," Virgil repeated confidently. "G for Geryon, this is our transportation and considering our situation we couldn't have asked for anything better."

"I can tell that you are confident that this Waa Pony can get us to the Tri-Dominion Caverns," Dan-te mused skeptically. "But are you sure that it can get us there?"

Almost in reply, the Waa Pony turned its head straight toward Dan-te and made a strange barking sound right into her face. The experience spooked her so much she fell over backward, pulling Virgil down with her as he laughed throughout the whole affair.

"First of all, this Waa Pony is a 'he,'" Virgil chuckled, standing back up and lifting Dan-te in the process. "Second, as you just noticed he is *very* susceptible to the feelings of the ones around him. Sensitive enough to feel you through the damaged Veil of Shadows. Waa Ponies tend to be solitary creatures. Even tame ones prefer to keep as far away from others as they possibly can. You remember what that Hammer in the sand bath said; 'All of the roads to the Tri-Dominion Caverns have been closed off.' This Waa Pony is the best chance we have of not only getting to the Tri-Dominion Caverns, but also getting there unseen. They are masters at traveling off-road on almost *any* terrain."

Dan-te looked at the Waa Pony again and *Knew* that Virgil was right.

Beneath his calm energy there is a natural instinct to keep as far away from other species as he possibly can, no matter what kind of ground he has to cover, Dan-te realized. *And he is very susceptible to the feelings and moods of anyone who gets too near him, almost as sensitive as a member of the Remnant or the Tribe of Shadows. The fact that he could sense me through the Veil of Shadows certainly proves that. Virgil might not have been getting overconfident about him after all. Regardless, we need to get going.*

Virgil knew that too, quickly making himself comfortable on the seat that was on top of the Waa Pony while still holding onto Dan-te's hand.

"Climb on and position yourself like I did and put your arms around my waist," Virgil instructed. Since Dan-te was taller than Virgil she found it easy to climb onto the Waa Pony. The hard part was making herself comfortable.

"I'm ready to go," she said, putting her arms around Virgil's waist and holding on tightly for what she realized was going to be an interesting ride. Dan-te had *Known* from the first moment that when Virgil identified the Waa Pony's name, he was familiar with them and had ridden them before. However, this would be her first time riding any kind of living creature, and she was both curious and excited at the prospect.

"Ok," said Virgil, undoing the rope binding the Waa Pony to a tree. "Here we go. Ok, boy, take us to the Tri-Dominion Caverns, and avoid as many people as you can."

Virgil used the heels of his shoes to gently bunt the Waa Pony's sides, and they were off. Dan-te guessed the Waa Pony would move fast, but he ended up running more quickly than she thought he would. From their shared position on top of the Waa Pony, it felt as if they were traveling on an extremely bumpy road, but the Waa Pony knew just where to go from the moment Virgil instructed him to take them to the Tri-Dominion Caverns.

He's been trained for this, Dan-te thought to herself as the Waa Pony quickly moved through the forest, changing directions periodically. *The pony is doing this to avoid other Hy-muns while making his way to the Tri-Dominion Caverns. Virgil was right about him. He is the best way for us to get to the Tri-Dominion Caverns.*

"Next stop, Tri-Dominion Caverns," Virgil cheered as they continued on their way; but one unsaid thought still hung on both of their minds. What would they find when they reached their destination?

Chapter 34

"Once we're over this hill we'll be able to see the tent covering the Tri-Dominion Caverns," Virgil eagerly exclaimed.

"Great," Dan-te whispered. "I'm going to be glad when I'm underground again and can get out of this Veil for good. It's served me well, but I'm getting tired of it. I also owe an apology to the Waa Pony, it does *Know* this area better than I thought."

"I told you," Virgil snickered followed by a whinny from the Waa Pony.

The Waa Pony easily traveled across the rough terrain of the Violet Plateau, avoiding all the roadblocks and checkpoints set up by the Hammers of the Orange Light on the paths leading to the Tri-Dominion Caverns. However, the Waa Pony suddenly stopped after cresting the hill overlooking the Tri-Dominion Caverns. Virgil and Dan-te could understand why.

"Is that really a *tent*?" Dan-te gasped.

Virgil understood Dan-te's surprise. Below them, the entire valley that housed the entrance to the Tri-Dominion Caverns was covered in a giant canvas tent. In that tent, the two of them could see a series of yellow-orange lights radiating from within it and illuminating the tent's interior. The same thought flashing through both their minds.

Lightning Lamps, Virgil and Dan-te thought.

Dismounting, and sending the Waa Pony on his way to keep him from being discovered, Virgil and Dan-te made their way on foot to the giant tent lit by the Lightning Lamps. As they were nearing it, a flap of the tent blew open in the breeze and suddenly bathed both Virgil and Dan-te in the yellow-orange light.

"No," Virgil screamed, moving faster than he ever had in his entire life to shield Dan-te from the Lightning Lamp's effects. Dan-te, frozen in panic as memories from the hospital suddenly flooded back into her mind, quickly found herself tackled to the ground as Virgil spread himself over her.

"Virgil," Dan-te coughed, the wind momentarily knocked out of her. "What are you doing to…"

Dan-te let the rest of her question hang in the air. She realized from the pink fear energy and look of shock pulsing and etched on Virgil's face, plus the simple fact that he *had* tackled her, she knew exactly what he was doing and also why he was doing it. The Lightning Lamp had made her visible, just like it did to the Tempter in the hospital, and Virgil had moved to protect her from being burned alive like the Tempter. He was terrified that something was happening to her right now, that she could be in pain unless he found a way to keep as much light from touching her as he could, using his own body as a shield.

"I'm alright," Dan-te said, putting her hand to Virgil's head. "I'm not burning, and I don't feel myself burning."

"But you are visible," Virgil countered, looking at Dan-te's now veiled but visible form, tinged blue-violet just like the Tempter in the hospital. "The Lightning Lamp neutralized the Veil of Shadows's ability to keep you hidden in my shadow."

"At least that's all it did," Dan-te replied, pushing Virgil off her and standing up. "The Veil is still protecting me from light, so as long as I keep the Veil on I should be protected."

"Monster," someone screamed, forcing Virgil and Dan-te to dive into a small grove of trees and bushes and search for the source of the commotion. Peering down toward the tent, they found it.

"There," Virgil whispered, pointing to a portion of the tent where another blue-violet figure was fighting his way out of a cut in the canvas.

"Another Tempter," Dan-te realized as the Tempter fought his way out of the tent followed by a team of Hy-muns carrying large hammers and wearing orange full-body suits with only a shaded glass panel on the front of their faces to keep their identities hidden.

"Destroy that monster," one of the Hy-muns ordered as they chased the Tempter down and pulled the Veil off him. As it was pulled off, the Tempter burned in the fading sunlight; just like the Tempter in the hospital. Virgil could feel Dan-te trembling violently and see the terror in her eyes as the Tempter burned to death and the Hammers cheered before going back into the tent.

I still remember my own past experiences with the Hammers, Virgil fretted, recalling the raid on the AAM's camp. *They haven't changed, they still think they are on some "noble" crusade.*

"They're the same," Dan-te squeaked. "Those Hy-muns, the Hammers, they're no different from the gladiators and warriors of Nis. They're lit with the same energy, the same passions. All they want is to fight 'their enemies.' I know I originally wanted to bring back a force of Hy-muns to stop Lord Tanas, the Tribe of Shadows, and the Third Great Attempt. But I wanted one that was better than the Tribe of Shadows. These Hy-muns…"

"We both know that these are *not* the kind of Hy-muns that you, or anyone for that matter, would want rushing through their home," Vigil replied, trying to comfort her. "And we can't let them learn about you or the Remnant. Somehow, they know about Tempters, and I'll bet they know the city of Nis is right underneath us as well. If they get underground and learn about your people then they won't stop with the Tribe of Shadows. They'll keep going until every last being underground is dead, unless they are killed first."

"I know," Dan-te sobbed, falling onto the ground over the sight she had witnessed.

"So, what do we do now?" Dan-te asked. "We can't just sit here, and we don't have the time to find another cave system. So, what do we do now?"

Virgil looked down at the giant tent again and the place where the Tempter cut his way out, quickly coming up with an idea. He did not like it, and from Dan-te's swift reaction it was an idea she liked even less.

"You can't go down there!"

"If you go down there with me you will be killed the moment you are spotted," Virgil argued. "That blue-violet Veil is nothing but a huge visible target for the Hammers. But if I go down there, there's a chance I can find some of those suits they're wearing. Then we can disguise ourselves."

"But if even one of the Hammers recognizes you," Dan-te countered, her voice racked with worry. "It will be you who's dead."

"That's why I'm giving you this."

Virgil reached into his jacket, took out his sword, and passed it to Dan-te.

"Like I told you before when the Hammers attacked the AAM, they never saw my face, but they did see my sword. It could identify me as the only survivor of the AAM far more than my face ever could. The scabbard also contains the pictures of me and my family, I can't risk the Hammers learning *that* information."

"Still, are you sure you want to give me your sword?" Dan-te asked. She understood what Virgil was thinking, but she still had her doubts. "What if you need it?"

"You'll need it a lot more than me if you are found and have to defend yourself," Virgil replied. "Besides, I can fight just as well without it. You *Know* that. Also, I can move in the light without burning up, you can't. I'll be alright on my own."

"But," Dan-te stuttered, the memory of the Tempter's death fresh in her mind.

"I know it's a bad idea, but it's the only idea we got," Virgil concluded. "If you have a better one, now is the time to tell me."

Dan-te looked hard into Virgil's face and eyes. She *Knew* he was afraid to walk back into the company of the Hy-muns who had murdered his friends before almost killing him; the pink fear energy was radiating steadily from him. But he was even more afraid about what would happen to all of them if he *didn't*. Virgil feared what would happen if the Hammers made it underground, or if the Third Great Attempt was successful, or what would happen if they found her, especially after seeing what happened to Tempters once they were captured and exposed to light.

"You're right, I don't have any better ideas," Dan-te conceded. "I want to tell you I have a better idea, that you don't have to take a crazy risk like this; but you're right, we have to take the risk. If we have a pair of those suits, we'll be able to blend in without being noticed, and you are the only one who can get them. But before you go, promise me a few things, first that you will come back."

"I promise," Virgil said with a smile. "I was always going to do that."

"Second," Dan-te continued, looking intensely at Virgil. "Promise me that the next time I come up with a bad idea that I want to go through with, you'll support me on it."

"I promise," Virgil laughed. "I just hope it's not too bad of an idea you come up with."

"Me, too," Dan-te smiled. "Lastly, can you promise me something if we live through all of this. Please, promise me one more favor later on."

"Ok," Virgil replied, a little curious about what kind of idea Dan-te might have had in mind, "I'll wait until everything is over for that promise to be asked. It will give us both good reasons to live through all of this and to succeed. Well, wish me luck, here I go."

Virgil took a deep breath and began creeping out of the bushes and toward the giant tent.

"Good luck, Virgil," Dan-te whispered as he took another look back before continuing on toward the camp of the Hammers of the Orange Light.

Chapter 35

"Let the Third Great Attempt begin," Tanas repeated into the camera before shutting it off. Since the capture of the "Hy-mun Horror," he had sent all of the servants away from Decca-Ju Tower and had been making numerous recordings of himself that could be played by him remotely from anywhere he wanted. The tapes were meant to serve as his proxy, programmed to activate under certain circumstances so he could leave the city and not arouse suspicion.

"Once the initial explosion is set at the Keyblast Point, every tunnel that the Great Tunnel and Nis is connected to is going to be filled with magma before the super volcano erupts," Tanas said to himself, reviewing the final pieces of his plan. "However, before escaping, I still need to finish my final and most magnificent performance for these savages.

"Now that the last recording is finished, I need to give these savages blood, more blood then they have ever craved. It's a good way to start the festivities. These first recordings should do that just fine."

Tanas's first recordings were designed to call together all the members of the Tribe of Shadows with Rodent-blood to the Great Coliseum in Wrath Eras. Once there, the gladiators of the Great Coliseum would then be ordered to massacre them in front of the entire city.

"A purging of 'Rodent-blood,' especially when they won't be declared martyrs, is something *everyone* in this city will enjoy. Once the spectacle is over, I can trigger my next set of recordings, announcing to Nis how, 'We have all struggled and lived through hardship, but we have endured and have constantly purged ourselves and have now purged our city further by ridding it of the Rodent-blooded ones. Now is the time to purge the surface of the Hy-muns and the Light and retake it as our own.' Once that's played, my last recording will be the announcement to, 'Let the Third Great Attempt begin!' From there, the detonator will be activated in Circle Emporium by the current Vice Pride, and if he fails, there are the backups that will trigger the explosion at the Keyblast Point, starting the magma that will finally wipe all these savages out and give me my freedom.

"I have spent thousands of years waiting for this moment," Tanas cried, gathering his belongings. "Planning how much magma was needed, how big and sturdy the tunnel needed to be to hold it once it started flowing so the tunnel wouldn't collapse in on itself; and if it did, calculating the force of magma needed to push through the blockage. Slowly shaping Nis to hold it and artificially create the conditions for the super volcano to erupt. Planning for what would happen if the detonator here in the city failed. Even preparing for any interference from the surface, I made a set of recordings for that, too. Not that those hybrid mutants could even mount any kind of attack if they made it here. My *preparations* would stop them as easily as they did that Rodent's Hy-mun Horror."

Tanas laughed at the memory of how helpless Reye was just from confronting him thanks to the genetic programming installed into the Hy-mun species. If the Hy-muns ever *did* invade Nis, he was sure his safeguards, paired with that programming would make their assault futile.

"I recorded instructions for the Tribe of Shadows if the hybrid mutants ever discovered and invaded Nis back during the Second Great Attempt, or the Great Rainbow War as they called it," Tanas remembered. "Back then, I tried destroying the Ziggurats themselves so I could escape. Unfortunately, that plan was stopped by the hybrid mutant who infiltrated Decca-Ju Tower. But with hybrid mutant technology at its peak before the attempt, I didn't want to leave anything to chance and decided to prepare for an attack if it came. Thankfully, those worries were for naught. The hybrid mutants all but destroyed much of their own technology, leaving the rest of it for the Tribe of Shadows to procure.

"Even if the hybrid mutants did invade the city, there would be nothing they could do at this point. Any entrance they could create would only form another vent for the super volcano. I calculated it can hold up to four vents before it could risk a problem, and the hybrid mutants can't make that many. There's no way they could unify themselves for that kind of undertaking. Not that I will be around to see anything that can or will happen anyway."

Tanas walked to the lowest level of Decca-Ju Tower, a level he used as his personal reflection room. He found what he was looking for easy enough, he was the one who had built it: a secret lift he had constructed centuries ago. When he was first banished, Tanas and his legions were only able to smuggle tools and enough materials to create more Veils of Shadows, this lift, and where it led to.

"I still remembered what the continent first looked like as I approached it from space, and what it looked like after my legions had virtually sterilized it. When Ash Addiel and the rest of the Nag-el arrived, they wouldn't even know that it was originally inhabited," Tanas mused, climbing into the lift and pressing a button. "The continent now has a large crescent shape, but when we first arrived, much of what the hybrid mutants would later call the Great Lagoon was filled with undeveloped fields and forest land. My legions were sterilizing that land when a large earthquake caused almost all of it to sink into the sea. I didn't see the event myself, but I did hear reports about it from my men. Especially the ship that sank with the land."

That ship was the real prize Tanas concerned himself with, the spaceship that was lost when the land sank centuries ago, the one he was now connected to thanks to his secret tunnel leading out of the city of Nis.

"Now to get going to the ship," Tanas chirped giddily, exiting the lift and entering a transport waiting for him. "That ship is my way off this planet and my ticket to freedom. It took a lot of work to secretly find and connect Nis and the ship, but it was worth it."

Over the millennia, Tanas revived the ship's functions and used its lab to figure out how to undo certain aspects of the Methuselah Drug. While he enjoyed being able to suck the heat out of someone with a touch and the longevity, he did *not* appreciate being devoid of warmth himself, nor did he want to feel lethal pain whenever his body touched natural light. Plus, he was completely aware and terrified of what would happen to him if the Ziggurat Security System was alerted to his presence on the surface. But after centuries of research, Tanas had finally figured out how to undo those specific effects so he could keep the abilities he wanted and lose the ones he did not. There was only one ingredient he still needed, pure, untainted Nag-el blood, and there was only one place he could find that.

"After the First Great Attempt, Ash Addiel took the remaining Nag-el back into space with him to enter a state of cryogenic hibernation while my virus burned itself out," Tanas remembered. "Thanks to this ship, I know Ash Addiel's ship is still in a geo-sync orbit above the planet. It's remotely keeping itself between the light of the sun and the planet, so it remains invisible to anyone looking for it. I also know Ash Addiel, and the rest of the Nag-el are still alive in the cryogenic hibernation that they put themselves in since they left the planet. I've been able to fool that ship's sensors so that it still can't determine whether the virus has burned itself out, so it's keeping everyone on board in suspended animation. Once I'm clear of the planet, I can dock with the ship, gain the blood I need for my cure, cure myself, and then destroy Ash Addiel's ship with everyone in it, leaving me free to go anywhere I want to with all the time in the universe. I will finally be free of this world and all the savages on it. And after all the time I spent locked in up in this underground prison, I need a change of scenery."

Tanas climbed out of his transport and into his ship, activating the charges that were set down the transport's tunnel in the process. Once the initial explosion was triggered from the Keyblast Point, another set of explosives would go off designed to collapse the passage leading from his ship to Nis. Once that happened, he knew his ability to activate recordings and his visual connection with the city would be cut off. Not only that but he would be committed to leaving the planet or remaining permanently locked in his ship at the bottom of the Great Lagoon for good. Tanas set to work getting the craft prepared for departure, using its monitors to watch what was happening in Nis. Thousands upon thousands of years have led to these coming hours, and Tanas knew his freedom was finally at hand.

"I've waited too long for this," Tanas mused, waiting for the ship to warm up and come to life. "But my wait is almost over, the Third Great Attempt is about to begin."

Chapter 36

What's taking him so long, Dan-te worried, gripping Virgil's sword tighter.

Dan-te was still hiding in the bushes. The Veil of Shadows, now blue-violet, lost all of its abilities to conceal her after being exposed to the orange-yellow glow of the Lightning Lamps in the Hammers' camp. The only ability it still possessed was that it protected her from the effects of sunlight. Dan-te clutched both the Veil and Virgil's sword as if they were her only lifelines left after Virgil snuck into the camp to see if he could find disguises for the two of them. A sound in the bushes almost made Dan-te's heart jump out of her chest, but a familiar voice ended all of her fears.

"Dan-te, it's me, Virgil. Are you alright?"

Dan-te could not even begin to say how she felt now that Virgil was back. Instead, all she did was embrace him harder than she had ever embraced anyone before. Dan-te *Knew* Virgil was surprised by her sudden show of emotion but was also happy to find her safe as well. She also noticed at Virgil's feet were two sets of the orange suits that the Hammers were wearing, and that Virgil's face was turning as blue as her Veil.

"You found our disguises," Dan-te cheered, quickly releasing Virgil who started rubbing his sides.

"Far easier than I thought it would be," Virgil coughed in pain, regaining his breath. "Now, let's get dressed. We can put these right over what we're wearing and then head down into the camp. I didn't see much activity, but it feels like something big is about to happen."

Dan-te took the larger suit and put it on. The Hammers suits were heavier then they looked. Dan-te quickly found that they were made with metal running through them. However, between both the outfits and the dark face covering, she realized the disguises worked. If not for his energy, she would not know it was Virgil until he spoke to her.

"Let's stay connected, so we don't lose each other."

"Agreed," Dan-te replied, retaking Virgil's hand as they made their way down to the tent concealing the Hammers' camp. Walking into the tent through the cut made by the Tempter, Dan-te did not know what to expect, only that it covered the entrance to the Tri-Dominion Caverns and their way back to Nis. What she saw took her breath away.

"How could they do this?"

The Hammer's camp was set in a depression carved out of the ground. Walking into it, with Virgil at her side, Dan-te did not need the ability to *Know* to realize that the crater they were walking into was not only artificially made, but also it was made recently. Dirt and rocks easily broke away under their feet as they stepped down the slope and into the camp, it was so loose that anyone would realize it had recently been dug into. The more solid pieces of rock that stuck out of the crater walls like jagged teeth were rough like someone had chiseled them down to make the crater smoother. At the bottom of the hole, the Hammer's camp rested like stagnant water in a pool. At three different points in the tent and around the valley, Lightning Lamps were set up which constantly projected the orange-yellow light that had revealed Dan-te and the Tempters in the hospital and the camp. Tents, box-like buildings, crates, and metal towers dotted the entire valley giving it the appearance of a small city. Throughout the encampment, people walked hurriedly in orange suits like the ones they were wearing. The dark face masks made it impossible to see who anyone really was. Lastly, in the center of the encampment was a huge terranaut ship supported by metal harnesses that directed it toward the ground; and everywhere was the symbol of the Hammers of the Orange Light.

"How could Hy-muns create something like this?" Dan-te asked.

"Not without a lot of outside help," Virgil answered, looking at that terranaut ship with renewed interest. "And I do mean, *a lot*. That terranaut ship is at least twice as large as the ships commonly used by terranauts. The largest ship I've ever heard of before now is the Arc, designed and built by Dr. Noah Heart, Professor Heart's father. But this one is twice the size of the Arc. And considering how much it cost to make the Arc, it couldn't have been constructed without a lot of help from highly placed persons in Hy-mun society."

Meaning persons like your father, or the other Virt Princes, Dan-te figured, remembering the luxurious ships the Virt Princes traveled in, and that four of them were in Tri-Dominion City. *I'll bet Virgil thinks the four of them, or at least someone close to them is involved in all this, too. Still, I'm surprised Virgil even managed to* find *our disguises, let alone get back to me. Everything in this camp looks the same and is crawling with Hammers.*

Everywhere Dan-te looked, Hammers dressed no differently from the two of them wandered back and forth through a camp filled with buildings that looked like simple boxes. From one look, Dan-te *Knew* they were built without feeling, radiating grey energy similar to the energy she first experienced on the Platinum Throne. The difference was *this* energy gave her a monotonous feeling—a dull sense that she was one out of a million similar types—instead of leaving her feeling like the place lacked belief.

"How were you ever able to find your way around this place?" Dan-te finally asked, "Almost everything looks the same, and there are Hammers everywhere."

"I was both extremely lucky and fortunate," Virgil replied, relief echoing throughout his voice. "When we came into the camp, did you notice a few tents at the right at its perimeter, just before all of these prefabricated buildings?"

"I did," Dan-te answered. "They were one of the few buildings that were actually *different* in this camp."

"When I slipped into the camp, I ducked into one of the tents and was lucky enough to find that it was filled with the suits the Hammers were wearing. I grabbed two and then made my way back to you as quickly as I could."

"Well, I'm glad you did," Dan-te said, relieved to have a little bit of luck on their side. "So, how do we get into the caverns?"

"Attention all Hammers of the Orange Light," a voice boomed throughout the camp. "Proceed toward the Antaeus for final briefing and boarding before beginning the invasion of Nis."

All at once, the Hammers stopped what they were doing and began making their way toward the ship in the center of the camp.

"I guess we are also heading toward the terranaut ship," Virgil sighed, a bundle of mixed feelings shuffling through him.

"Do we really have to head for the ship?" Dan-te asked nervously. "Why don't we just enter the Tri-Dominion Caverns and make our way back to Nis from here?"

"For starters, we'll look suspicious if we don't head for the ship," Virgil replied. "Second, we're technically already *in* the Tri-Dominion Caverns."

"What?" Dan-te asked. She did not know what was surprising her more, what Virgil just said or his reaction. Virgil was a chaotic mix of feelings. She *Knew* he was angry, scared for himself and for her—having seen exactly what the Hammers would do to Dan-te if they ever got their hands on her—protective of the both of them, and resolved over what they still had to accomplish. His energy radiating, swirling, and turning so many different colors Dan-te did not know how Virgil could hold himself together. Now, she had to consider what Virgil had just said, that they were already *in* the Tri-Dominion Caverns.

"I *Know* this camp was carved deep into the ground," Dan-te whispered, looking around at the walls. "Do you mean the Hammers dug into the cavern's main entrance just to set up and position their terranaut ship so it could reach Nis?"

"That's exactly what I'm saying," Virgil answered with a sigh.

"Then I guess we *have* to head toward the ship," Dan-te grumbled, gripping Virgil's hand tighter as the orange-yellow light from the Lightning Lamps continued shining down on them.

I almost wish I was back in the "Reversed State," Dan-te thought.

While Dan-te might have been disguised in one of the Hammers' suits, making it impossible for anyone to realize who, or what, she was, the lamps made her nervous. The memory of the Tempters from the Tribe of Shadows was still fresh in her mind. She could almost hear the Hammers calling her "monster," capturing her, tearing off the Veil and cheering triumphantly as she burned to death in the light.

"They won't get you," Virgil assured her, placing his other hand on top of Dan-te's hand; making her realize she wasn't just holding his hand, she was clutching it. "As far as anyone can tell, we're just a couple of Hammers in the crowd. They won't find you."

"I hope you're right," Dan-te replied. She could hear the care and concern in Virgil's voice; but *Knew* from the multicolored energy swirling around him, especially the fearful pink energy, that he was just as scared as she was. Rounding a building to get closer to the terranaut ship they quickly found themselves part of a large crowd of similarly dressed Hammers of all sizes; all indistinguishable behind opaque masks, and all heading toward the terranaut ship at the center of the camp. The crowd was so big that both Dan-te and Virgil had to tighten their grips on each other to stay connected. They realized that in a group of this size if either one of them got separated, there would be little to no chance of finding the other again without potentially alerting the Hammers to who they were.

"This is it." Dan-te and Virgil said in unison, causing them both to look at each other and share a small laugh, breaking a little of the tension they both felt. Taking a deep breath, they held on to each other's hand like it was their lifeline and made their way with the crowd to the terranaut ship; their ride back to the city of Nis.

Reunions, Reflections, and Reconciliations

The Story Concludes in: "The Second Coming"

War comes to the city of Nis as the Hammers of the Orange Light invade intent on wiping out the Tribe of Shadows and anything they consider a "threat" to Ash Addiel. Meanwhile, amidst the chaos, Virgil and Dan-te return to Nis aboard the Hammers' ship intent on finding the means to prevent the initiation of the Third Great Attempt. Elsewhere, Reye, Ann, and the captured members of the Remnant put their own plans into motion to stop the Third Great Attempt, while Stella attempts a final desperate bid for freedom and the Tribesman encounters an unexpected ally in the Great Tunnel on the way to the Keyblast Point. In the chaos, a face from Reye, Stella, and Virgil's past will appear before them again for one final reunion. While far from Nis, Tanas, hidden from the battle, waits to trigger the Third Great Attempt safe in his escape ship. Paths converge in the explosive conclusion to the story that first began in "The City of Nis."